The Eaglet in the Americas

Titles by John Mariner

The Eaglet at the Battle of Minorca
The Eaglet at the Battle of Lagos Bay

The Eaglet in the Americas

Book Three of the Eaglet Trilogy

JOHN MARINER

To Richard.
J Mariner.

© Copyright 2005 John Mariner.
Previously published under ISBN: 0-9726303-1-7
All rights reserved. No part of this publication may be reproduced, stored in a retrieval system, or transmitted, in any form or by any means, electronic, mechanical, photocopying, recording, or otherwise, without the written prior permission of the author.

Printed in Victoria, BC, Canada

Note for Librarians: a cataloguing record for this book that includes Dewey Decimal Classification and US Library of Congress numbers is available from the Library and Archives of Canada. The complete cataloguing record can be obtained from their online database at:
www.collectionscanada.ca/amicus/index-e.html
ISBN 1-41204537-1

TRAFFORD

This book was published *on-demand* in cooperation with Trafford Publishing. On-demand publishing is a unique process and service of making a book available for retail sale to the public taking advantage of on-demand manufacturing and Internet marketing. On-demand publishing includes promotions, retail sales, manufacturing, order fulfilment, accounting and collecting royalties on behalf of the author.

Offices in Canada, USA, UK, Ireland, and Spain
***book sales for North America and international*:**
Trafford Publishing, 6E–2333 Government St.
Victoria, BC V8T 4P4 CANADA
phone 250 383 6864   toll-free 1 888 232 4444
fax 250 383 6804   email to orders@trafford.com

***book sales in Europe*:**
Trafford Publishing (UK) Ltd., Enterprise House, Wistaston Road Business Centre
Crewe, Cheshire CW2 7RP UNITED KINGDOM
phone 01270 251 396   local rate 0845 230 9601
facsimile 01270 254 983   orders.uk@trafford.com

***order online at*:**
www.trafford.com/robots/04-2345.html

10   9   8   7   6   5   4   3   2

Contents

Santander	9
'Enemy in sight!'	19
'Hoist Battle Ensigns!'	29
The Taste of Victory	39
Rear Admiral Charles Saunders	47
Boston and a Bad Business	55
Southward Bound	65
Commodore John Moore	75
'Our Day of Destiny'	85
The Taking of the Guns	95
Mayhem and Death	103
'A Damned Good Drubbing!'	113
The Black Pit of Hell	121
Pirates All	131
'In Peril of Our Lives'	141
'A Nest of Vipers'	149
The Mandinka of Guadeloupe	159
The Hanging	169
The Revenge of the People	177
Petite Tempête	187
'Pickle 'em in Brine'	195
Retribution	205
The Loss of a Legend	213
The Homecoming	221

CHAPTER ONE

Santander

The imposing home of Commodore Daniel Winchip sat upon a rise above the Falmouth Quays. It was a square building of Cornish granite blocks with large windows on two levels and a solid roof of oak and Welsh Porthmadog slates. Above all that towered the tall chimneys, reaching skywards as if seeking to add height to the building. Creeping ivy had found its way to the upper floor, dressing the windows and moving imperceptibly upwards as if to attack the stone guttering. There was no ivy on the weather side, allowing dark green moss to cling to the granite and to the pile of stacked winter logs that grew with each passing year. The only ornamentation could be found in the portico, its white pediment surmounting the span of white columns, all of which gave shelter to the large, black oaken door and to the great brass lion's head that was the knocker.

'Santander' dominated the high ground and overlooked the whole of the Quays and the Carrick Roads, from the River Fal and the village of Flushing, to Pendennis Castle. The gardens climbed up to the house in terraces, the gravelled path zigzagging its way upwards among the flower beds. At the top, level with the house, was Poppy Meadow with its dew ponds and granite outcrops and behind that was the great field, worked to supply vegetables for the market. Beyond even that was the copse of Cornish Elm, Hawthorn and Elder, with an underbrush of hardy ferns and brambles, the whole having an aura of the mystic; fungus on shady boughs, dew ponds teeming with life and the pungent tang of decaying timbers – and the feeling that one was not alone. The place was unvisited but for the gathering of firewood; and had been for years and was looking to remain so. It had all been husbanded by Jonathan, the Commodore's ageing coxswain, a man who now lay in his bed, racked with pain and with a rasping and bubbling cough that gave mind to but a single thought – consumption.

Daniel Winchip opened his eyes to the new day, aware that Madeleine's head was resting on his shoulder. He looked down upon her with the same passion that had engulfed them both, before sleep had overcome them. Strands of her long black hair were entangled across her beautiful face and gathered between the contours of her small but exquisitely naked breasts. He saw, too, the ghost of a smile that lingered upon her relaxed features as if she were the sole possessor of a much coveted secret.

He looked upon her with a passion that made him draw breath and in the instant of expelling it he decided that this expedition with his squadron to the Americas would be his last. As it was, he felt lucky to be alive, the memories of moments past crowding into his mind; moments when death had seemed far more likely than deliverance.

'Of what are you thinking, beloved?' Madeleine rose lazily on one elbow, ignoring her own nakedness. 'Have you been long awake?' She pulled her flimsy nightgown lightly about her shoulder and shivered in the chill of the air, yet still smiling as he leant down to kiss her.

'No, my darling, just long enough to realise how much I love both you and our little Richard.' Winchip rose from the bed, removed his woollen nightcap and then reached for the large fire poker. With a slight shiver he disturbed the small coals until a bright flame made a solitary pirouette in the centre of the large grate. It was enough to offer the essence of heat; though the temperature changed not one jot.

'Daniel, it is snowing!' Madeleine pointed to the window. 'Look how it falls – and how steadily.' She looked at Winchip. 'There is no wind, my love, you cannot sail!'

Her joy may have been absolute; but her knowledge of the elements was sadly lacking. 'We have to do what we can, my love, even if it means towing the ships out of Falmouth to seek the wind offshore. Besides, when the sun gets up, so then shall come the chance of a wind. Warm air and cold, they never mix and the cold air always seems to get the upper hand.' Winchip plucked two small logs from the large wicker basket and placed them upon the growing flame. He then donned his blouse and breeches before taking the china jug from the washstand. 'I shall get hot water for your ablutions, my dear, for Beth will be busy, that is for certain.'

It had distressed Winchip that he had come home to find that Beth's husband, Jonathan was confined to his bed with a cough that seemed to have no end to it. He had called in the doctor the previous evening who, having examined Winchip's ailing coxswain, had only a sad shake of his head to explain Jonathan's obvious pulmonary consumption. He had recommended broth and bed rest, slipping Winchip's guinea into his pocket as he had stepped out into the dull red of the evening sun.

As the bedroom door closed behind her husband, so Madeleine laid full length on her back and stretched her arms above her head. She knew she should be sad, not only for Daniel's imminent departure but also because of Jonathan; and yet she deemed it far more important that she should make the most of the few hours that she and Daniel had left to themselves before he returned to his flagship, the sixty-gun Bellicus. On an impulse, she rose from the warmth of the bed and strode to the window that overlooked the slate roofs and smoking chimneys of the houses behind the Falmouth Quays. She also took in the grey stone tower with its four plain pinnacles that was the Church of King Charles the Martyr, where she and Daniel had been married more than two years previously. As she watched the snow fall lazily onto the terraced gardens that ran down to Church Street, so she remembered those early days when she and Daniel had drawn closer with every passing day – and those walks in the gardens where their love had been rekindled with cuddles and kisses on each of his homecomings, sometimes among the daffodils and then among the roses – and even once when the snow was falling as it was at this very moment. At long last, marriage had sealed their private pact.

With a shudder that was like the return of a forgotten fear, she remembered their first meeting on that early dawn, near the Island of Aix as she arrived on *Eaglet* with the horrid spy, Foche, now dead and consumed by the sea – but killed by whom, she had no idea; and neither would Daniel speak of it. The treacherous little man had taken advantage of her on that island, threatening to have her brother, Stephen, killed if she refused to yield to his evil desires. She had confessed it all to Daniel on the way to Gibraltar, on hearing that Foche was to make the journey with them. She shook her head in wonderment that Daniel had not only forgiven her instantly but had since made no mention of Foche, nor of the events that must surely have brought about the spies' terrible demise. Madeleine wiped a tear from her eye; a tear that laid claim to a confusion of feelings, all churning away at her insides, none seeking nor finding precedence one over the other. At this moment and for a few hours to come, she would have Daniel to herself – and that was enough. She turned to sit by the fire, now bright and giving out warmth, the logs crackling and spitting as if to chastise her for her moment of weakness. She dashed the terrible memories from her mind and dispelled her hatred in a moment, determined that, like her husband, she would banish the memory of Foche from her mind for all time. He would certainly not spoil her final moments with Daniel before he was once more gone to sea – this time to the distant Americas.

She found him in the study, once more making arrangements for a protracted absence, writing notes to the agent of Cox and Company, the new bankers of Albemarle Street in London, letters that would allow Madeleine to draw funds as and when she required. He looked up and rose to his feet as she entered; now wearing a light silk gown over her flimsy nightdress.

'Am I to be forsaken for the writing of a few letters, my love?' She melted into his arms, grateful for the sanctuary of his private study where no one entered unless invited; and for the warmth on her back from the flaming log fire. His hand cradled her breast and his lips pressed on hers with the same earnest desire of the previous night. Had it not been so obvious, she would have led him upstairs by the hand; for her loins ached and her knees were surrendering to a familiar weakness. She knew that her legs would have borne her no distance at all. Sensing her feelings, he lifted her up bodily in his arms and took her to the chaise longue, her squeak of protest lost in the moment and certainly not repeated. As he laid her down, so she stared into the smiling brown eyes of the man she loved so deeply, taking in his tanned face with its weather lines and his black hair, tied in a queue that lay upon his shoulder. As they came together, so she gave a deep moan and grasped him tightly, whispering words into his ear, feeling his breath warm upon her breast and never wanting him to stop, knowing that it would be many months before she could once more hold him in her arms with such perfect intimacy and whisper such words of blatant desire and encouragement as she was doing at that very moment.

The two carriers bundled Winchip's sea chest onto the hand cart and guided it down the winding path until they were but faint shadows in the falling snow. Master and Commander Peter Pardoe, Winchip's son-in-law, together with Winchip's daughter, Emma, had gone before them, clinging to each other as if every one of their last moments together was to be their last, down the gravel path to Church Street and along to Wynns' Coffee House. The bowed window of Wynns' Hotel projected onto Church Street like the quarter window of a First Rate, whereas the rear window offered up a view that encompassed the whole of the Carrick Roads. It was a good place for saying goodbye, when words of love could not be overheard above the loud and companionable chatter.

Winchip had released Jonathan's hand and had risen from the chair beside his coxswain's bed, well aware that he had been taking his last look at his old and faithful friend. No longer aware of his surroundings or able to speak; and with the racking cough tearing at his very insides and with the need to wipe blood continually from his chin, death could only be an hour away. Yet the tide deprived him from spending even that length of time with the man who had served him so well and for so long.

Winchip had also comforted Beth, Jonathan's wife of many years, expressing his sorrow at her loss and assuring her that 'Santander' would always be her home. It had been a conversation balanced between hope and the fear of uncertainty, yet he knew from Beth's tears that she understood the truth of things and was comforted by the fact that Jonathan would rest in the graveyard at the foot of the hill, as Winchip had arranged with the Reverend Walmsley.

In half an hour, Winchip's barge would be at the steps, alongside *Eaglet*'s jolly boat; a short time in which he had so many words of love to convey to Madeleine and yet so little to offer in the way of promises.

In the portico, Madeleine's sister, Alice, wished Winchip a safe voyage, at the same time reminding him to take care of her husband, Douglas Munro, now Winchip's secretary. She held little Richard up in her arms so that Winchip could kiss him – but the child found interest elsewhere as he stared in wonder and attempted to catch the floating snowflakes.

They sat together at the rear window of Wynns' Coffee House, Winchip and Madeleine, together with Pardoe and Emma. The glass panes of the window had long since become opaque in the dampness of the warm atmosphere. Their voices had need to be raised to be heard above the clatter of dishes, the scrape of chairs and the blasphemies of those who brushed snow from their coats; and those who demanded the door be hastily closed. The raging log fire in the great hearth of Wynns did more to encourage than dispel the vapours that rose from every quarter. Captains and officers alike, both Dutch and English from the packet boats in the shallows off Flushing, had exchanged their mails and now waited for slack water, each in his customary way.

'Shall you be in danger, my dearest one?' Madeleine almost whispered the words in Winchip's ear and her hand gripped his arm as if she dreaded the answer he would give.

'Danger is never far away, my dear – but take heart, for this time we are sure to be on patrol duties where danger seeks to avoid us. Smugglers, contravening the Navigation Acts, do not readily give themselves up; and slave ships, of which there will be plenty, seek only to reach their destination and deliver their human cargo before they have only skeletons to sell.' He patted her arm. 'I also have much to look forward to on my return, my love.' He smiled benevolently, knowing that all he had said before was lies. Before he could speak another word there was a sudden hubbub at the door and a chorus of abusive shouts.

Hellard and Pender entered together, two formidable coxswains, dusting the snow from their pea jackets in the open doorway, ignoring the shouts from those sitting in close proximity. Thus they waited, jeered at and threatened, as both captain and commodore, together with their ladies, wended their way towards the flurry of whirling snow that surrounded the two grinning petty officers.

Outside Wynns, Winchip gathered both Madeleine and Emma to his side, drawing his cloak about their shoulders to protect them from the snow. He looked into their enquiring eyes and smiled as he held them tight.

'Take care of yourselves; you are both very precious to me. Mind your steps on the return to the house, tread small and flat and you cannot slip.' With that, he kissed each of them on the cheek, spun on his heel and strode into the darkness of the 'ope' and then downwards to the quays and his waiting barge.

On board *Eaglet*, Master and Commander Peter Pardoe sat in the same depression in the stern seat that had comforted Winchip's posterior over the last few years. From that position he could see down the larboard side of *Eaglet* and, by virtue of that, have sight of all those who approached the entry port.

As one bell in the forenoon watch gave out its solitary ring, so Lieutenant Bowes, his first officer – and the son of an admiral – put his head round the door.

'One bell has just rung, Sir – and we have slack water!'

'Thank you, Mr Bowes – are the men at the capstan...'

'They are, Sir; the boats are ready to be swung over should the need arise; and their crews have been mustered.'

'Then have the anchors brought to short stay until we are ordered to depart, for you can be sure we shall be sent out ahead. I shall be up directly.' As Bowes disappeared, so Pardoe closed his journal. It would be a long time before *Eaglet* once again dropped anchor in these waters, just as he knew how long it could be before he saw Emma again. She had waved to him until he was out of sight, her white kerchief contrasting with the dark blue of her bonnet and cloak, now totally obscured by the snow and the great bulk of Winchip's sixty-gun flagship, *Bellicus*.

Winchip came on board *Bellicus* with due ceremony, the fife and drum band playing a catchy tune which he recognised but was unable to name. The presence of canvas hoses spread about the deck explained the absence of snow on the boat tier and guns. He expected that the work would continue once he was out of the way. For the sake of the musicians and the shivering marines, he quickly exchanged courtesies with Niven and the side party and then ushered the first lieutenant to the welcome overhang of the poop. He shook the snow from both his hat and his cloak before passing through to the great cabin with Niven close on his heels.

Booth, Winchip's manservant, brought out hot rum toddies and laid the silver salver on the table. The vapour rose from the tankards in the cold of the great cabin and the smell of the rum mixed with spices hung like nectar in the air.

'Thank you, Booth – a thoughtful gesture. Take what remains to your galley mates and remain there for a while.' Winchip sat down heavily on the stern seat and gestured to Niven to take a chair. The thought of taking his squadron of five ships across the Atlantic did little to raise his spirits. Like *Bellicus*, the two fifty-gun ships, *Cassius* and *Incensed*, would have little trouble, come what may. His worries were for *Eaglet* and for *Trial*, both sturdy craft and well manned; yet that would count for little in some of the mountainous seas that would surely rise to meet them. His fingers beat a tattoo on the table. There were times to *trust* in God and moments when one needed to feel the grasp of His hand.

'We have much to discuss, Mr Niven but time and tide have beaten us to it. Firstly we must find a wind and, if there is no wind to be found, then we shall tow the ships out of harbour with the beginnings of the ebb, we can do no more than that.' Winchip wrapped his hands round the toddy and stared from the quarter window. As he looked across towards Flushing, so he saw the surface of the sea shiver before his eyes, changing back and forth from silver lustre to blackness and back again in the blink of an eye. The shimmering effect on the water was painting imaginary channels the width of the Roads and the snow was now falling at a shallower angle. 'We have the beginnings of an easterly, Mr Niven. I'm damned if I'll not take that for an omen!'

'My word, you are right, Sir.' Niven looked across Winchip's shoulder. 'I had better attend to my duties…'

'So you should, James – but first, let us drink to a safe journey.'

They held their glasses high, each knowing in his own heart that luck or providence would play little part in what was to come.

The squadron had provisioned at Plymouth and had taken on spare canvas, each ship lower in the water than Winchip would have liked when all was said and done. He knew that he was echoing the fears and trepidation of a thousand captains before him, yet it left him feeling no better. He stared at the falling snow and saw that that, too, was easing, as though a curtain had been raised to hasten their departure. It was at that moment that the sun burst through the breaking clouds to bring a cluster of diamonds to the waters of the Roads and flashes of brilliant light that reflected from the compacted snow. Already, the vapours were beginning to rise from soaked timbers beyond the stern windows and the gulls were screeching in an endless chorus as they resumed their circling overhead.

CHAPTER TWO

'Enemy in sight!'

Commodore Daniel Winchip shivered as he sat at the large polished table in the great cabin of his new command, *Bellicus*. He had received the vessel – and a squadron to boot – at the same time that Admiral Boscawen had told him of his promotion from Post Captain to his new rank. Considering the number of Post Captains who were far more eligible and certainly more senior to him, Winchip had to assume it was as much to do with his last command, *Eaglet*, as it had to do with him. The thirty-two-gun frigate had served at the Battle of Minorca with distinction, coming to the attention of Admiral the Lord Hawke with the Western Squadron; and of late she had played her part at the Battle of Lagos Bay, following the orders of Admiral Boscawen.

As he closed his journal with hands stiff from the cold and replaced the quill in the silver writing tray, so he counted his blessings – yet, like all good things, the good Lord found it hard to dispense his bounty without making a charge for his munificence. He rang the small brass bell on his desk with gusto, pleased to see Booth, his manservant, appear like a cannon shot from his new – and larger – cubby hole. The ageing Booth had been with him for many years, yet still the wiry and diminutive sailor endured.

'Find me something hot, Booth – toddy or broth, it matters not.' He nodded his thanks to Booth's retreating figure, at the same time rising to peer through the increasing opaqueness of the stern windows. The notorious Canadian snow had stopped and in its place, sleet was driving across the turbulent wake of *Bellicus*. The sky was a murky grey and promised to remain so. Having left Gibraltar in mid October, sailing to Plymouth and then on to

Falmouth, he could expect little else now that the winter had set in and their landfall nigh. He felt his hair brush the deckhead as he turned back to the table, a hazard, even in a ship-of-the-line. Booth came from his cubicle with a steaming bowl of broth on a tray. Its provenance was uncertain – but by the gods, it smelt good. The knock on the door came before he could even take up his spoon.

'Enter!'

Second Lieutenant Guy Percival came into the cabin, bringing with him a draught of cold air. He was hatless and the front of his deck cloak was speckled with raindrops. His face glowed red from the wind. He looked first at the broth and then at Winchip. 'I am sorry to trouble you, Sir; but the wind is rising and Mr Niven requests permission to reduce sail, at the request of the master, Sir.'

'Very well, Mr Percival, if Mr Blackstock considers it prudent to do so, ask Mr Niven to act accordingly and inform the rest of the squadron with a general signal, if you please.' If *Bellicus* was feeling the blow, it was certain that the other ships would be feeling it the more so.

'Aye, Sir.'

Percival turned and was gone, the closing of the door leaving Winchip in peace once more. Percival had been one of Admiral Boscawen's aides at Gibraltar, looking to get to sea before the war ended; chasing the chance of promotion before it was too late. He had also taken a hand in strapping Foche's broken and blooded body to *Eaglet*'s tether, leaving the man sitting on the buoy with his smashed face nodding at the waves – all of it a gesture, implying that *Eaglet* had been responsible for the man's death before a trial could be convened by the admiral. Winchip found a wry smile; it may well have been true but it could never be proven. In any even, Percival was proving to be a good officer, confirming his first thoughts about the man.

Winchip devoured the fish broth with relish, the barley giving it substance and the salted fish its texture. He downed the French Chardonnay Burgundy in two gulps and dabbed at his mouth with the napkin. It was now time for him to go to his cot, the long box that acted for a bed – or his coffin should the occasion arise. He had given himself four hours before he would need to rise; to take the deck once more, in the forlorn hope that the weather had taken a turn for the better.

In his nightgown and with his woolly nightcap drawn down below his ears, he settled down to sleep. Booth would raise him for the second dogwatch, of that he could be certain; but he knew it would be a good half-hour before sleep overcame him.

His thoughts immediately turned to 'Santander', his house of stone that overlooked the slated roofs of the Falmouth Quays. With its great chimneys and large windows; and the three hectares of land that comprised 'Poppy Meadow' and the expanse of terracing that led down to the Church of King Charles the Martyr. It was now 'home' indeed. Alice, the sister of Madeleine, his wife, would now be well ensconced there and Emma, his daughter, would at last have good company with whom to pass the winter days. Emma's husband, Peter Pardoe, was now the master and commander of *Eaglet*, once Winchip's own command.

Winchip's thoughts turned to Madeleine with consummate ease, his beautiful and regal wife whom he had left behind with such reluctance. With closed eyes he could picture her olive skinned face, set in a frame of long black hair and with brown eyes that had such a depth to them. It was if she were with him now, lying at his side, glowing with that special countenance that spoke of both pleasure and happiness, just as she had done on the morning of his departure. He remembered too, their love making. It had been a torrid affair, gathering intensity as every moment sought to eclipse the last until, exhausted, they had lain together, unmoving and unwilling to move and joined as if only an act of God could pull them asunder.

Captain Peter Pardoe stood on the quarterdeck of His Britannic Majesty's thirty-two gun frigate, *Eaglet*, out of Rotherhithe in seventeen fifty-six; a forerunner to the 'Southampton' class frigates of the same year. Pardoe was wrapped in his deck cloak with a woollen muffler wound about his neck and lower face. The northerly breeze on the starboard beam had all the promised trappings of Canada in winter, one moment snowing and the next bringing needle-sharp sleet that brought a numbness to the face and hands. To this was added a continuous mist of freezing spindrift, coming across the bulwarks in a cloud, leaving a rime of frosty ice on cordage and timber alike, invidious and dangerous, akin to a boarding enemy, persistent and seemingly unstoppable. His feet danced a few steps where he stood as another deluge of foaming and freezing water swirled about his shoes, the scupper drains belching forth sea water from a vicious and choppy quarter sea. The sun was a pale orb on the weather bow, approaching its low zenith, appearing and then disappearing, embraced by a great halo, yet leaving no shadows and promising no warmth. It had been warmer in the great cabin, out of the wind but he felt the need to share the elements for a while with those who had no other choice but that of enduring it – his people.

In the tops, eyes were directed to the west and to the north, to where the English fleet under the command of Rear Admiral Charles Saunders would be guarding the mouth of the great St Lawrence River. Eyes were also to the south-east, to leeward, where signals could blossom out at any moment from the halyards of *Bellicus*.

Pardoe glanced astern, to where the two ships, *Cassius*(40) and *Incensed*(40), sailed unperturbed with angled yards, in line ahead and on a starboard tack. Pardoe had been comforted by their presence, always there, making a flotilla into a squadron, all under the broad pennant of his father-in-law, the commodore.

Pardoe turned his face away from the bitter wind and was glad of the momentary respite. He spoke directly to John Hartley, the eighteen year-old and sandy haired, second officer. 'Noon is nearly upon us, Lieutenant. Have the midshipmen muster for the master's lesson while we still have a sun for their sightings and a horizon from which to measure, if you please. When that is done, have the lookouts replaced once more.'

'Aye, Sir!' The newly appointed Lieutenant John Hartley touched his hat and quickly left the quarterdeck.

It had been a long and arduous westing from England, discovering on each clear noon just how far their preordained latitude of 45 degrees and 15 minutes had escaped them to the north, their drift to the south being so insidious. Each day they had beat back to the north knowing that on the morrow the whole process may have to be repeated. The journey had been particularly arduous for *Trial*, the sloop-of-war that was accompanying them, braving Atlantic storms that had been frightening in their ferocity. Her captain, Master and Commander Horace Culpepper, had done well to regain his station. Often, during a gale or caught in the doldrums of still water and sea mist, she had lagged behind or gone from their sight, only to come into view again with added sail as she recovered her track. The squalls had raced down from the north-west, one upon the other, riding the narrow Labrador Current, enveloping the sloop of war in rain of huge proportions that blotted her from sight, yet, when the squalls had passed, so she once more appeared on the horizon, undaunted and with her suit of sail complete.

It was well known that there were other dangers for English ships bound for British North America. In North American or Canadian waters, a large French force could be waiting for those who braved that latitude. Fortunately, this time, it would seem they had been lucky. Now, well into the Cabot Strait, the small island of St Paul lay off the larboard bow and the lookouts in the tops had been doubled, searching for the squadron frigate that would surely challenge them as they moved towards the mighty Gulf of St Lawrence.

'*Deck there, flag's signallin'!*'

Pardoe looked up to the tops and waved a hand in acknowledgment. Charles Dundas, the duty midshipman, would come down to him as soon as he had filled his slate. He knew what Commodore Winchip's signal would be now that they were approaching waters that could be controlled by the French or the English, dependent upon who held the seas at this critical time.

Midshipman Dundas came down to him at the run. 'The signal is to "take station ahead with all safe sail" and "remain in sight", Sir.'

'Thank you, Mr Dundas. Keep alert, young man and remind the lookouts that their sightings could just as well be French as English and that we require to be properly informed.' Pardoe had hopes for the new and strongly built midshipman, his abundance of black hair already tied in a queue. He was an addition to the ship's company, a sharp fifteen-year-old with great promise, finding his way to *Eaglet* whilst seeking a berth at Gibraltar. 'See that the signal is acknowledged, if you please.'

'Aye, Sir' Charles Dundas dashed away, his expression crowned by his usual frown of worry as he sought so hard for correctness in all things. Pardoe knew that the master's mate, Longdale, had heard the message and was already sending men aloft. Longdale was the replacement for Claridge, now gone with the commodore to *Bellicus*. The staysail booms came out with a rattle; and the new, square stays'ls crackled open in their turn.

'*Deck alow – frigate – away on the larboard bow – she aint signallin*''

'Up you go, Mr Archer and look for yourself. If indeed she *is* challenging, then send up our number and tarry a moment – she may give us directions, you never know.' Pardoe watched the fifteen year-old Godfrey Archer snatch the bunting from the locker and spring to the shrouds, as keen as mustard, his black widow's peak cleaving his forehead. Slightly built but as agile as a squirrel, he took the ratlines, the safer route in the cold and blustery wind.

The sudden activity was bringing the ship alive to events, as if the journey from England had been but a deep slumber from which they were now awakening. Pardoe knew otherwise but could find no better way to explain his feelings, so long and so arduous had been the crossing of the Atlantic, each mile a step further from both his home and his wife, Emma – Commodore Winchip's beautiful, raven haired daughter by his first marriage. His thoughts were interrupted as the burgeoning twelve year-old

Midshipman, the Lord Guy Pickering, ran up to him from the backstay and stopped with a jerk.

'Mr Archer reports, "enemy in sight", Sir – she is a French frigate, now making off to the west, adding sail and signalling as she goes.' Guy Pickering frowned, knowing full well what would follow.

'Inform the flagship, "Enemy frigate in sight, beyond Cape North – making signals to the west"; and then wait for the response from flag.' Pardoe's shoulders sagged. The thought of doing battle after such an arduous and debilitating journey did not sit well with him. His people were tired – no, exhausted – as recent gun practice had proved. The other captains of the squadron would soon be watching with mixed feelings and expectation, just as he was, staring through the glass at *Bellicus* in anticipation of the signals that would be exchanged between his command and the flagship.

The acknowledgement from *Bellicus* was not long in coming.

'Signal from Flag, our number, Sir. "Give chase, report numbers and 'ratings' and wait in sight for orders", Sir.' Pickering's eyes grew larger with every second as he related the lengthy signal.

'Thank you, Lord Pickering. Acknowledge – speedily, if you please.' Pardoe turned towards John Hartley, the second officer. 'Tell the divisional officers we may be going to quarters, Lieutenant.' To the master, he said. 'Proceed with all safe sail, if you please, Mr Ramblin.' Pardoe took in wind and compass, quick to realise that *Eaglet* was sailing seven points off the wind. 'Let us have the weather leeches off the t'gallants and sail 'full and by', Master; we shall be the faster for it!' He grunted as the master nodded his agreement.

Close hauled and with her yards well angled, *Eaglet* headed west by north, set to clear the headland and gain a sight of the French. As he watched, so the French frigate was blotted out by the land, yet he knew that *Eaglet* could sail no closer to the wind, no matter how sharp her yards were braced up. There was always the lee shore to consider and an increase in wind didn't bear consideration. He snatched a glass from the rack and went aft, to the taffrail. *Bellicus* had closed on them, now a mile distant, coming up to them with all speed with *Cassius* and *Incensed* following in line astern. He returned to the binnacle and replaced the telescope in the rack.

'We shall come about, Master, as soon as we have knowledge of the enemy.' Pardoe gave a wide smile. 'We are going to count them, not fight them.'

'I thank the Lord for that, Captain!' Mr Ramblin moved his clay pipe from left to right by articulating his mouth, allowing the wind to cause havoc with his white hair and beard, both of fine gossamer in the light from the background.

As *Eaglet* came onto Cape North, so the promise of a view of the whole of the Gulf of St Lawrence would be laid open before them. The wind could now be read by the travel of the sea and the white horses that were building from the north as if racing to escape from whatever chased them southwards.

Already, *Eaglet* was plunging among the white-caps, close hauled with the wind forward of the starboard beam. In his mind's eye he could conjure a fleet of French men-of-war awaiting them, their admiral's broad pennant streaming out to leeward for all to see. The cocky attitude of the French frigate had given birth to his dread; what lay beyond Cape North could confirm it.

'Top men up! Prepare to wear ship!' The young and lanky master's mate, Longdale, was in good voice, already hastening the topmen up the ratlines.

'Wear ship!'

Pardoe peered through the glass from the fo'c's'le, waiting impatiently for the western passage to be opened up to him, the high ground of the cape taking an age to pass astern. When it did, it was as with the sudden lifting of a theatre curtain, jerked away to reveal nothing but dark waters under an ashen sky. Then, as the Gulf of St Lawrence offered a view of her ankle, so he saw the frigate, the wind up her tails; and beyond were four ships-of-the-line, each of forty guns if he were not mistaken, four leagues distant and with the appearance of adding sail. Beyond them, two colliers, each ship rigged, were scrambling to do likewise. The whole scene smacked of ships in hiding; waiting until the English squadron had passed – but it was too late.

'Deck there, four ships-o'-the-line…due west…they'm French – and two beyond!'

Lieutenant John Hartley smiled and threw up a hand of acknowledgement to the lookout and then turned to Pardoe. 'A bit late; but you have your answer, Sir.'

'Indeed, we do. Have the guns checked and secured, Mr Hartley, a loose cannon is something we can do without, today.' Pardoe caught Mr Ramblin's eye. 'Bear away, Master – we have no more business here.'

CHAPTER THREE

'Hoist Battle Ensigns!'

Commodore Winchip paced the quarterdeck of *Bellicus* with sleepy eyes, knowing that the impatience he felt was futile and served no good purpose. He had seen *Eaglet* round North Point and since then the fo'c's'le bell had rung out twice. He was aware of the lee shore beyond the point and how easy it would be for an enemy to use it to advantage just as he was equally aware that his son-in-law would have to beat back beyond Cape North before he found a friendly wind. In the end he turned to face both the master, Walter Blackstock, and First Lieutenant James Niven.

'Signal to *Cassius* and to *Incensed*, Mr Niven, "form line of..."'

'Sir, *Eaglet* has rounded the point and is signalling.' Second Lieutenant Guy Percival regained his breath. 'She reports. "Four French ships-of-the-line, each of forty guns or more and two colliers beyond, all making sail" and "query slavers", Sir.'

'Thank you, Mr Percival, is she being pursued?'

'Not as yet, Sir, as far as we can tell; and she is well round the point.'

'Thank you, Lieutenant.' Winchip walked to the mizzen shrouds with his hands linked behind his back, tucked beneath the tails of his coat, knowing he would not be disturbed. That his son-in-law had given the precise ratings of the enemy was more than welcome, it was inspirational. Had they been Second Rates, then he would have been quick to announce it. Already, his mind was painting a picture; seeing events as they were most likely to unfold. He glanced up at the wind pennant and then at the run of the sea, his mind's eye telling him that in order to be best placed for what was to come, he would need to be to windward. He made a hasty decision and strode slowly back to the quarterdeck and spoke to Mr Blackstock in casual tones.

'Come as close to the wind as is safe, Master and beat up to the north on a larboard tack, if you please; and as quickly as you are able.' Winchip turned to Niven. 'Have the divisional officers spur their men on, Mr Niven. If we do not get to windward then things may not go well for us.' He smiled as Niven's eyes flashed in anticipation. 'Make a general signal for a larboard tack, James; seven points off the wind should do it – that should wake them up.

Niven grinned and turned away, grabbing at Costly as he paced towards the boat tier before sending a loblolly for his sword.

'All hands to wear ship – and smartly now!' Midshipman Paul Claridge, lately the master's mate on *Eaglet*, shouted through the trumpet at Mr Blackstock's bidding and then hung the instrument on its hook.

The whistles and shouts rang out, urging seamen to their masts as they gathered in their divisions, seamen and marines alike. The knowledge that the enemy was in sight had brought new life to the ship, whilst the general signal that rose in jerks up the gaff halyard brought fear to some and bewilderment to others.

Winchip watched as *Cassius* and *Incensed* came onto their new course 'full and by', each presenting a wall of straining sail. For a moment he felt arrogantly proud-hearted, almost covetous of his small squadron; but he knew he was being hasty. When this engagement was done with – then that would be the moment to count his blessings. He turned to Midshipman Claridge. 'Make a general signal, Mr Claridge: "Hoist battle ensigns", if you please.'

He continued watching, seeking that unspecified spot in the ocean where everything would change, for better or for worse. Cape North was sliding down the larboard side, moving from the bow to the beam, some two leagues distant; and still the enemy had not appeared. *Eaglet* had obeyed the general signal and was now well ahead, leaning from the wind, battle ensigns blossoming even as he watched. The cheer that rang round *Bellicus* did not surprise him. The huge ensigns cast fleeting shadows over the deck as they burst out, thudding and cracking, cavorting in the wind as if rejoicing to be free – for the first time, since Lagos Bay.

At last he had the measure of things. He scanned full circle with the telescope and then turned to Niven. 'The squadron will come into wind, Lieutenant and captains to the flagship, if you please – and with haste, lest we miss our chance.

The great cabin of Bellicus had been filling with arriving captains and masters, called there to hear the words of Commodore Daniel Winchip. As the chairs were pushed back to the hull, scraping noisily across the chess board of canvas decking, so the company stood before the great table. Winchip knocked on the polished oak with his knuckles and the cabin fell silent.

'I have called you here for a reason, Gentlemen. I can assure you that what I have to say is important and that it will be said without preamble and without recourse to discussion.' He let his words sink in, knowing he had their attention. 'We may shortly be engaging a superior French squadron and I am well aware that you will do your duty. However, having been at Minorca and knowing something about French tactics, there is much I can do to help us defeat the French. I shall be issuing orders as things progress and these orders *will* be obeyed instantly! I know, as do you, that there is the matter of the "Permanent Fighting Instructions" to consider, a standing order that I am about to cast to the winds, whatever the consequences.' He stopped there for a moment, seeing that their faces were aghast, yet still allowing them to take in what he had said. 'I am assuming that each master here is aware of the tactic of 'lasking', using 'a soldier's wind', one that allows us to sail directly down upon our enemy without the adjustment of a single yard.' Winchip grunted his approval as each of the three masters nodded towards him with understanding – and also to each other. Both Boyce and Nathanson looked at him as though he were mad. He stared back at them. 'If you fail to do my bidding you will see the rigging of your vessel torn asunder by the French – and on that you have my solemn word. They will wait for you to show your profile before they systematically dismantle you with their broadsides.' He let that sink in, hearing his own footsteps resound on the deck as he paced to the stern windows and back again. 'Every captain shall take his ship through their line, firing bar-shot into the fore-rigging of the one and round-shot through the length of the ship by firing into the stern of the other.' He looked at each in turn. 'Am I understood, Gentlemen?'

The master of *Bellicus*, Walter Blackstock, stepped forward a pace. 'We masters, the three of us, are aware and willing, even eager to comply, Commodore – but it is to our captains we must look for orders.'

'What say you, Captains – are you willing to carry out my orders?' Winchip swung round, staring at Boyce and Nathanson in turn.

'You have my support, Sir. I see penury staring me in the face; but, by God, you must realise the consequences of such an action, brilliant as it may be, in its concept.' Nathanson shook his head, surprised at his own frankness.

'My only thought is to win, Captain, as should be yours; and by any means possible.' Winchip looked pointedly at Boyce. 'What say you, Captain Boyce?'

'I shall consider your proposition, Commodore. The concept of blatantly defying the orders of Their Lordships at Admiralty does not sit well with me – and *never* will it!' Boyce stood abruptly and turned on his heel, nodding to his sailing master as he did so.

Winchip watched the captain of *Cassius* pass through the door to the quarterdeck, his sailing master close on his heels. It was with a mixture of anger and sadness that he indicated the others should do likewise. Winchip turned away and stared out of the stern windows, his hand beating on his thigh and remaining that way until the sound of retreating footsteps had faded into the noises of the ship.

Lieutenant James Niven stood at the binnacle of *Bellicus*, waiting patiently for the signal from the tops that would warn him of the presence of the French. With the ship sailing close hauled, 'full and by', the taut rigging was setting up a howl that seemed to transcend all other sounds.

The captains and sailing masters of the two Third Rates had long since departed, piped off ship as one departure, leaving the 'Spithead nightingales' and marines in disarray.

As the master returned from the captain's cabin, so Niven relaxed, yet it was another five minutes before the Commodore appeared and came down to him.

'Our course is west of north, Sir, wind out of the north and we are sailing 'full and by', the enemy to the west not yet in view.'

'Thank you, Mr Niven.' Even so, Winchip glanced at wind, course and weather out of pure habit. 'Shall they come out to us, Lieutenant, or go about their business?'

'They are a superior force, as their frigate has no doubt reported, Sir.'

'And the wind in their favour.'

Niven's eyebrows qualified his puzzlement. 'In their favour, Sir?'

'Remember Admiral Byng at Minorca, Mr Niven. The French were happy then to let us come up to them out of the south-west. An hour later, most of our ships were tattered in the tops with spars coming down like ninepins. If these French captains are of the old school, then they shall already know that we have come to windward – as usual.'

'The master has told me of your plan. Is that why you considered lasking, Sir?'

'If they come to us, then yes, I shall give that order and cut their line in three places, firing left and right. With good gunnery we should bring them to their knees.'

'It has a good ring to it, Sir.' Niven looked to the tops. 'It brings back memories of the past – a time when miracles seemed to grow on trees. I wondered whether your promotion would change you, Sir – but with respect, it hasn't.'

Winchip turned his face towards Niven. 'Then you approve?'

'*Deck alow – Five ships comin' around the 'eadland – and they'm French!*'

'You were right, Sir, damn me if you weren't! Niven snatched a glass from the rack and raised it to his eye. 'They've turned to

The Eaglet in the Americas

the south, Sir, the four Fourth Rates in line of battle and there is a broad pennant on the third ship. The frigate is to the north.' Niven leaned forward as if to obtain a better view. 'By heaven, they have gathered their mains! They have gone to battle canvas – they're challenging, Sir!'

'As I thought they would, James; and we shall not disappoint them.'

Pardoe lowered his telescope, seeing events as they transpired. He judged *Eaglet*'s distance from the stern vessel of the French line and dashed the glass from his eye. He turned to First Lieutenant Bowes, standing at his side. 'Come to quarters, Mr Bowes, we have a godsend, a fortuitous opportunity should we be given our chance.' Pardoe strode the width of the canted deck to Mr Ramblin who remained stoically by the wheel. 'Master, I would like to cross the stern of that last Frenchman and put a few shots through the length of her – can it be done and have we time enough?'

Mr Ramblin stared out to sea, across the army of white horses that continued their charge to the south. After a minute he raised his deep and booming voice, sufficient enough to transcend the noise of the ship going to quarters. 'With ease, Captain but you'll only get the one pass. When we come up into wind, after the event, the French will be beyond your reach.'

'Fair enough, Master, allow us time for the guns to be secured again and then give your orders.' Before Mr Ramblin could reply, Pardoe was gone, pussyfooting down the cavorting deck to catch Bowes at the guns.

Winchip stood with Mr Blackstock by the mizzen shrouds of *Bellicus*. 'We shall adopt a parallel course until we are half a league apart, Master; and then we shall wear ship in unison and go down amongst them.'

'A general signal will suffice, Commodore, now that they know what is required of them.'

Winchip gave a cynical nod and returned to the binnacle. Time was getting short.

'Guns are secure for the evolution, Sir; and the signal is bent on, though not yet raised.'

'Then raise it, Mr Niven, for that looks as much like half a league as it ever will and we are ahead of them.'

'Aye, Sir, I will indeed!'

Winchip watched as the general signal jerked up the halyard and then blossomed out with a rumble and a snap. Casting his eye to Nathanson's vessel, he thought for a moment that the order would be disobeyed. Then, with as much grace a forty-gun ship can muster, there was a flurry of action in her tops and the sprit of *Incensed* came round, her acknowledgement standing out proudly from the mizzen truck as if it were meant for the whole world to see.

Winchip clapped his hands. 'She makes a fine sight, Mr Niven.'

'Indeed, she does, Sir. Perhaps we should hope that *Cassius* does even better.'

'We should wear ship, Captain!' The voice of Mr Blackstock brought them back to the present.

'Then do it, Master!' Niven, his smile still lingering on his face, nodded his confirmation to an impatient Mr Blackstock.'

Winchip's face had lost its smile as he looked astern, to *Cassius*. The forty-gun Fourth Rate ploughed across the run of the white horses, sending up great waves of spuming water from her bows. Yet, still she maintained her course. Winchip was about to slap his hand down on the taffrail when he noticed a change. A flurry of activity in her tops and a heave on tack or brace had changed her profile. The great yards came round until her sprit swung slowly to larboard to confirm her proposed evolution. He heaved a great sigh, knowing in his heart that Boyce had made a decision that had been forced upon him by Admiralty Orders; a decision that might come back to haunt him when all was said and done. On the other hand, Winchip was surprised; and it was in that state of mind that he turned away. Boyce would not be led by the nose – that was for certain.

The French maintained their course and speed, a sedate progress under topsails, in line of battle with the broad pennant of a commodore plain for all to see. Each ship was leaning with the wind, not enough to draw them round but enough to give elevation to their guns – the equivalent of an extra quoin to despatch the chain-shot high into the rigging of the enemy they were about to meet.

The moment that *Incensed* wore ship, so Pardoe obeyed the general signal, knowing full well that *Eaglet* had not been foremost on Winchip's mind. He nodded to Mr Ramblin and on a signal to the master's mate, Longdale's voice roared out the required orders, his hands gripping the trumpet, watching results and chivvying the laggards along. *Eaglet* wore as if she were mimicking Nathanson, coming round to face the enemy with her own plan of attack.

Pardoe drew his sword and rested it on his shoulder. He marched the length of the larboard line of guns, his shoes crunching on the sanded deck, encouraging the captains to choose their balls with care, calling for the guns to be double shotted with balls chosen for their shape. It was too early to open the ports; but nevertheless, the double cordage was already being held by men determined that it would be done first time and done right. Others laid out the breechings, the five inch rope that would stop the recoiling gun in its tracks; and prepared the tackles, the two inch rope used to run out the guns – or stop the gun from running itself out in a rising sea.

Pardoe returned to the binnacle, glancing at sea, sail, compass and wind in one long sweeping movement. The French were drawing closer and already *Incensed* had opened her ports. The French did likewise, even as he watched the ship in the rear; the ship moving slowly southwards under tops'ls. She would receive *Eaglet*'s bounty, her guns never likely to find an angle to fire upon *Eaglet*, she being more intent on *Incensed* than a puny frigate.

The distance was three cables and *Cassius*, too, had opened her ports. Pardoe knew that the French would be waiting for the English to tack – an expectation that would be denied them. It was at that moment that the ship in the French van fired her broadside, a crash of thunder and a cloud of smoke that passed away to the south like an avalanche of powdered snow, yet Pardoe was unable to tell where her shot had gone as *Incensed* blocked any sight of events. He tore his eyes away and marched down to the twelve-pounder at the bow, where he turned to look towards the stern at the line of the *Eaglet's* great guns, his mind suddenly crowding with memories, few of them pleasant and most with abject horror.

'Open your ports!' Bowes voice had acquired a treble note. As the clatter of the ports ceased, so he shouted. 'Run out!'

Pardoe held his sword high. The rumble of the carriage wheels against the run of the deck was deafening; but it was the raised hands of the gun-captains that took his attention.

Pardoe shouted. 'Fire as you bear, lads! Drive the captain from his cabin!' The cheer warmed his heart and so it might. There would be few deaths on *Eaglet* today – unless fate dealt them a wicked blow.

The Frenchman was looming large, her guns run out; and as Pardoe watched, so she fired her broadside, as did the other two ships in the line. The foretops'l of *Incensed* shuddered and then split from top to bottom; but Pardoe had no time to watch. The frustrated Frenchman was on the larboard bow, a cable distant, with Eaglet about to pass through her wake. Pardoe could see her name in gilt, splashed above the window and below the great lantern that hung above her taffrail. It was *'Belle de Gironde'* – a name to be wiped from the French list, given the opportunity.

The bow gun fired and recoiled in its breechings, snapping the rope taught with a loud crack, jerking Pardoe back to events. The smoke seemed to loiter, choking and blinding until the wind carried it away. The second gun crashed out and the third followed. All down the line the guns roared, each shot raising a cheer. Pardoe wiped his smarting eyes and looked to the Frenchman's stern. What he saw appalled him. The stern windows were gone, as were the ornate frames, her gilded name and the big lantern. Yet, it was the smoke that attracted his attention, plumes of it, black and on the move, pouring out as though the whole ship were afire. Then, he saw the flames, licking out from the gap where the windows had been, the fire ferocious in its intensity. He watched in fascination, walking aft to maintain his view – until he was suddenly blown backwards by a huge explosion and a blast of hot acrid air.

CHAPTER FOUR

The Taste of Victory

Winchip judged the distance to the French to be less than half a league, telling him that the French could fire at any moment. They would be wondering when the English would wear ship and offer their profiles to the French guns, no doubt already loading with dismantling shot. How confounded they would be when the English passed through their line, firing larboard and starboard, one gun upon the next until their sterns would be turned to matchwood and their rigging into tatters.

Incensed opened her ports as he watched; and beyond Nathanson's vessel, *Eaglet* was flying, under full sail towards the stern of the Frenchman in the rear. How he wished he could be there, with Pardoe; but those days were over. He looked to larboard, his body still tensed, waiting for the inevitable. What he saw confounded and distressed him. Boyce had ordered his *Cassius* to wear to larboard; to present his side and the full weight of his guns instead of passing between the enemy ships. The fifty-gun vessel had her ports open the moment the turn was completed and, as he watched, so her guns were run out – but it was too late. The French line opened fire as one. The hum and whine of dismantling shot twisting through the air was akin to the sound of angry bees – and yet the tops of *Bellicus* had escaped any shot sent in her direction.

Winchip glanced down at the upper gun deck, gratified to see that Niven was in full control, as Percival would be with the eighteen-pounders on the deck below. The distance to the enemy had already been reduced to two cables and the wake of the French ships could be seen sparkling on the waters before them.

Having those moments to spare, he looked once more to *Cassius*, his anger rising within him as he saw the tattered sail and fallen foretopmast being dragged by its rigging alongside the ship, dragging the vessel round to face those who would be cheering at the ship's demise. Another broadside swept through the remnants of *Cassius*' top hamper like a tempest, further dismantling her maintopmast and smashing down her driver to collapse onto her poop and quarterdeck. Her broken mainmast stood like a rotten and stunted tooth, devoid of form and bedecked by her own maintops'l to give it the appearance of a bell tent.

Winchip would have dwelt upon Boyce's bullheaded stupidity were it not a blast of warm air that caught him unawares and caused him to stagger back and then trip over the whelps of the capstan.

Pardoe scrambled to his feet and retrieved his sword which was swinging to and fro, the point of the blade deeply embedded in the planking of the deck. Others were getting to their feet around him, scrambling to the bulwarks as the men on the lifts let the main yard drop swiftly to the deck. A dozen men dashed forward to douse or beat the line of flames that threatened to devour the whole sail. As Pardoe stepped briskly towards the quarterdeck, ignoring the throbbing pain in his back, he noticed Longdale was already giving orders, at the same time emptying the contents of a slow match tub onto the last of the embers with a triumphant shout. The master's mate stared at the charred canvas and ordered the spar raised on its lifts, the black edges of the sail casting charred and blackened scraps as it flapped in the wind.

'We thought you were dead and gone, Captain.' Mr Ramblin displayed a wide and rare smile that contorted his whole chubby face, so rare was the occasion.

Pardoe allowed the master a wry grin. 'We shall come about, Mr Ramblin; as soon as the guns are secured and we are well beyond that mess.' Pardoe stabbed his finger towards the wreck that now lay astern, enveloped in thin wraiths of smoke and licks of flame that looked certain to get worse. 'We shall beat to windward, Master, on a larboard tack and as close to the wind as you dare – we are of no more use to the squadron here.'

The ship's gunner, Mr Wellbeloved, had lost little time in seeing the guns secured. The warrant officer touched a forelock to his captain and was gone the moment Pardoe acknowledged him with a smile and a nod of thanks. Mr Wellbeloved was one of many who had survived in *Capable*, the only ship that had the commodore had not brought home. It had been during a reconnaissance of the inlets and river mouths of the French shore with the Inshore Squadron when the sixty-gun *Frenchman* had come out of the mist. The single ship engagement had seen both vessels stricken and without leeway, drifting apart to heal their wounds. *Capable* had been driven onto a sand bar to prevent loss of life and then burned to prevent looting by the French. Rescue had come later; and never was the sight of a friendly relay frigate greeted with such enthusiasm.

'All hands up to wear ship!'

As *Eaglet* came round, leaning from the wind, so Pardoe crossed to the starboard bulwarks and looked more closely at the damage done to the forty-gun Frenchman. The smoke was getting thicker by the minute and flames were now seeking to escape through her gun ports, licking at the open covers. Around her, a platform of timbers and spars, cordage and canvas, rose and fell with each shallow wave. Upon the nest of jetsam lay many bodies, spread out where they fell, some limbless and others with their clothes still smouldering on their unfeeling backs. As *Eaglet* came closer, so the horror gained clarity, made all the more horrific by the staring eyes of the dead, rising and falling with the oily swell in her lee until their dead weight allowed them to slip clumsily through the wreckage to the deep.

It was evident that one of *Eaglet*'s double shotted twelve-pound guns had struck the ship's hanging magazine. The bulk of *Belle de Gironde* was sinking slowly where she lay with the licks of flame still encapsulated within the increasing clouds of smoke that now poured from every orifice. She was settling like a broody hen onto her nest. Her headway was lost to her and already the seawater was pouring through her gun ports, denying those who tried in vain to use them as a means to escape. There was no hope for her, or for her crew. The water about her hissed as her flaming shreds of sail touched water and then – even that stopped. She went down a with a sucking gurgle and much blowing of trapped air, accompanied by the cries and screams of those few of her crew who hung to spars and other remnants of timber that had lost both their shape and their form, waving their arms and crying out in French for rescue. They passed down the starboard side of *Eaglet*, arms stretched out in a vain appeal, their plaintive French cries turning to screaming curses as the powerful English frigate passed them by. As Pardoe stood and stared back at the unfortunates he felt no remorse; not even pity for those who slipped beneath the waves as their wounds or the water consumed them, their curses still on their lips, unable to swim or too weak to hold on. He turned away with a shrug of his shoulders; there were others with a far greater claim on his services.

Pardoe checked wind and compass as a matter of course and, on looking to starboard through a glass, he was delighted to see that the French had been bested – their plan thwarted and the result for them – disaster. The sound of gunfire came to him from the starboard beam and he swung round to convince himself it was not directed at *Eaglet*. *Bellicus* sat on her reflection as if the battle had never been; and around her, ship's boats plied between *Incensed* and *Bellicus* like bumboats. Both ships appeared unscathed, save for *Incensed*'s tattered tops'l. Pardoe swung himself onto the mizzen shrouds and climbed the ratlines until he could see far beyond *Bellicus* to the south. Boyce's *Cassius* was a floating wreck, with not a stick above the mains. She was too far to the south to have cut the French line – and that was when Pardoe realised the terrible truth. Boyce had decided not to obey Winchip's order and had paid the price for his obdurate decision. There were holes in her that looked to be betwixt wind and water and others that had peppered her tumblehome and brought ruin to her bulwarks and nettings. Her ports were smashed and blood was already darkening the timbers below her tumblehome. The French ship that had done the deed, together with one of her companions, was drifting towards the shore, leaving a flatness of the surface of the sea that was their leeway. Already, English ensigns were flying over the French from their gaff halyards and boats containing the French officers were plying their way across the open waters to *Bellicus*. The French crews would be battened down by now and the scarlet tunics scattered about the ships gave rise to assume that the bullocks had taken charge. Of the colliers or the frigate, there was no sign; and it took little imagination to assume that they, too, had sailed close-hauled to Cape North and then free to westward with the quarter wind.

The fourth French ship had her tattered courses gathered and had suffered terrible damage in her tops. Pardoe assumed that she had come under Winchip's bar-shot and had been dismissed from the commodore's mind. The English ensign fluttered above her flag; and that was all that mattered. Forty of *Eaglet*'s crew had been taken off the ship to help man the prizes; and that, too, mattered. All in all, it had been a great victory against the odds; and would have been even better had Boyce not been so obstinate. For a moment he feared he might be speaking ill of the dead – but then, characters such as Boyce never endured. They, like their name, simply slipped into history – and from ones memory. Pardoe turned as Archer's voice interrupted his thoughts.

'Signal from flag, Sir: "Captain to repair on board". The midshipman's face was drawn and pale as he looked back at the stricken dead on their platform of detritus that was now too far away to discern whether any still lived.

'Stop gawking Mr Archer. Would you have us put men over the side to help those devils, when a French squadron could appear at any moment? Have a boat put over; and buck yourself up young man, the men in your division seek heroes, not mice.'

'Heroes not mice, Aye, Sir.' Archer drew himself up and strode manfully away to seek the boatswain, his expression giving no voice to his thoughts and his demeanour as inscrutable as ever.

The great cabin of *Bellicus* reeked of dampness and gun smoke and of sweat. Already the great guns and the accoutrements of war had been secured or stowed. Every chair was taken and the only face missing was that of Post Captain Boyce. Booth was distributing welcome glasses of mulled wine. The moment Booth disappeared into his galley, so Winchip held up a hand for silence.

'Gentlemen, may I congratulate you all on a great victory today? At the same time, I regret to tell you that Captain Boyce has died of his wounds. As it was impractical to prepare him for a return to England, I have just committed him to the deep from *Cassius*. His passing will be a great loss to our squadron, as will those others of our people who died today.' Winchip coughed and gathered himself together, giving any of those present who considered his actions regarding Boyce were unfair, the impression that he had just unburdened himself of a fearful conscience. 'We shall make what repairs we can, at sea. I wish to find Admiral Saunders at the earliest opportunity in order to receive my orders and deliver our prizes. Those men chosen from other ships to work the prizes will remain with them until we have met with the St Lawrence Squadron.' Winchip let his eyes roam round the faces before him. 'We won a battle because I broke the rules, gentlemen. My report shall contain the truth of matters and you shall not be held to blame – and on that you have my solemn oath.'

The low murmur of grateful acknowledgement gave him a hint of satisfaction. Whereas they had followed him once, it seemed hopeful that they would do so again.

Winchip made his way down to the cockpit and the orlop, where he knew that the ship's surgeon, the sharp featured Mr Lockheart, would be busy. He had seen four seamen taken below; but that might not have been the total number who had received wounds on *Bellicus*. He went forward by the light of three glims and already the moans and the curses were reaching his ears. The danger had been more from splinters than high flying shot; but he, as well as any captain, knew that splinters took a heavy toll. He came onto the orlop with his hat beneath his arm, his other hand staying those who would rise on sight of him.

The surgeon was wiping his hands as a man was carried away to a corner with fresh bandages round his head and upper arm. As Winchip came under the light of two lanterns, so Lockheart offered him a hard stare.

'If a battle is to be measured by its wounded, Commodore, then you have made a poor fight of it; just four this time – and one with the loss of his leg.' Lockheart pointed to the offending article, white and unreal, the toes of the foot curling upwards, thrown into a dark corner, beyond the eyes of those still awaiting their fate.'

'I came down here because I care, Surgeon – and I'll thank you to keep a civil tongue in your head. What is the count and how many dead?'

For a moment Lockheart was stunned. In a more civil tone he said. 'Four have bad splinter wounds but will live. I have just removed the leg of the fifth and his fate is in the hands of God.' The surgeon nodded towards the opposite corner to the one taken up by the leg.

Winchip went over to the bulkhead and saw the man lying on a straw palliasse, his eyes closed with his arm stretched across his face as if he had no further use for his body or for the world. Winchip realised that it was for another reason than that. The man was crying silently, the tears coursing down his cheek – and he wanted no man to know of it.

'I shall leave you to it, Surgeon, they are obviously in good hands.' Winchip turned and was gone before Lockheart could utter another of his curt replies. It was as he came up onto the deck through the main companion that he realised he hadn't noticed the seaman's stump, where that morning it had been a leg.

Eaglet beat northwards in clear water the whole of the next day. Close hauled, she had progressed towards the St Lawrence on a starboard tack, the damage done by the explosion having been hastily repaired at sea. At latitude forty-six degrees and thirty minutes, the Labrador Current that had sought to put them onto Breton island, had left them. It had eased with a suddenness that gave Pardoe the impression it had simply cast them away - given

The Eaglet in the Americas

them up as a shark would disgorge a blow-fish. In the absence of the current, so the wind had backed to northerly.

Pardoe, wondering if the wind would ever become conducive, looked across to Mr Ramblin. 'We will wear ship, Master – due west, if you please.'

As the pale orb of the morning sun rose in the east and cast its bright tentacle in *Eaglet*'s direction, so Pardoe strolled to the taffrail where a seaman hurriedly touched his forehead before removing the last stern lantern. Now, they were plying north-westwards, directly towards the great river that was the St Lawrence with the wind on the starboard beam. To the rear, a mile distant, Winchip's squadron kept pace, the prizes in the centre, clear for all to see.

'Excuse me, Sir; we have been challenged by a squadron frigate.' Archer stood erect at Pardoe's side, trying to disguise his shortage of breath with the journey from the tops.

'Thank you, Mr Archer; send up our number and then inform flag, if you please. Pardoe's shoulders sagged with relief at the news, having been tempered by the knowledge that another confrontation with the French could even yet be joined.

The newly promoted Second Lieutenant Hartley held the glass to his eye as the challenging frigate remained at her station with reefed tops'ls, no doubt seeking to inspect the newcomers, fresh from England, as they passed her by. As *Eaglet* eventually passed down her larboard side, so Hartley saw her ensign dip smartly and then recover – surely a gesture of welcome. A moment later a signal gun commenced the salute to the commodore's flag.

'The frigate has dipped her colours, Sir!' Hartley shouted to the quarterdeck in general.

Pardoe heard Hartley's shout and turned to the lieutenant. 'Dip ours in response, Mr Hartley – sharply, if you please!' Pardoe raised his glass and stared at the frigate, noticing at once how salt stained was her hull. Also, she was newly painted with black stuff from the waterline to her bulwarks, glinting in the sunlight where the salt had not found her.

So, they had arrived at last. Somewhere out there to the west, beyond the sea mist that was beginning to blur the horizon, would be the mighty land of Canada, cloaked in pine trees so it was said, some as tall as a church steeple.

CHAPTER FIVE

Rear Admiral Charles Saunders

In the first grey light of dawn, Commodore Daniel Winchip sat in the stern sheets of his barge as it coursed swiftly through the off-shore waters that were now shrouded in mist and as still as a mill pond. Above the squeal of leather on thole pins as the oars worked in unison, the raucous screech of 'keow-keow' rent the air as the huge black-backed gulls swooped for scraps across the calm leeward waters of Rear Admiral Saunder's anchored fleet.

Winchip wore his new dress uniform and the two-hundred guinea sword, the glittering weapon awarded to him by Their Lordships at Admiralty in recognition of events at the time of Minorca. The sword lay openly across his lap, more for safety than ostentation. Munro, Alice's husband and Winchip's secretary, sat across from him, attired in smart walking-out clothes.

Winchip looked upon his oarsmen with a degree of pride – men who, not an hour since that moment, had been busy in the tops or employed elsewhere, dressed in coarse canvas waistcoats or woollen shirts, ducks and petticoats. Now, each was garbed in a smart suit of dark blue trousers and a jacket, together with a blue and white shirt, striped athwart the chest. Winchip had been quick to notice how the uniform had brought a sense of pride and a proud stiffness to the backs of those men chosen to man his barge. Though, truth to tell, the barge itself was no more than a pinnace with a touch of panache.

Winchip winced as his new coxswain, Pender, shouted the response to the challenge from *Neptune*, the Second Rate ninety-gun ship of Rear Admiral Charles Saunders.

As Winchip came up onto the main deck of *Neptune*, a smile came to his face on hearing the ostentatious presence of a fiddle, fife and drum band that took up a tune the moment his head rose above the deck. The trill of the pipes prompted him to raise his hat, deferring to the band and the salute from the marines and boatswain alike. He removed it once more as Admiral Saunders stepped forward to receive him, the fresh complexion of his face defying his advancing years; and yet wreathed in smiles.

'Welcome on board *Neptune*, Commodore.' Saunders glanced away from Winchip and gave Munro the most cursory of nods.

'Thank you, Admiral.' Winchip's smile brought deep creases to the swarthy Hispanic look of his skin and a twinkle to his dark brown eyes. His only prayer was that his queue of jet black hair was not lying on his shoulder with its black ribbon dancing in the wind as it was wont to do. 'It is a pleasure to be here and to meet you, Sir. My name is Winchip – I doubt I am yet even gazetted – and this is Mr Douglas Munro, my secretary.' He liked the admiral's face – it had a bright awareness to it, despite the short periwig that protruded from beneath his splendid gold-laced hat. He and Munro followed in Saunder's steps to the great cabin.

Winchip saw nothing in the place beyond that which he would expect. The tang of pitch and black stuff was in the air as usual, as was the whiff of beeswax and lamp oil. He took the proffered seat and placed his hat upon the large polished table and then unhitched his sword, accepting with alacrity a glass of claret from the steward's silver salver that flashed in the light from the stern windows. He had declined the offer of tea, which he had always found to be obnoxious.

'How was your journey, Commodore, not too wearing, I hope?

'It was tiresome, Admiral and somewhat stormy but little beyond that. Two days of repairs and 'clean ship' would not go amiss, unless your need of us is urgent.'

'As to be expected then – and of course you must put yourself to rights.' Saunders nodded to the flag lieutenant who occupied a chair by the door, scribbling feverishly in his 'vade mecum'.

The Admiral then wrapped both hands round his tea-bowl and sipped at the contents with relish. Almost with reluctance, he lowered the dish and shook his head, looking Winchip squarely in the eyes. 'I have no use for you *here*, Winchip.'

Winchip was shocked. 'But that cannot be possible, Admiral – my orders and…and the despatches?'

'They are no longer of importance, Commodore. Quebec was taken on the thirteenth of September.' Saunders rose from his seat, beckoning Winchip to stay seated. He strolled to the stern windows as if using the moment to gather his words. 'It is no reflection upon you, Winchip, my word upon that. Their Lordships continue to act as if my last despatch holds good for three months – a month to get to England and a further month in discussion; and then there is the matter of a further month until your arrival.' Saunders turned slowly on his heel. 'We have *won*, my dear Winchip! In three months from now there could be a daisy-chain of victorious English ships on their way back home, you mark my words!'

'Well, that *is* good news, Sir!' Winchip held his tongue lest he showed his anger. He was aware of the difficulties that had faced the English, in that Quebec would be a hard nut to crack with its fortifications and the natural barriers, such as the mighty St Lawrence River and the precipitous cliffs through which it flowed. 'I am compelled to ask how it was done, Sir, having studied the terrain myself – from the news sheets, I hasten to add.'

'It was done, my dear Winchip, by scaling the cliffs from Fuller's Cove by means of a meagre track. Four and a half thousand troops scrambled up there, two abreast; and God help he who faltered – and two brass cannon came up behind them, pulled up by our navy lads, God bless 'em!' Saunders face suddenly became serious, almost embarrassed at his own excited outburst as he mentally re-lived events. He shook his head from side to side. 'We lost a great man, Winchip. General Wolfe was given the task of taking Quebec and for his pains he was taken by two balls in the body, shedding half his blood and guts on Canadian soil. He died soon after the event but I thank God he was told of his great victory before he breathed his last.'

'He will be a great loss, Admiral.' Winchip dropped his head for a moment and closed his eyes in a second or two of genuine sadness. It was cruel that good news always had to be tempered by bad. England would have received news of the victory, the rejoicing only to be cut short as the death of Wolfe became known. He changed the subject lest they dwelt upon it. 'What about the French, Sir, are they now finished – or have we indeed arrived too late?'

'They have moved upriver to Montreal in a disorderly fashion, where they appear to be regrouping. They *may* make a stand there – in fact it is almost a certainty. A large group, numbering two-hundred or even more, escaped to the south.' Saunders gave a tired sigh. 'Another group, all French deserters, have fled towards the coast, looking for a vessel in which to escape, I'll warrant, although their numbers are no more than fifty, I am informed. We cannot afford to have half a battalion of armed French soldiers wandering loose in the vicinity, yet it will take a regiment to pursue and capture them.'

Winchip held up his hands in despair. 'It is not exactly a naval matter, Admiral but if you think we can be of any help, you know you have only to give the order.'

'I know that, Commodore; and I thank you for it. General Amherst has a great strategy in mind for the capture of Montreal when the time comes, something about attacking on three fronts with General Murray coming down from the north, Brigadier Haviland coming up from Lake Champlain and Amherst, himself, from the south. He will need all the troops he can muster to execute his plan and it leaves precious few men for the defence of Quebec should the French gather enough men for a counter attack.'

'My squadron could readily apply itself to a defensive line across the St Lawrence, Sir, without a doubt – and their guns to boot.' Winchip enthused to the idea even as he spoke. 'A thousand men would not go amiss, that I'll warrant!'

'Indeed, they would not, Commodore; but there is much to be taken into consideration. There are diseases on this station and I, for one, would not countenance the loss of three ship's crews through scurvy, dysentery, typhus or desertion, at a time when we have no idea if, or whether, the French will attack. Many of our men have hardened to those diseases – better they keep them to themselves methinks – and as to desertion, should you loose sight of a man then he is gone forever, for you will never find him in this land, Commodore and that, *I'll* warrant!'

Winchip could not gainsay the wisdom of Saunder's words, even if they did end with a hint of amusement, just as he was aware of his own naivety and lack of local knowledge. As he could find no answer to Saunder's logical and undeniable argument he kept his mouth firmly shut.

'So, there you have it, Winchip. While you are here you will need to be victualled and your ships cleaned at the very least. At Louisburg, the dockyard is hard pressed, with ships waiting a month to be refitted. In short, your squadron would be surplus to my needs and somewhat of a liability and, if that shocks you, then you have my sincere apology.'

Winchip was stunned, quickly recalling the long cold days and nights during which they had struggled gainfully to make speed towards their destination – and all for nothing. He kept the bitterness from his words.

'I shall await your orders then, Admiral. If we might be allowed to provision at Louisburg before we return, I would be most grateful.'

'Of course you shall provision, Winchip. I shall see to it that you have my authority.'

Winchip was about to rise from his seat when the flag lieutenant gave a meaningful cough. Saunders spun round from his position by the stern windows.

'What is it, Mr Hornby?' There was a hint of annoyance in the Admiral's question.

'There is the matter of the missing Guinea-ships, Sir.' It was more of a question than a statement, said in a manner that indicated a task that someone else had found distasteful.

Saunder's hand flew to his mouth. 'Well, I'll be damned!' He turned to Winchip as if the idea, whatever it might be, had suddenly become his own. 'There is one possibility that might keep you here, Winchip, though you may not care for the task.' He turned to the lieutenant. 'More claret, if you please, Mr Hornby! Commodore Winchip and I have much to discuss.'

The three captains and Winchip sat haphazardly round the six legged, polished table of *Bellicus*. The blackness of the stern windows gave a feeling of confinement to the great cabin with only the reflections of the lamps to give the glass substance. The meagre warmth in the cabin emanated from the bodies of those present. Smoke drifted below the deckhead and the sniff of brandy had become part of the heady atmosphere. Winchip had not felt so snug since they had left England and he was in a mind to let things be. He laid his brandy glass on the naked table and wiped his mouth with his napkin before tapping the glass with a spoon.

'Gentlemen..,' he waited until he had their attention, '...there was a moment today when we were about to be told to heave up our anchors and return to England, unwanted and a burden to our hosts.' Suddenly he had their rapt attention. 'Under the circumstances of England's victory here, as we have just been discussing, I think I would have issued that order myself, just as Vice Admiral Saunders had a mind to do.' Winchip relished the look on their faces as they perceived there had to be better news to come. Culpepper's pipe draped from his lips and his tipsy eyes were as wide as crowns as he stared into space. 'As it is, we are ordered to depart – but upon a different mission. We are to proceed to the south, to investigate the disappearance of several Guinea-ships bound with their cargo of slaves to the sugar islands, Havana and places in Florida.' Winchip sipped his brandy as the cabin resounded to the voices of those who were already in warm southerly waters, giving great expectation to the unknown.

It was at that moment that he realised he had been given a task that had become anathema to Rear Admiral Saunders, tied down with Quebec and now wondering what the French would do next. The man had too much on his plate as it was. Winchip had been given the order meant for others, of that there was no doubt. He gave a wry grin. What he knew about slaves he could print on a thimble.

'At least we shall be warm, by George!' Nathanson rapped the table with his bony knuckles, followed by the others in quick succession.'

Winchip grinned and let the din continue for a moment. At last he raised a hand. 'You shall not be surprised when I tell you that most of the shipping hereabouts is slave traffic. The Navigation acts as we understand it, deny trade with the Americas by any country – other than the Dutch, I hasten to add. It is safe, therefore, to assume that the ship you see on the horizon is, likely as not, a slaver. 'Winchip peered down at his written orders to refresh his mind. 'Rear Admiral Saunders requires that I search and eventually report my findings and that I make every attempt to recover the missing ships and apprehend those who stole them. My orders are explicit, Gentlemen, however – Rear Admiral Saunders made it very plain to me that our overriding task is to sink all things French; and that is what we must keep uppermost in our thoughts. We shall sail at first light, with *Eaglet* remaining on the inshore station to windward…for the present.' Winchip glanced at Culpepper, 'And *Trial* shall remain to seaward.' Culpepper lowered his eyes as if he had been expecting nothing less. 'We shall hopefully provision, scour the casks and water at Louisburg, giving you an opportunity to make and mend and clean ship according to your needs. From there we shall call in at Boston to deliver despatches to the Navy Office.' Winchip pushed his chair back and stood. He saw no reason to mention that it would also be an opportunity for him to visit his agent, Seth Burke and enquire after Stephen, his wife's brother. Stephen had sided with the spy, Foche, under the threat that Madeleine would be killed if he refused to assist the little Frenchman. Winchip had rescued

Stephen from Foche's clutches and, to avoid his being arrested, had sent his brother-in-law from Gibraltar to Burke at Boston, in a fast trading vessel.

As the captains rose in unison to a clatter of chairs, so Winchip nodded to Booth, allowing his ageing manservant to bring out the cloaks and hats, piled like a mountain in his small but wiry arms. Winchip opened a stern window a mite to release the stifling air before following his captains out onto the quarterdeck to see them from the ship.

When Winchip returned to his cabin he yawned involuntarily. He had every reason to hope that he would be in his cot within minutes, where even God would have trouble in waking him.

Pardoe took another sip of his commodore's finest French Claret as Winchip tried to outline *Eaglet*'s role in what was to be their first task on the Americas Station. Through the open deck light, the sound of the ship's victuals being swung inboard left little space for speech. The occasional thump of a victualler's hoy against the hull of *Bellicus* brought a wince from both of them.

Bellicus lay at anchor, fore and aft, in the harbour mouth at Louisburg, together with *Incensed*, positioned beakhead to stern so that no ship of any size could proceed into the harbour without leave. As a further threat, all gun ports to seaward remained open, giving air to the lower decks and relief from the unexpected warmth of the day. As his father-in-law had said, the harbour appeared to be ripe for an attack and he was already well aware that the French were not yet done with. Pardoe watched the gig and jolly boats of the other two captains separate as they returned to their ships. He smiled as the rakish figure of Culpepper bobbed up and down in the stern sheets like a fishing float as his gig plied though the choppy shallows. Beyond Culpepper, the low wooden houses along the Louisburg Hard appeared as one long dwelling, built so close to each other as they were in the limited and valuable space. Besides the few red-brick buildings, only the warehouses stood above the mass, their shingle roofs reflecting the brilliant sun. The calm sea seemed to be sprinkled with jewels that glittered anew with the passing of every shallow and oily swell. Ships were at anchor and small vessels plied between them, leaning from the wind, intent on their daily business.

CHAPTER SIX

Boston and a Bad Business

The morning sun was well up in the azure sky to the east, bringing with it a heady warmth that cheered the heart, drying out canvas and timbers alike and frustrating the low hanging mist, bringing annoyance to those who cast pails of water across *Eaglet*'s decks while the rasp and scrape of the holystones continued without end.

Deep into the great basin that stretched from Cape Cod to the settlement of Gloucester, *Eaglet* and the two great ships that were with her lay in the almost empty naval anchorage, before the hard at Boston, open to the sea and with few defences. A signal from *Bellicus* had sent Culpepper back out to sea in *Trial*, no doubt satisfying Commodore Winchip's need to have eyes where they would matter most. To the north lay two East Indiamen, one Dutch and the other English and to the south, lying together as if seeking safety in numbers, were three armed single decked ships, each under the same 'letter of marque' and showing the Portuguese flag as a canton in the upper quadrant next to the staff. To Pardoe, through the glass, they warranted nothing but a nodding awareness, though he assumed they were escorts for the slavers. Only the eight menacing gun ports in the line of each of their strakes held his interest. The smell that was coming up from the southern shore on the warm breeze had the tang of sweat and the stench of faeces in it, though from which vessel, he had no idea, though he would wager it was the stench of slavers and all that that implied. He took the glass from his eye. The only ships to the south were whalers, benign and clear for all to see. He knew then that there must be vessels beyond his line of sight – some of them slave ships for certain.

'*Deck there, Commodore's barge approaching!*'

Pardoe saw Bowes acknowledge the call and then found the commodore through the glass. He knew he had five minutes to find his new hat from his trunk and buckle on his sword. He afforded himself a smile to think that he and the commodore would be going ashore in street clothes, as would Hellard – a fine looking bunch, bobbing towards the hard in the Commodore's fine barge.

To Winchip, Boston Harbour appeared to be a busy place that had the appearance of being set apart from the mainland. The great marshy area of reeds and mud flats to landward in the south gave rise to the question as to how the harbour and mainland were linked. The lush green fields in the distance beyond the town and the sparse forest with its sea of tree stumps before it were as a backdrop to the mess of buildings that fronted the hard and beyond. Warehouses, shipyards, the Excise House and other important buildings dominated the frontage of timber-clad earthen wharfs, timber quays and slipways. Behind the trading edifices lay the houses of the bourgeoning town, interspersed with church spires of various denominations, reaching up as if to escape the loitering smoke from the multitude of chimneys in the early morning air.

The anchorage was large enough, with 'House' tethers clearly marked as to ownership. The shallows, too, were marked by old and anchored casks, each painted in buff and with a tattered red flag prominent on a staff. In deep water, two tea-ships sat proudly together as if they had arrived in company, while a newly arrived whaler sat alone, her decks being washed with sea water that gushed through canvas hoses. There were other ships, mostly benign, as if waiting for a cargo, or held slaves, waiting to be landed or to be shipped.

Further into the harbour, a mighty earthen and gravelled timber wharf sought to reach out to sea, so long did it appear; and was, even now, crowded with workers, bent on increasing its length. On the wharf, houses had been built with a planned regularity, one after the other in a great line, the whole seeking to form a barrier that denoted the inner harbour from the outer.

The inner harbour – for indeed, that was what it was close to becoming – appeared to be charming from a distance. The red-brick houses were interspersed with those of stone; houses whose whiteness glared their importance above all others. Among the houses were dispersed a number of large deciduous trees that would throw many dwellings into a pleasing shadow come the spring and gave substance to their being. Timber buildings to the north stood out as warehouses, their shingle roofs reflecting the rays of the sun. This whole backdrop enclosed the busy harbour itself, which was long if not large, yet still filled by a press of bumboats, wherries, luggers and punt-ferries that criss-crossed between shore and shore and ship and shore. They even traversed the gaps between the protruding timber piers spread along the hard, hiding even that from those who approached by water. A small barquentine lay just inside the harbour environs, her fore main yard swinging inboard as she loaded for sea. Further south, weeded and tidal marked, appeared the only stone mole in sight. A sloop of war, her canvas furled and in gaskets, lay against it in quiet solitude. She bore no flag and no pennant betrayed her house or origins. Her name was *Céleste*.

Sitting complacently in the stern sheets of the barge, Winchip hoped that Stephen had kept his promise. His brother-in-law had given his word that he would stay in Boston under the eye of Seth Burke until such time as his return to England would be unnoticed. Burke and Winchip had met in England many years previously. Although the man had not impressed him, his honesty in monetary matters had seemed good enough for Winchip's fellow officers and that had been sufficient.

'The steps are approaching, Sir!'

Pender's warning jerked Winchip upright. He secured his sword and gathered himself. His coxswain had chosen the long, Custom House wharf and he had no reason to contest his choice.

'Easy oars...toss oars!' Pender's curt commands were timed to perfection, allowing the barge to glide up to the slippery and weeded stone steps without so much as a bump.

'Thank you, Coxswain.' Winchip looked the man in the eye. 'Nobody is to go ashore, Mr Pender, trusted or otherwise.' With an assuring nod from Pender, Winchip climbed the steps with care then placed his feet firmly on American soil.

After walking the length of the long wharf, it was but a short step to reach King Street. The clatter of carts and iron shod hooves over the cobbles was joined by the cries of the vendors, heard above all else. Shops and stalls abounded and the raised and cobbled sidewalks were crowded to capacity, speckled by coloured parasols in the morning sun. The large houses were grandiose, with small verandas and large windows, similar to those that could be seen in London, looking down on the plebeian traffic with distain. The traps of the gentlefolk worked their way along the wide street, each to the right of the road; some with an attendant black boy, gaily dressed, trotting barefoot at its side. Near the junction, in front of the tall water pump, a small troop of English dragoons allowed their mounts to slake their thirst at a long wooden water-trough to the side of the road. Guzzling greedily, the horses' tails lazily swished away the flies in orchestral union.

Buildings that were of brick seemed to be of the modern English vernacular style, imposing themselves among the lesser dwellings with their windows of large square panes, in frames of timber that were less heavy and painted white – or black – against the red brickwork. On the roofs were Welsh slates as opposed to shingles; and gutters that led to the end of the building to discharge their contents to the side of the house.

The premises of Seth Burke were not hard to find. A large shingle hung from brackets on a protruding beam that was driven into the wall and denoted in four lines the business of: 'S.Burke/AGENT/to/His Majesty's Navy. The shingle swung with an interminably loud squeaks in the light wind that fanned the length of the street. Prominent and grand, the sign may have once been but, facing the prevailing weather the chocolate brown of the base-paint and the once gold lettering of the wording had faded enough to render it almost unreadable.

The old two-storey dwelling was timber framed and uninviting, with a large padlocked gate of vertical planks attached to the side of the house, conjoined with the next dwelling as if that, too, were owned by Burke. The heavy door that was wedged-open beneath the sign gave the impression that much toing and froing was expected – or that it was to be a hot day.

Winchip stood at the door and, indicating that the others remain outside, he strode into the gloom of the interior. Even in the bright shaft of light from the window there was dimness within the large room. Dust hung in the sunlight from the unwashed windows and papers in many forms abounded on shelves and a table, as well as on a large desk set against the far wall – all scattered as if discarded. At a tall and far more meagre desk, placed in the path of the sun's weak rays, a man sat upon a tall stool and remained scribbling, his feet doubled beneath him to allow the heels of his shoes to hook onto a rung. He raised his head and squinted hard at Winchip, a stranger, standing with the light behind him. At last he spoke. 'Can I help you, Sir?'

Winchip recognised Stephen immediately. 'Yes, Stephen, you *can* help me. I am looking for Mr Burke.'

'Good God, is it you, Sir?' Stephen unhooked his heels and for a moment looked at Winchip aghast. On being certain that it *was* Winchip, he ran a hand through his shaggy dark hair and stepped down, his large frame striding towards him with his hand outstretched. 'It is a delight to see you, Brother-in-law. Pardon my language but you were the last person on this earth that I expected to see.' Loxley's brown eyes sparkled in the light from the door.

'It is good to see you, too, Stephen – and I am glad to see that you were as good as your word and stayed to make an honest living.' Winchip shook Stephen Loxley's hand with both a will and a conscience. He would have bet a goodly sum that the man would have moved on, to leave Madeleine fearing for his whereabouts and safety. For once, he was glad to be wrong.

'I could do no other, Daniel; you did for me what few men would do for another, family or otherwise.' Stephen, having recovered his wits, suddenly appeared to be very nervous. 'I...I cannot talk to you here, not in this place, Daniel. There is a tea house at the end of the street..,' Loxley gestured the direction with a finger. '...can I meet you there in a little while? I would stop to explain but...'

'Of course you can, Stephen.' Winchip interrupted with an understanding nod and then turned and left the place without another word. He realised immediately that Loxley would have a good reason for not wishing to be seen with him and he respected the fact by leaving on the instant, knowing it was not the moment to seek reasons.

They sat together at a vacant table in the corner of the expansive and popular tea house, their four hats hooked onto wooden pegs above their heads. Loxley had entered after a searching look to ensure that, in his eyes, the place was safe to enter. Now, he sat with them, nursing a cup of tea that remained untouched.

Winchip sipped his coffee and then lowered the dish to break the silence. 'What is troubling you, Stephen?'

The question hung in the air for several seconds before Loxley replied. 'I am in a fix, Daniel – a terrible fix.' Loxley held up a hand as Winchip made to speak. In a hoarse whisper, he added. 'I have discovered that Mr Burke is trading with slaves illegally. I have known it for some time; but to have told of it would have caused me, myself to be implicated. I have no way out, my word upon it.'

'What exactly is Mr Burke doing that is illegal, Stephen?' – Winchip, knowing nothing about slaves, wondered if he would be any the wiser if Stephen explained to him. – 'Tell me everything if I am to help you.'

Loxley looked about him like a hunted fox and in the same guarded whisper, said. 'When the slaves come up for sale they each carry a silver tag about their neck to denote that tax has been paid.' As Winchip nodded his understanding, so Loxley continued. 'The slaves he sells have come into Boston in the dead of night; and they are from places far and wide and that is most unusual. Not only that, they have been held somewhere in poor conditions, not fed and put to rights after a long journey, as is usual. They are badly marked and many have the first signs of illness; even their necks are marked with excessive use of the halter – and the silver tags are false, I know that for certain! On top of all that, they are not sold at Mr Burke's regular auction. Instead they are passed on again as a single purchase, taken into the night and never seen again.' Loxley came to a stop with a shake of his head and spread his hands in a desperate appeal to Winchip.

'What do you mean when you say they are from different places?'

'The slaves that were locked in the ware-room came in two days ago, in the early hours. Many were Mandinka from the James Island Fort on the Gambia River, while others were from Senegal, Sierra Leone, Dahomey, the Congo and also Guinea. None comes from further north than Senegal because Moslems are very hard to sell.' At last Loxley took a sip of his tea but still he hurried on. 'I have spoken with these slaves, Sir and, except for the Mandinkas, one hardly knows another and they certainly never travelled to their first destination together, except for a few. They all speak of having been on board ships that have been captured by other ships. They have then been taken to Tortuga, at San Domingue, where there were many more slaves, housed in huts. They were badly fed, the women were used and many had been mistreated; and that is *before* they spent more than two weeks at sea to get here.'

'Good God! They then came all the way to Boston I take it, from this island of Tortuga, a dozen or two at a time to avoid suspicion.' The point was a rhetorical one. Winchip was trying to conjure a picture of events and put reason where confusion seemed to hold the higher ground. 'So, the slaves that came in last night have already gone if I understand you.'

'They were purchased by Mr Burke for twenty thousand guineas and a Captain Pascal came to take Mr Burke and the slaves to the West Indies. They left together in the early hours of this morning and were placed on board the collier, *La Mouette*.'

'That is the French for 'The Seagull', Sir.' Pardoe spoke without taking his eyes from Loxley.

'You can be sure that that was the ship on which they embarked – the slaves and Mr Burke – of that there can be no doubt.' Loxley looked crestfallen. 'I have not seen Mr Burke since – and I have every reason to suppose I shall never see him again. He has cleared his account at his agency and taken every penny piece, together with all my savings, stolen from my drawer. His baggage, too, is gone. It is my belief that he has left Boston with the ship, the slaves and his benefactor to boot.'

'Good Lord – Martinique!' Winchip sat upright in his seat and raised a hand to prevent Loxley continuing. Burke was the ideal person to act as an agent for such an audacious subterfuge, so far from the Caribbean or not. The inferences were overwhelming and Winchip's duty in the matter came to him as plain as a pikestaff – but that could wait, as could the unfolding of his knowledge to his captains – for now. He leant back in his chair with a false smile and a raucous laugh, trying to avoid the four of them appearing to be huddled together as if planning some devilish plot.

Loxley shook his head from side to side. 'Mr Burke is not coming back, Daniel, of that I am positive. He is going south with the slaves, that I *do* know, for they represent his wealth for the future.' Loxley's shoulders seemed to sag with despair as he realised the implications of what he had just said, despite the knowledge that he would no longer be compelled to fall in with Burke's nefarious plans. 'He owes a large amount of money in Boston and certainly has no intention of paying it. He also made me sign for the slaves in my own name instead of that of the agency on their arrival. That is unusual and it gave me cause to worry. Usually, he signs the manifest in the name of the agency, which leaves my head on the block for I am now totally responsible for slaves that have been taken from under my nose. It won't do, Daniel – it won't do.' Stephen hung his head. 'It will not be long before his creditors realise he has gone, leaving me responsible for the agency – 'tis me that they will hang for his sins, for they will want to hang someone, of that you can be certain!' Loxley uttered the words in a hoarse whisper. 'When you came in, I was writing a letter to Madeleine, to explain things, you understand, in case she never sees me again, for I am now in fear for my life.'

'I understand perfectly, that is why I want you to collect you baggage and come with us, there is nothing left for you here but trouble. You will go on board *Eaglet* with Mr Pardoe, where you will be safe. Then, we will get down to planning what to do next. How does that suit you?'

'It would be the saving of me; but I must come penniless, except for the money you advanced me, which is sewn into my breeches.'

'Good heavens, man! Do you mean to tell me it is still intact?'

'Not a penny spent, I worked hard for the five-hundred guineas that were stolen by Burke – the money is yours – and my word, you shall have it back on the instant.' Loxley's face brightened as he went to tear at the small, hidden pocket.

'You keep it, Stephen; the debt is cleared and, although you don't yet know it, you have earned it, my word upon *that*.' Winchip nodded his assurances and reached up to the peg for his hat. He then fished into his pocket and handed Hellard a coin. 'Return to the agency, Coxswain and help Mr Loxley recover his belongings and remove any sign of his having ever been there. Then, find an eating house and take your dinner there. Keep your eye on the agency and, if Mr Burke *does* turn up, detain him and have Mr Loxley pass the word to Mr Pardoe. At midnight, you are to return to *Eaglet*, the pair of you, without further ado. Am I clearly understood?'

'Aye aye, Sir, I understands ye as clear as a bell.' Hellard nodded vigorously and then added. ''Twould be as well to have a boat at the steps early, Sir. You never know what *might* happen.'

'The boat will be there.' Winchip turned to Loxley. 'Do whatever Mr Hellard tells you, Stephen – your life may depend upon it.'

CHAPTER SEVEN

Southward Bound

Winchip sat at his desk, wondering in his heart why treachery and devious dealings seemed to follow in his wake. Soon, Mr Burke would be wishing he had stayed in Cornwall all those years ago, at a time when he confided that he was going to 'chance his arm' in the Americas. Winchip would see him to his destiny, that was for certain; but at what cost?

He drew a quill from the silver stand. He would write to Madeleine, knowing she would be overjoyed to read that Stephen was safe. He would also tell her other things; words that needed to be composed rather than dashed onto the paper. He took out her 'likeness' from his pocket and propped it against the ink stand, seeing her face and that of little Richard, conjuring in his mind's eye the thought of them both, sitting there before him. With a contented nod, he counted what few blessings he had left to him.

Sometime after seven bells in the evening watch, Winchip heard the challenge from the entry port, just as clearly as he heard Hellard's stentorian response. The sea beneath the counter was lapping at the exposed rudder and pintles with a rapid tattoo indicating calm, if not choppy, water. He dusted the page of his journal, blew away the excess and closed the book with a sigh. He felt there would be much to follow what he had already written and little of it to his liking. The knock on the door flung his thoughts to the winds.

'Enter!'

Niven entered wearing neither hat nor coat and his blouse was open at the neck. He looked down at himself and then at Winchip before speaking. 'I am sorry, Sir, I was about to retire.'

Winchip smiled. 'I take it Mr Pardoe and Mr Loxley have arrived on board?'

'They have, Sir but there is also a lady with them. It seems she is an old friend of Hellard's and is in poor straits by all accounts. Hellard made mention of her being put on the muster, Sir and I promised him I would speak with you on the matter.'

'Hell's bells, Lieutenant, for a moment I thought…never mind, have Mr Pardoe and Mr Loxley enter the cabin, if you please.'

Winchip indicated that Pardoe and Loxley should sit at the great table, while he remained at his desk. 'Is everything in order?' The question was so open and direct that for a moment it seemed that Pardoe was lost for words.

'Mr Loxley and Hellard did as you asked, Sir. The Coxswain is sure that nothing has been left to involve Mr Loxley in Burke's treachery.'

Winchip looked at Loxley. 'Are you happy with that, Stephen?'

'Oh, yes, Sir, except for one small point. As we were talking with Stephen, it transpires that you misunderstood him on one point. The slaves had not *come* from Tortuga but were *going* there in their original ships. It seems they were all taken at sea – that was why they spoke of being taken off one ship and put into another. Your man, Burke, will be collecting his ill gotten gains instead of the original and real owners. It is a nasty business all round, Sir, if you ask me.'

'Well, it answers the questions posed by Their Lordships at Admiralty and a few queries that were coming to my mind, Peter. At least we know where Burke is going and that has to be an advantage I'd say.'

Stephen raised a hand. 'Also the origin of the slaves in the first place – though the number of ships he has sent to the bottom is any man's guess.'

'You are right in every instance, both of you, which suggests the reason why Admiral Saunders was tardy in appointing a captain for the task – Their Lordships at Admiralty will be quick to ask why so many vessels were sunk and lives lost before efforts were made to obey their orders – and he with no answer. The admiral has a subordinate who does ill by him in my book – but no matter.' Winchip gave a deprecating sniff that would have made most men cringe. 'We can do no more. Get to your beds, both of you.'

Stephen fumbled in his inner pocket before he turned away. 'I have found the original signature of which I spoke, Daniel, it was in my belongings.' He passed the piece of paper over, the smile on his face a mixture of relief and confidence. Here is also a piece of paper in Mr Burke's hand; it is a list of the ships from which the slaves were taken and the number of slaves on each – he was meticulous with his own accounts.'

'Thank you, Stephen.' Winchip looked at the paper in his hand, wondering how so small a thing could convey so much greed, misery and desolation. 'I shall place it in my drawer on *Bellicus*, Stephen, where it will be safe, for you have little else to support your story should you be called to answer you accusers.' Winchip brightened. 'Send in Hellard and his new-found lady, if you please – they require no escort.'

Mrs Higgins, for that proved to be her name according to Pardoe, was making a vain attempt to appear coy as she stood behind Hellard's shoulder. She was a handsome lady, dark eyed and with a face free from rouge. Her dark hair, prettily touched by splashes of grey, was tied in a bun like that of a washerwoman, yet she had the look of a lady of many parts and prepared for any eventuality – a match made in heaven it would seem. She still retained much of the beauty of her youth; the look that had obviously smitten Hellard. She also had the courtesy to remain silent as Hellard spoke, his hands held humbly together before him.

'Mrs 'Iggins is known to me, Sir, just as I know 'er 'usband is long gone and that she is now a free lady, Sir.' Hellard had plotted his course well. 'We knew each other in Falmouth, Sir. We met during *Eaglet's* early days, that time when you gave me a guinea for the men's grub and a wet, Sir – you'll remember.' Unplanned or not, Hellard had made his point.

'Are we speaking of romance, Hellard?' Winchip declined to notice Mrs Higgins dig Hellard in the ribs.

'She do bake a good loaf o' bread, Sir – and aye, Sir, we do 'ave an understandin', Sir.' Hellard raised himself up another inch.

Winchip decided that Hellard's lady saw in her new found man a means by which she could escape her life of uncertainty – an aspiration for which she had his every sympathy. 'In that case, Mrs Higgins may stay on board *Eaglet*. You will obey the rules, both written and unwritten, as will Mrs Higgins. Your lady will be mustered as your wife, so there will be no talk of hanky panky, Hellard. I shall talk to Captain Pardoe and see that Mrs *Hellard*, as she will now be called, is placed on the muster as cook's assistant and *you* will make arrangements as to your sleeping space together, if that suits your good lady?' Winchip posed the question by raising an eyebrow.

'It do, Sir, it do!' Mrs Hellard replied with gusto in a falsetto voice.

'Then that will be all.' Winchip allowed himself a faint smile as Mrs Hellard's shy, tinsel giggle faded with the closing of the cabin door. There were already two women on *Eaglet's* muster; a third would make little difference.

The squadron left Boston in the early mist of the morning, dousing sails to gather the light overland air from the west. Out to sea, the t'gallants of *Eaglet* billowed out with a succession of crackles and thuds, dispersing the gulls that still swooped for morsels in the ship's wake. As the ships of the squadron departed from the naval anchorage, the staccato sound of lesser vessels discharging their salutes echoed out in their turn to Winchip's broad pennant and carried to *Eaglet* on the fitful air as she loitered to take up the inshore station.

At one bell in the afternoon watch of the following day, the two ships-of-the-line were twenty miles off shore with Culpepper's *Trial* further out to sea and Pardoe's *Eaglet* to windward, well within sight of land. *Bellicus* and *Incensed* loomed large against the horizon, their presence bringing security to those who wondered what the future might bring. The course of due south had been set, the moment *Eaglet* had navigated both Cape Cod and the great coral reefs of Martha's Vineyard; accorded by Mr Ramblin to be the haunt of whaling captains.

Master and Commander Peter Pardoe removed his hat and wiped the inner band with his kerchief before replacing it fore and aft upon his head. As the squadron had left Boston, Pardoe had noticed that the sloop of war that had lain quietly against the harbour wall had departed. He had noted the fact with interest and considered that it could be no coincidence that *Céleste* had departed at the same time as *La Mouette* – perhaps as escort. He found satisfaction in having sent a lengthy signal to *Bellicus* to that effect. The fact that he could have boarded *La Mouette* and had been in a position to later investigate *Céleste* found no place in his conscience. It was simply a matter of bad timing, in that it had all happened before the amazing revelations of Stephen Loxley.

The westerly wind had veered to north-westerly, still coming off the land but settling abaft the starboard beam of *Eaglet*, her canvas now filled and her deck canted towards the foam flecked water that rushed down her larboard side. Spindrift floated across the quarterdeck in a mist, only to catch in the wind and be driven over the larboard bulwark and back into obscurity. It was a fine day for sailing, yet still there had been no sign of *La Mouette*, nor the sloop of war.

It was on the third day that the call came from the tops, the words shouted through the hailer whisked away by the wind. Pardoe waited for Bowes to come down to him.

'Well, Mr Bowes?'

'Two ships against the land, Sir. One is reported to be a collier and the other a sloop of war.' Bowes stood with a beaming smile pasted onto his face, knowing it was what Pardoe wanted to hear.

'Have it relayed to the flagship, Mr Bowes; it appears our rogue has been found at last.' Pardoe turned to Mr Ramblin. 'Are you familiar with the land hereabouts, master?' He nodded towards the western shore.

'Aye, Captain, I am, though it were a few years ago.' Mr Ramblin sucked on his tooth. 'You have the Albemarle River to the north and Pamlico Sound and Raleigh Bay to the south – both good places to hide in, should there be the need.'

Pardoe grinned at Mr Ramblin's additional information; and the fact that he was aware of his captain's train of thought. 'And what of the ground there, Master?'

'There was a time when it would be safe enough for some; but no place for others.' Mr Ramblin pointed his old clay pipe to the west. 'We'd do well to take soundings afore we commit ourselves, I'm thinking – should the occasion arise.'

'Thank you, Master, I feel we are about to find out for ourselves.'

Bowes came up to the binnacle from the shrouds. *'Bellicus* has signalled, Sir: "Proceed as ordered"'

'Thank you, Mr Bowes.' Pardoe smiled grimly, at the same time gripping his hands tightly behind his back in his sudden anger. He could have gone into the bay and taken the pair of them, given the chance. Now, that chance was gone. He sighed with despair as the water continued to jet through the larboard scupper drains and the drone of the wind through the rigging spoke to him with both urgency and impatience.

Mr Ramblin sucked on his tooth. 'You should know better, young sir. When the Commodore says to follow them vessels, then that's what he means. Take 'em now and what proof could the Commodore show at a trial, I ask, if we don't catch your Mr Burke with his hands dirty?'

'You are quite right, Master, as always.'

'Not at all, Sir, t'is my duty to ensure you are kept rightly informed, just as I have about the island of Tortue, off San Domingue; and how it's the French for tortoise, as is Tortuga – the more common name, and how pirates once had a fortress at Tortue, as you call it.' Mr Ramblin glared at the helmsman who had been looking at each of them in turn as they spoke. 'Keep yer eye on the card, Mister, or answer for it later!'

Pardoe, ignoring the rebuke of the helmsman, looked long and hard at the old master and then grinned. 'What would I do without your perspicacity, Master – you tell me that!'

'Age and time served do have certain advantages, Sir.' Mr Ramblin snatched up his trumpet and bellowed an unnecessary admonition to the tops, promptly bringing his overlong conversation with his captain to an end.

At two bells into the afternoon watch, a cry came from above. A few moments later Midshipman Godfrey Archer came up to the binnacle at the run, addressing himself to Pardoe.

'A signal to us from *Incensed*, relayed from flag, Sir: "*Eaglet* to close on the flag at four bells in the first dogwatch", Sir.'

'Thank you, Mr Archer. Acknowledge and then attend your division, if you please.' Pardoe pondered over why there should be a delay of several hours before he approached the flagship, until he suddenly realised that if the squadron hove to, then it would be obvious to the collier and sloop that they had been seen. He cursed himself for a fool – something he had cause to do too often of late.

At the allotted time, Pardoe paid his respects to James Niven as he came on board *Bellicus* and even managed to exchange a few words with the man who had once been his senior officer in *Eaglet*. They parted in fraternal good spirits at the double wheel, where Pardoe stepped past the sentry and entered the great cabin. Winchip was not alone. The massive figure of Douglas Munro was sitting at the end of the table, a chart before him, together with an untouched glass of claret. Pardoe deduced that their conversation had been a serious one, sufficient for Munro to neglect his nectar.

'Come in, Captain and sit yourself down.' Both Munroe and Winchip shook Pardoe's hand. Winchip nodded to his manservant, Booth and then at Pardoe – coffee or claret?'

'Coffee would go down well, Commodore, if you please.' Pardoe felt that he had lost the initiative. Whereas he was about to be expansive over the sighting of *La Mouette,* he had the distinct impression that it was no longer of any importance. The large French chart, spread across the table, was that of Hispaniola and of the Isle de la Tortue.

Winchip looked up from the table. 'You must have been bursting at the seams to chase them into the bay, Peter?'

'I was, Sir, you can be assured of that. Your signal to proceed as ordered came as a disappointment.' Pardoe gave a self-effacing grin as he spoke to disallow any thought of impertinence.

Winchip laughed. 'I want to hang the man, if not both of them. I can only do that when I can prove their intents and purposes. With luck the collier and sloop shall think we have passed them by – and *that* is how I want it to appear.'

Pardoe looked up from his coffee. 'If I may speak, Sir, having spoken to Mr Ramblin about the island of Tortue, the place mentioned by Mr Loxley, he is of the opinion that the island of Tortue, the name given to it by the indigenes, is pronounced Tortuga by others and is off the north western coast of Hispaniola, as Stephen said.' Pardoe drew himself upright. 'He also said that it was once the haunt of pirates, Sir, and that there was a fortress and other buildings there at one time.'

'Thank the Lord for Mr Ramblin!' Winchip closed his eyes as if to give thanks for his deliverance. 'That is the confirmation I was seeking.' He looked at Pardoe directly. 'What else did the master have to say?'

'You can ask him for yourself, Commodore. I took the liberty of bringing him with me, considering he knows far more than I do on the subject of tortoises.'

Winchip and Munro laughed in concert. At last, Winchip said. 'Thank you, Captain; you have saved us valuable time.' Winchip maintained his eye contact with Pardoe. 'I have already decided that we shall be making our way directly to Tortuga, Captain, providing we do not come into contact with Commodore Moore, at present in waters to the south of us. The Commodore's squadron must not be missed, for it is from him that we shall receive up to date information about the French and the war situation.'

Winchip drew breath – things were becoming more complicated by the minute. 'Prepare to return to your ship, lest it sinks in the absence of both her master and her captain and then take the van, showing stern lights. Keep your lookouts sharp and report *all* your sightings, in detail, after sunrise. I shall speak with Mr Ramblin shortly and return him to you in the stateroom. If you both wait for Mr Niven, he shall see you both off the ship with due ceremony.'

At that moment the sentry's head appeared round the door. He announced Niven and Mr Ramblin and then stepped aside, allowing Pardoe to depart.

Pardoe waited for Mr Ramblin in the stateroom, satisfied with his own actions. The evening sun was low on the western horizon and already the stateroom was bathed in red, as were the sails of *Incensed*, squatting with her foretops'l against the mast, shortly to be swallowed by the great red orb as it sunk into the ocean. He felt no disappointment that he was to be excluded from what whatever plan of action his father-in-law had decided to make. He knew that *his* presence would already be raising questions in the mind of Nathanson of *Incensed*.

Eaglet sailed in the van, due south into the waning light, Pardoe well aware that three hundred leagues of ocean lay before them, due south to the twentieth line of circumference – and Hispaniola. The likelihood of another sail was hardly worth the consideration. There was still warmth in the timber casing of the binnacle as he laid his hand upon it. In fact, the deck beneath him still exuded the heat of the day from its timbers and the smell of tar still stung the nostrils. Pardoe knew that the warmth would not last; and that soon, the setting of the sun would warrant the warmth of a cloak.

'Deck alow!'

'Where away?' Lieutenant Hartley called up though the trumpet.

'*Ships to the north-east, hull down – three o' the line and a frigate – sailing south by west – and they'm French!*'

As Bowes waved a hand in acknowledgement to the shout, so Pardoe turned to the twelve-year-old Lord Pickering and said. 'Send to flag: "ships in sight to the north-east – two French ships-of-the-line, plus one frigate, course south by west".'

'Aye, Sir!' Pickering wasted no time in repeating the message as he rifled the signal locker and then raced to the gaff halyard.

Pardoe watched *Bellicus* intently and grunted his satisfaction when the acknowledgement jerked up her halyard. He turned to Bowes with either excitement or apprehension filling his chest but he knew not which. In the end he spoke without equivocation.

'Call our people to action, Mr Bowes, guns attended but neither loaded nor run out, if you please. Also, relieve the lookouts and get some fresh eyes in the tops, the French will have seen *Bellicus* by now and will be sure to shy away, probably to south by east.'

'Aye, Sir.' Bowes grabbed the hailer and shouted his orders from the rail athwart the quarterdeck. Whistles blew and marines darted below or stood at each companion. The young drummer at the fo'c's'le fumbled to hitch the lanyard of his drum about his neck while gripping his sticks between his teeth.

Nothing had changed; and never would it. Pardoe watched without seeing, thinking of other times in different places, when Winchip had stood at the very same spot, watching and noting, yet saying nothing. There was but one difference, *Eaglet* had recently seen action and come through unscathed, the gunners now more aware of what was required of them and knowing that they had the means to take the battle to the enemy. Pardoe knew it had much to do with the old hands, from gun captains, quarter gunners and through to the ship's gunner, Mr Wellbeloved, demanding and cajoling, teasing and praising until the curses turned to grunts of acceptance and those to willing nods. There had been gun practice aplenty; and for that he thanked the benefit of Winchip's teachings; but likely as not there would soon be a boarding and that was what worried him. The *Eaglets* had never been bested once *Eaglet* had been placed alongside her enemy and, by virtue of that; the law of averages was unjustly set against them.

CHAPTER EIGHT

Commodore John Moore

In the chill of the evening, Pardoe waited by the binnacle of *Eaglet* as the young Lord Pickering came down the deck towards him.

'A signal from flag, Sir. – "Come into wind and maintain station".' Pickering's eyes were open wide and seemed doomed to stay that way, while a dewdrop hung precariously under his long aristocratic nose.

'Thank you, Lord Pickering – remain on the quarterdeck, young man.' Pardoe allowed himself a smile of approval at the twelve-year old peer's keenness to do well. It seemed correct to address him by his title at their first meeting of the day; and by his name only from that moment on. He looked across the quarterdeck to Mr Ramblin who nodded in his turn but with raised eyebrows. Already, the master was sending men aloft.

'Hands to braces – prepare to wear ship!' Hartley's shouted instructions through the trumpet carried on the breeze.

Midshipmen Archer, Smithers and Dundas arrived red-eyed on the quarterdeck as if they had anticipated the call, each tipping his hat and immediately squinting towards the distant and empty line that was the north-eastern horizon.

Pardoe acknowledged their arrival collectively with a nod of his head. 'Three French ships have been observed to the north-east with the coming of dusk. Mr Archer will remain here, on the quarterdeck, while the rest of you attend your divisions.' He turned away and raised his telescope to look into the north-east for the Frenchies. There was little else to be done – for now. Why his father-in-law had chosen to allow the French free passage

– or to appear to decline battle – was beyond his imagination; but there would be a good reason, of that he was now certain.

Eaglet's sail was being taken in, even as he watched. The great yards swung in unison as seamen trudged the deck with the heave, interspersed with marines in brown canvas ducks and vests of varying colour and origins. The foretops'l suddenly flapped like an angry swan as it lost the wind, bucking and cavorting until it finished up plastered against the foremast, the impression of the mast clear to see. The t'gallants'ls were being punched into shape and gathered by grasping hands. Pardoe would have expected a chanty but there was none – evidence of uncertainty in the air. The fores'l, now stuck to the mast as if pinned there, was painted the deep red shade of the sunset, bright against the darkening sky to the east. The sun was taking its final plunge, leaving a bloody reflection that came down to them, twisting and turning with the gentle swell, soon to be snuffed out until the dawn, when yet another uncertain day would be upon them, fraught with danger – or the likelihood of it with the sighting of every sail.

Even with a stern window open to the November night, there was still a trace of warmth in the great cabin of *Bellicus*. At least the gossamer layers of smoke that usually loitered below the deckhead had vanished; sucked through the window like departing wraiths.

With the sumptuous meal now over and the loyal toast delivered by a seated Culpepper, it was time to circulate the brandy and get down to business. With Pardoe remaining on watch in *Eaglet*, there were but two captains at the table, each well aware that something was afoot; but their commodore's short visit to Boston had offered few clues. It was therefore of no surprise to Winchip that, at a time when the chatter would normally begin, the only sound was that of water slopping beneath the ship's counter with a monotonous regularity.

'Gentlemen, allow me to remind you that my orders direct that I use my squadron to apprehend and deal with any vessel bound for the Americas or the Antilles for the purpose of trade that is contrary to the Navigation Acts. I am also required to proceed to the south for the purpose of making enquiries into the whereabouts of several neutral and British slavers that have gone missing in southern waters. I am required, if possible, to determine who is responsible and to deliver those persons into the hands of the British Authority at Basse-Terre at Guadeloupe.' Winchip allowed a murmur of comment to pass before continuing. 'I hasten to add that I have evidence that piracy is involved; a word not much used in His Majesty's Navy of late. I also believe that that pirate has been – and still is – capturing Guinea ships and their cargoes and sending them to a holding place where the slaves are mixed with others, given a stamp of authority and then sold on to the French at Martinique – and at a good price, you can be certain of that.' Winchip looked at his small audience. 'I also believe that French Guinea ships heading for Martinique have been taken by this buccaneer, their cargoes stolen and, when they have taken sufficient crew members to take the captured ships onwards, then the ship – and the rest of the crew are sent to the bottom, for none has been found, nor crew to tell of it, except those that have volunteered to join with their captors.'

'May I ask if this has anything to do with the clandestine coming and going of yesterday evening, Sir, from *Eaglet* in particular?'

'You may, Captain Nathanson.' Winchip allowed himself a smile, knowing something about favouritism and 'interest' and the connotation of Pardoe's visit. 'It so happens that my own agent at Boston, a Mr Burke, has chosen to take his skills – and the authority of his position – to this pirate for the purposes of gain. He, alone, can authenticate these stolen slaves, with the necessary papers and discs of taxation, a business he has abandoned at Boston, leaving many traders penniless into the bargain. His assistant, a Mr Loxley, a man who is completely innocent of any wrongdoing, is now on board *Eaglet* and is related both to me and to Mr Pardoe.' Winchip afforded Nathanson the slimmest of smiles. 'Does that satisfy you?'

'It does, Commodore; but where is this pirate now and how shall we know him for who and what he is?'

'He is probably within two leagues of us at this moment, sailing south as we are, heading for the Ile de la Tortue – or Tortuga, off the northern shore of Saint Domingue, or Western Hispaniola; a place well known to Mr Ramblin, the master of Eaglet.' Winchip raised a hand to prevent interruption. 'I believe that Tortuga is where the slaves are being kept, from where they can be shipped in small vessels at night, to arrive at Martinique at a place and time to suit themselves, all legally tagged and with the 'correct' paperwork to hand, courtesy of Mr Burke.'

Nathanson shook his head 'It must involve a great deal of money, with some of these slaves fetching a hundred guineas or more, I am told – so why are we not preparing to take him to task, even as we sit here gossiping?'

'Yes, Captain, it does involve a great deal of money – and with money comes danger; and with that danger can come death in its most secret and brutal form – you have my word upon it.' Winchip paused, disallowing anger to dress his words, yet letting what he had to say sink in. 'As to our sitting here, gossiping as you so wrongly call it, I am seeking to allow all concerned in this dreadful trade to come together at Tortuga. In this way it is possible we shall have them all in one place, caught in the act and with the evidence to hand.' Winchip caught Nathanson's eye. 'How is that for gossip, Captain?'

'I apologise, Commodore – I had no idea...' Nathanson shook his head, lost for words.

Winchip continued. 'I might add that Commodore Moore may soon be in the offing.' Winchip saw their eyes brighten, knowing that that would cheer them and boost their moral into the bargain. 'Should we meet him, then there is a chance that he will add to our strength – but we cannot take that for granted, having no knowledge of his orders.' Winchip laid his hands on the table, a sign that conveyed an end to the conversation and the dinner, both. 'You now know as much as I do. I suggest you return to your vessels and then await events, gentlemen – just as I must. Keep your lookouts sharp and your eyes always on *Bellicus*.'

After seven days and six nights of calm seas, a warm sun, dazzling dawns and majestic sunsets, the midshipmen, under the tutelage of Mr Ramblin, declared at noon that they had arrived at the 22nd line of latitude. A signal gun was fired from *Bellicus* and her three attendant vessels each acknowledged with their agreement. It was from the maintop of *Eaglet*, sailing in the van on the next chilly dawn that the sighting of an English Squadron to the south-south-east came down to those on the quarterdeck.

The Squadron of Commodore Moore, feared by Winchip to have been missed on the passage south, soon came into view to Winchip, who was squatting at the cross-trees of *Bellicus* like one of the Barbary apes at Gibraltar with a telescope to his eye. Moore's squadron was on a westing, like a flotilla of swans on a lake of sparkling white diamonds that flashed red in the low sun out of the east. Winchip closed the glass with care and took the ratlines down to the deck. At the binnacle he looked once more towards the large squadron, seeing the tops'ls of Commodore Moore's ships hurriedly come about in the light air, waiting for Winchip's ships to do likewise to windward, with *Eaglet* remaining to the north-east. Winchip raised his glass once more before the view would be lost to him during the evolution. He recognised several ships, including *Rippon*(60), *Burford*(70), *Lion*(60) and *Norfolk*(74), as each came into view. There were also some fifty-gun ships, obscured in the rapid changes of sail. It was the large Third Rate, *Cambridge*(80) that displayed Moore's broad pennant, its swallow tails at odds in the rising breeze and the bright sun.

Winchip had been quick to lower his own broad pennant, well aware that any commodore afloat would be his senior. As the salute ended and men scuttled from their parts of ship, their duty done and Mr Blackstock contented, so Winchip removed his hat and used it to fan his face, now tanned even more deeply by the relentless sun.

'Deck there – flag is signallin' – our number.'

'Flag requests your presence, Sir.' Midshipman Costly stood in breeches and blouse, the permitted dress in the heat of the day.

'Thank you, Mr Costly, acknowledge, if you please.' To Niven, Winchip added. 'Have my barge put over, Mr Niven – smartly, if you please – at this moment I think I have the rare benefit of being an unknown quantity.'

The eighty-gun ship, *Cambridge*, had stood above Winchip's barge as he arrived, as a cat would look down upon a petrified mouse. Now, arrived on deck, he strode towards Commodore John Moore, feeling less intimidated and more his own self. The fife and drum band had disbanded and already the marines were being hustled back to the fo'c's'le. Winchip raised his hat. 'I am newly appointed, Sir. I am Commodore, second class, with the name of Daniel Winchip, yet to be gazetted.' Winchip smiled broadly. 'You, Sir, need no introduction – and may I congratulate you on your taking of Guadeloupe in May?'

Moore smiled infectiously. 'You are very welcome on board *Cambridge*, Commodore but your praises are too kind. I have recently heard of *your* exploits and wonder if we are not as two peas in the same pod; let us retire to the cabin where I assure you, it is far cooler than here, on this sweltering deck.'

The great cabin of *Cambridge* offered no more than Winchip expected, except for the cool breeze that seemed to be diverted through the open stern windows by a couple of old triangular stays'ls draped on a line from the taffrail and inverted, a device he would keep in mind. He handed the two-hundred guinea sword to an attendant lieutenant, together with his hat and then unbuttoned his coat, following Moore's example. He passed his orders and journal across the table, accepting at the same time a large glass of lemonade, which he drank as Moore read the contents of Winchip's pouch with care, his eyebrows rising as he quizzed the contents. Moore appeared to be of a similar age to Winchip and seemingly well established in his rank of Commodore. His countenance displayed the worries that must surely be attending him as events seemed to have come upon *him* rather than being of his own volition. Yet the man had shown his true self with the hearty welcome and lack of the need to impress. He would do for Winchip and that was sufficient.

'It is a devil of a task you have been given, Winchip, reminiscent of years past; and providing little return, except for the satisfaction of a damned good hanging or two. Having said that, I suspect your prizes in the Gulf of St Lawrence shall bring you and your people a pretty penny.'

'My orders reflect a task left unfulfilled, Sir, though at the same time it leaves the perpetrators thinking they can do as they wish. As for the prizes, they have yet to be bought-in.'

'They will be, Winchip; and with grateful thanks, you can take my word for that, together with the healthy headcount.'

'My people worked for it, Sir; *my* word upon *that*.' Winchip took another glass of the cold lemonade and, with as winsome a smile as he could muster, he posed his question to Moore directly and without preamble. 'I intend to become acquainted with the island of Tortuga and, depending upon what I discover, I shall take all necessary steps to accomplish the task given to me. If I need to increase the strength of my squadron, can I rely upon your support?' Winchip took up his lemonade and looked away; he had no desire to appear the beggar.

Moore spread his hands; his tight lipped face expressing his regret. 'I have my own orders Winchip; and they do not include Tortuga. At home, Mr Pitt has insisted that we make yet another attack on Martinique and, God willing, this time we shall succeed. The damned sugar island is worth its weight in gold to England, whereas its value in terms of brave English lives seems to have no limit!'

At that moment Winchip felt a sudden anger, not so much towards Commodore Moore but for Boyce and his lost *Cassius*. 'I submit, Sir, that the release of just one of your Fourth Rates will give me the edge that I need to bring the French to their knees. Once I have them all bottled up at Tortuga I can clear up this piracy problem once and for all and reward your generosity two or three times over in terms of prizes.' He hoped he hadn't shown himself to be over confident, a dangerous trait when dealing with other people's lives.

'Ah! So that is why you allowed that French squadron to pass unhindered – bees into a honey-trap, so to speak?'

'As you rightly say, Sir, it was exactly that! Had I engaged the French, then I would have lost Seth Burke, together with a large number of slaves and slave ships to boot, making good their escape while the battle raged – I couldn't do one thing without losing the other; the evidence I need to advance my case at Basse-Terre.'

There was a moment of silence, during which Moore drummed his fingers absent-mindedly on the polished table. 'Very well, Winchip, I shall place *Responsive* under your temporary command, which infers that I require her to be returned in one piece, Commodore, though, God forgive me, I could raise a smile if the old tub foundered, were it not for her people.' Moore smiled and looked Winchip in the eye. 'She is commanded by Post Captain Conwy Madoc, a Welshman who has done good service in His Majesty's Navy and is now feeling it in his bones, Winchip. He missed his chances some years ago in a débacle with the Dutch – he is destined never to attain flag rank.'

'Alas, from what you say, he is lucky not to be on the beach.' Winchip stood and nodded to the servant to retrieve his coat and sword. 'I shall not burden you further, except to thank you for having the courage to change your mind, Commodore. However, I would be greatly obliged if I might seek any spare charts your master may have of Tortuga; and details of a passage through the corals?' Winchip respected Moore's position and felt himself lucky at getting a fifty-gun ship and all that that entailed. As for Conwy Madoc, well, he would soon find out more about the Welshman with a shady past. As to the charts, that was a different matter. The whole area abounded with coral reefs; the grave yard of a thousand wrecks if tavern gossip were to be believed.

'Of course you may have the charts, Commodore and I wish you well in your enterprise.' Moore gave an instruction to the lieutenant and waited for the man to leave the cabin before handing Winchip's orders and journal back to him with a smile. Moore made to return to his seat but checked himself and turned back.

'Should you have occasion to send men ashore, Commodore, there are one or two things you should know...'

Winchip waited, aware that every word uttered by Moore could only add to his knowledge of Tortuga and probably prevent a disaster if he conveyed this knowledge to those who were soon to venture onto the islands shores.

'...Tortuga is a place of many identities, Winchip; and has a very violent history going back two centuries or more, to the days of the first buccaneers. The island has been attacked by the Dutch, the Spanish, the French – and the English and I can tell you it has been a bitter pill to swallow on every occasion. When the Spaniards finally overcame Le Vasseur's fort in the south-western harbour and took the island, they had to abandon the place eventually to the very buccaneers from whom it had been taken – but that was long ago. Now, with Hispaniola divided between the French in Saint Domingue and the Spanish in Santo Domingo, things have quietened somewhat. Tortuga is now at peace, building up a large slave population, hence allowing the planting of tobacco, sugar, rum, coffee, indigo and cotton.' Moore swallowed a long draught of his lemonade and took up a kerchief to wipe his brow. 'The economy of Tortuga has multiplied by many times in contrast to the frugal efforts of earlier planters who took over from the buccaneers. The place is at peace with itself, though there is much barbarity towards the slaves who have been brought in from West Africa and elsewhere.' Moore stared Winchip in the eye. 'Leave the place alone, Commodore. That is my suggestion, unless you want a bloody nose and a sore rump to boot. There is not a man alive on that island who will give you the time of day – and why should he? If you want to capture your man Burke, then I suggest you do not go on shore but consider a cutting out expedition, find out where the man is and then take him in hand.' As for your slaves, you must decide who has ownership and pass them over; you can do no more than that. Or you could take them to Guadeloupe, to Basse-Terre, where they would be more than welcome, together with your report and the man, Burke.' Moore sat back in his seat. 'As for the French ships in the bay, that is for you to decide, for I would never presume to remind you of your duty.'

'I shall take your advice on board, Sir; you can be assured of that.'

'Good; and as to your passage through the corals, I would suggest you take station astern of my own squadron and follow us through the Canal de la Mona, for that is your best route to Hispaniola, north or south. However, watch the current in the Caribbean Sea, it can be a feisty devil and could drive you onto Jamaica twixt one bell and the next; and it will not serve you well as you pass between Cuba and Hispaniola going north, abetted as it is by a fierce easterly wind on your beam.'

'I am obliged to you, Sir.'

Moore shook his head with a wide smile. 'You are certainly the man for the task, Winchip – I can see Henry Morgan turning in his grave, even as we speak.'

CHAPTER NINE

'Our Day of Destiny'

As the last of the setting sun painted the darkening cabin of *Bellicus* in a dull red hue, so Booth lit the lanterns with a flaming wick, adding a soft yellow light by which the captains could more easily the chart on the table before them.

Winchip, Pardoe, Nathanson, Madoc and Culpepper pored over the chart of Hispaniola – or 'Little Spain' as Columbus had once named it. The dark haired Madoc affected the appearance of being a shy man, small in stature and self effacing, yet he had a quick eye for those about him and took in more than one would assume. Beyond the open stern windows only the slopping of water beneath the counter could be heard, monotonous in its regularity – that, and the discordant screech of attendant gulls. Winchip looked up from the chart with a satisfied sigh. He felt he had learned many of the Island's topographical features; and even more about the location of her gun emplacements and areas of occupation, gathered to update the chart over the years. He quaffed the last of his claret and wiped the bottom of the glass with his kerchief before replacing it on the polished table. All had been said that needed to be said and he considered that to continue would be akin to flogging a dead horse. He rose from the table to the accompaniment of scraping chairs. A difficult journey lay ahead of them – and most of that in strange waters. What he needed now was sleep; and a great deal of it...unless circumstances decided otherwise

The squadron of Commodore Moore had led Winchip's command through the Canal de la Mona until the shores to larboard and starboard disappeared below the horizon, bringing them out into the Caribbean Sea before the night caught up with them. Winchip had felt a moment of loneliness and a stab of longing as he watched *Eaglet* add sail to take station behind the sternmost Fourth Rate. The southern horizon loomed large, spreading from east to west in a deep blue sea of utter tranquillity. He knew himself to be in strange and dangerous waters, just as he was aware that his own squadron could well prove to be inadequate for the task that lay ahead. He had appreciated Moore's generosity and only hoped that Conwy Madoc would not be found wanting. The French ships he had allowed to pass them to the south so many days previously could, by now, be but a small part of the force that had gathered at Tortuga to share the spoils of Burke's wicked yet lucrative plans. For the moment, however, he cursed Boyce and his unmitigated stubbornness, though he knew that the man meant nothing to him, like many other arrogant and pig headed captains in the King's Royal Navy. It was the loss of *Cassius* that tormented him most – that and the loss of so many brave and helpless Englishmen.

For three days and nights the squadron had endured an easterly wind that had the heat of an oven and was as dry as dust, both during the day and in the bright star-lit hours of the night as they progressed from the Canal de la Mona to Cape Carcasse, the most westerly point of Hispaniola. The land to the north had come closer and then faded into the mists of the horizon before coming in sight once again as seen by *Trial*, patrolling to the north. Now, the wind was from north of east, still retaining much of its warmth; but gusting as it came off the very land that was the centre of the commodore's interest. The waters in which *Eaglet* had found herself had appeared in colours that defied the imagination; light green in the shoals and a thousand hues of blue in the great deep, the colours changing in their turn as seen from the tops, where the pale forms of pre-natal islands sought to pop their heads above the surface of the sea; and where dolphins leapt from the water, two by two, cavorting in pairs while other, smaller, fish flew to the height of a man, winging and flashing in the sun more quickly that the eye could count, over trough and wave before vanishing once more into the depths.

With *Bellicus* in sight to the south-west, *Eaglet* entered the Windward Passage from the south; the northern exit from the Caribbean, separating Cuba and Hispaniola. With the change of course to the north-east, so the wind had come before her larboard beam.

With canted yards and canvas reduced to tops'ls and stays'ls, *Eaglet* made slow progress, close-hauled as she was. The only difference in her appearance was the French ensign that stood inboard from her gaff halyard, flapping like a trapped bird, as were the same ensigns on every vessel of Commodore Winchip's squadron.

'Excuse me, Sir, the Cap-à-Foux is reported on the larboard bow.'

'Thank you, Pickering.' Pardoe spoke as he peered through the telescope. He could just see the top of the lush hills that were the cape, rising to two hundred feet or more from the sea, shimmering in the haze sent up by distance and the water in between. He was sufficiently sure that they were close enough for what his father-in-law had in mind. He looked round at Midshipman Pickering. 'Send up a signal to flag, Pickering – "Cape à Foux to the north-east".' With a fulsome grin of great satisfaction, Pardoe turned to Mr Ramblin and said. 'Come into wind if you please, Master, we shall await the squadron here.'

Every stern window in the great cabin of *Bellicus* was opened wide to catch the air; and two worn and discoloured stuns'ls guided in the cooler air of the rising easterly through the quarter lights, as Winchip had seen on the flagship of Commodore Moore. Two large jugs of lemonade graced a linen cloth on the large polished table as Winchip, Pardoe and Mr Ramblin conversed over the chart that depicted the island of Tortuga.

Winchip dabbed a finger at the chart. 'It is a large island, Peter, craggy and mountainous according to this description, with a good harbour in the south-west – sufficient to shelter a squadron of third rates, together with a great fort, built high upon a large and craggy flat topped mountain and overlooking the bay. ' Winchip removed his finger from the paper.

'Any enemy ships would also become prey to guns sited on the shallow ledges around the place, Sir. 'Pardoe nodded at his own words in the conviction that he was right. 'They would also be without hope of finding enough elevation to return fire.'

Winchip nodded his agreement. 'But any ships there at present could be blockaded with no difficulty at all – just as certainly as none could enter.'

There was silence for a good two minutes, each contemplating the hand-drawn sketch that was their reason for being there, a sketch that included the Admiralty's new contour system showing heights that he had read about in the gazette, yet finding no solution as to how they were to proceed. Pardoe, being temporarily lost for words, suddenly closed his eyes for a moment as he realised the dilemma in which his father-in-law found himself – there would have to be a reconnaissance and his commodore was unable to find the words that would send him once more into the dangers of the unknown.

'I would like to take a party on shore, Sir, if you would allow me to. We know nothing about the place and it would seem to be the wisest course open to us.' Pardoe took a good swig of his lemonade as if his request held little importance beyond the inconvenience of its necessity.

Mr Ramblin coughed to attract attention and then spoke with a conviction that forbade argument. 'You'll have no trouble at all, Captain. There's more than a few English families in Saint Domingue and on that you have my word. Chances are that I know a few; every one of them bein' retired naval folk, though they could be dead by now, I'm thinkin.'

'Dead, Mr Ramblin?' Pardoe's eyebrows were arched in surprise.

'Aye, Sir – of old age, I'd say.' The master looked nonplussed as the laughter rang out, not to know that it was more in relief than good humour.

Winchip held up his hand with a smile. 'You are ahead of me, gentlemen.' His face resumed the serious countenance with which he had opened the discussion, enough for Pardoe and the master to sober up on the instant. He looked Pardoe in the eye. 'There will be no reconnaissance, Captain – and no more subterfuge. I have made up my mind on the matter. Saint Domingue is French; it is as simple as that. As she is French, so I must assume that Tortuga is also.'

'Are you intending to attack Tortuga, Sir?' Pardoe was careful to keep the surprise from his question.

'I am contemplating it, Peter, although Commodore Moore gave thought to a cutting-out operation and I am tempted to agree with him. Firstly, however, we must find out just how many ships are in the bay, their size and their armament. We cannot remain in our present position for too long less we attract too much attention. I require Culpepper, in *Trial*, to sail between the mainland and Tortuga, to the east. She will put her officers in the tops and make a note of the shipping in the bay. She will then come about to return to us, forty miles due north of this position, having confirmed her findings on her second pass of the bay. She will do all this under a French flag.' Winchip drew himself up in his chair with a sigh as if glad to have given voice to what he had intended to do all along. 'Get along with you, Captain; and call *Trial* in and give her these orders, for Culpepper must be certain of what is required of him – and no more than that.' Winchip handed a small pouch to Pardoe with a smile. 'Tell me that you didn't think of Mr Basson when we talked of reconnaissance, Peter.'

'I did think of him, Sir – and would have been very glad of his company had the occasion arisen.'

'Good, I am glad to hear that you have a better opinion of him than hitherto. Men of the ilk of the master-at-arms are the backbone of our English navy – never forget that.'

In deep water, the squadron maintained its position in the prevailing easterly, forty miles north of Tortuga. Pardoe's *Eaglet* patrolled to the south, back and forth over the same waters, with Tortuga on the southern horizon and the squadron to the north.

The sun had been up for two hours and thankfully no longer destroyed ones vision as it danced on the choppy water in a dazzle of flashing light as it had done with the coming of dawn.

Pardoe stood impatiently at the binnacle, dressed in blouse and breeches with even his stock long since abandoned. Bowes stood with him, similarly dressed, their animated conversation together after their breakfast now diminished to idle chit chat – and still there was no sign of Culpepper. The decks had been 'holystoned' and watches had come and gone, with only the raising up of the crew to their divisions, ready to come about, to break the monotony and the vision of emptiness about them.

Pardoe straightened his back at the sound of a call from the tops and then spun on his heel at the sound of Archer' shoes on the poop deck.

'Trial has been sighted to the south, Sir. She has acknowledged our challenge.'

'Thank you, Mr Archer. Send up: "Captain to flagship" and then send to flag; *"Trial* in sight to the south – ordered to flagship"

'Aye, Sir' Archer was at the locker in three strides, knowing what he needed and taking-up the bunting in a trice.

Pardoe relaxed, knowing that there would be a long wait before *Trial* came up to them. His mind wandered back to the early days of *Eaglet*, to times when the sighting of any ship gave cause for apprehension. He thought of those who had died, often at his side – and of those of their enemies who now languished in English prisons – or on the sea bed. He thought, too, of Minorca, Lagos Bay and many other dramatic times in between when *Eaglet*'s crew had diminished in manpower with every battle, boarding, short engagement or cutting out. It was without difficulty that his mind turned to his father-in-law, Commodore Daniel Winchip, the man who had brought upon them all those things in the cause of duty. He was a man apart, a man for the moment, a brilliant tactician and a good commander – but he was changing. Pardoe was beginning to notice small quirks in his everyday speech and actions that gave him great concern. He remembered the French sixty-gun ship *Aventurier* in the Strait of Gibraltar, how they had taken her – and how Winchip had received a powerful blow to his head when her foretop had come down with a crash. Perhaps Culpepper's news would change all that, enough to make it essential that a party went ashore, and bring an end to this business that was causing his father-in-law so much worry.

Pardoe ran his hand through his curly golden locks as the breeze tossed it into his eyes, reminding him that he was hatless. Oh, that he had had a father like Winchip, or a father at all when his own had been killed at sea, in the service of His Majesty, unlike the Godforsaken step father who had rid himself of a twelve year old by sending him to sea as an unwanted burden when he married his mother, now, herself, dead and gone, destroyed by the man who had wasted the whole estate – and Pardoe's inheritance.

'Flag has acknowledged, Sir.' Archer stood beside Pardoe with his face bland but his eyes expectant.

'Thank you, Mr Archer, remain on the quarterdeck, if you please.' Pardoe shook himself free of his melancholy. 'I shall be in my cabin if required.' That he would be called to the flagship was more likely than not; to be dressed and prepared would be an advantage.

Winchip, his four captains and Captain of Marines Monk, of *Bellicus*, sat around the large table in the great cabin of the flagship. Coats had been discarded and swords were laid across the width of a large oaken chest as if they had been surrendered to mother comfort. Through the stern windows the ships of the squadron lay on calm waters in close proximity to the chains, ready and close enough for a mad dash of ship's boats were a gun to be fired, declaring the presence of a French ship on the flat horizon.

Master and Commander Horace Culpepper commenced his report at a nod from Winchip. 'On the first pass of the entrance to the bay, the ship being under tops'ls and close hauled, I observed two colliers at anchor in the centre of the bay, together with a sloop of war, and an armed barque – and two French ships-of-the-line tethered against a long jetty that projected from the shore under a great fortress that was some one hundred feet or more above the bay.' Culpepper paused for breath. 'The fortress consisted of extensive walls and a large number of embrasures that suggested heavy guns – though I saw none. These guns could be used to cover the whole bay – yet there were other guns, either side of the entrance to the bay that faced each other across the water and covered any ingress or egress of the bay. These, too, were heavy guns and may well have been thirty-two-pounders.' Culpepper took a deep breath, glanced at his piece of paper and looked again towards Winchip. 'I saw nothing on the return journey to change the fact that it would be a formidable task to even approach the enemy, let alone defeat him.'

'Thank you Captain.' Winchip afforded Culpepper a wide smile. 'So, there we have it, gentlemen, a difficult place to enter and an even more difficult one to leave.' Winchip put his arms into the air as if his plan were already in ruins. 'I see no immediate prospect of taking this place; not without a great loss of life and perhaps even the possibility of the loss of the squadron and our being captured to boot.' He sat back with an impatient grunt, daring any man to contradict the obvious. It was not in his nature to accept a defeat that was already staring him in the face – let alone admit it.

'May I speak, Sir?' Pardoe sat back in his chair with his right arm lying lazily across the chart before him as if its information no longer served any purpose.

'Of course, Captain.' Winchip's brow expressed first puzzlement and then a hint of hope.

'If Captain Monk agrees, his marines could take the guns either side of the entrance by stealth, perhaps at dusk tomorrow. These could be held until we ran up to twenty boats into the harbour and cut out the colliers and the armed barque before they knew what was happening. I submit that the fortress guns would be reluctant to hit the French men-of-war and, in any event, you would be beyond the harbour entrance with the squadron to cover the withdrawal of the boats and take off the marines.' Even as Pardoe finished he saw danger at every point; but then it had always been like that.

'It sits well with me, Sir.' Captain Monk was nodding his head, even as Pardoe was speaking. 'We shall have to take the guns without a shot being fired, or both the fort and the vessels in the harbour shall be standing to arms before we could blink.'

'Yet you think the plan has merit, Captain Monk?' Winchip was leaning across the table as he posed the question.

'Yes, Sir, I do. If I know the French they shall all be the worst for drink – and you can be sure that they have been inactive for a long time and inactivity brings on neglect as we all well know, Sir.'

Winchip turned to Pardoe. 'There we have it then! Tomorrow we shall lay our plans.' Winchip looked at both Monk and Pardoe in turn. 'As this operation is being undertaken by the marines, Gentlemen, 'twould be better that Captain Monk were in charge. What say you, Captain Pardoe?'

'I concur, Sir, without a doubt.'

'Good, then that is settled. *Trial* shall make another pass immediately and get a view of the gun emplacements at the entrance from her tops. Far better we know what they are made of – and their size, for that will tell us the strength of the opposition.' Winchip rested his hands on the table. 'Tomorrow could well turn out to be our day of destiny.'

CHAPTER TEN

The Taking of the Guns

The squadron stood off to the south-west of Tortuga, close to the land and silhouetted against the early evening sun, each ship with a French ensign flapping at the stern and riding to two anchors in the longshore current. Winchip and Pardoe stood at the fo'c's'le rail of *Bellicus*, the fiery trail of the setting sun coming down to them from aft, akin to a stream of molten iron spitting flashes of sunlight in their eyes, each red and rolling wave seeking to dominate the one before it. Like a cauldron, the sky above seemed to reflect the heat of it, the underbellies of the thin clouds of the heavens were tainted by it, yet the soft cool touch of the evening breeze shattered the illusion in its concept as it rustled the ensign above their heads.

'There, Sir!' Pardoe stabbed a finger towards Tortuga.

'Ah! The fishing boats – just as they were at Toulon, two lanterns, one above the other.' Winchip turned to Pardoe and slapped him on the back. 'Am I becoming so befuddled that *I* didn't think of the fishing boats? Now, we at least know how to approach the island without causing suspicion.'

'Indeed we do, Sir, once night has fallen and the wine has been flowing, though there shall be no need for lights if the moon is absent, for it will be as dark as pitch. May I suggest that the change of the dogwatches would be a good time to launch the first boats, the ones that will seek to destroy the barracks, for darkness will be looking to descend at that time?'

'Let it be so, Captain – and have the main force leave soon after their return.'

The stocky and sandy haired Lieutenant of Marines, Barry Barnes, of *Eaglet* stepped boldly ashore onto the sandy beach, sword in hand and with two horse-pistols stuck into his belt as a last resort. The night was darkening with the setting of the sun, yet the pale moon gave shape and form to the rocky escarpment that faced him. He looked up to the summit of the slope and found little there to daunt his men. It would be the rattle of muskets on rock and the curses of those who floundered that would give them away. He fervently prayed they had listened to his lecture back on *Eaglet*, extolling the need for caution and silence. At the point where they had arrived, they were at least two hundred yards from the gun-emplacement, far enough away to group and to gather their wits, yet not so far that they could not be heard as they approached.

'All the men are ashore, Mr Barnes.' Pardoe's whisper was hoarse and subdued. 'They are now yours to command, Lieutenant.'

'Thank you, Sir, I'll have them up that escarpment and gathered at the top, if you would be so kind.' Barnes knew that his men had been deprived of real action and for that reason alone he had told Sergeant Haggler to tell them the truth of things, distasteful as it was sure to be in any man's army; and remind them of past deeds when they had distinguished themselves with honour. It was now up to each man to do his duty, like it or not. In the moonlight his pale face broke into a wry smile – they had never let him down yet – but at that time they had carried their muskets loaded. Now, they were to use only their bayonets – the task to be completed without a single shot fired.

Lieutenant Niven counted the marines as they rose above the escarpment to the east of the entrance to the bay. Even with muskets it had been a silent affair, save for the odd grunt as a foot had been carelessly planted. Fortunately, there had been neither shale nor loose rock or else things could have been very different. Niven leaned forward to grasp the hand of Captain Monk who drew him upwards onto the safe soil at the top.

'If you will go ahead and report back to me, Mr Niven; numbers, defences and the state of the guns are all I require. When you are set to return, we should not be far behind you.' Monk saw Niven away and then turned to his stocky figure towards his men. 'You must work quickly and with bayonets alone. Thrust them deep and move on – let none of the enemy leave this place lest the bastard raises the alarm – I want them all dead; and I would prefer them to go quietly.'

The coastal path on which they stood was wide and open, interlaced with the ruts from wagon wheel that had bitten deeply into the soil; yet further inland the grass was higher, with shrubs dispersed at intervals and the vague shapes of small trees. It was the ground that Monk preferred and was certainly their safer option.

'Follow me.' Monk's whispered order was enough for the marines to melt into the scrubland. Two minutes later Monk's heart missed a beat as Niven appeared before him out of the semi darkness.

'There is a small barracks ahead, Sir, with a door at each end.' Niven's whisper was almost inaudible. 'Through a window I could see that most were asleep; but there are two men awake by the landward door and they have a woman with them – a black woman. I'd say; they total twenty at most'

'Did you see the guns?'

'There are two large ones, benign and unattended and with round shot and tools to hand; and a bunker for the powder - unlocked. There is also a furnace for heating shot; and it is not yet cold – methinks they light it to keep warm of an evening.'

'Thank you, Mr Niven. Shall you take the door to landward while I take the other?'

'Just as you wish, Sir, when I hear you go in, then we will do likewise.'

Monk was gone without another word, taking ten men with him into the darkness. Niven hastened to gather his half of the force and with a curt gesture bade them follow him. Laughter sounded in the silence of the night and the soft but joyful giggle of a female cautioning the attackers that women were present. The door was a flimsy thing with light showing through the cracks in the dry and twisted vertical planks. Niven beckoned to Corporal Wheeler, a marine of huge stature; and as the man approached him so Niven bade him prepare himself. The sudden crash of the door at the other end of the barracks came as a shock, expected or not. Niven nodded to Wheeler – just the once.

The landward door burst open with a loud crash and the rending of timbers, sending Corporal Wheeler deep into the interior, the bayonet on his musket rising and then plunging, time after time, thrusting at all that moved. Behind him, Niven launched himself inside the building, feeling the marines passing him as he thrust his sword into the chest of a man wide-eyed with fear and struggling to rise from his chair. Another came at him without a weapon before Niven could release his sword. The first lieutenant kicked him in the groin without a thought, feeling his sword come free from his first victim as he did so. As the marines continued to rush past behind him, so he thrust his sword into the stomach of a man who stood paralysed with fear and surprise. The fear that was in his eyes grew wide with abject terror as he looked down at the blade protruding from his body. At that moment Niven was attacked from behind as an arm was wrapped tightly around his neck, pulling him downwards and backwards, nails digging into his throat. He grabbed at the hilt of the knife at his waist, twisting and thrusting in one movement, feeling the blade enter flesh. With a wrench of his arm he drew the knife upwards, feeling it jar on a rib, at the same time feeling the offensive heat and wetness of gushing blood as it soaked his breeches. He withdrew the weapon and plunged again, higher and with more venom, hearing his attacker's breath belch from his throat, the ensuing blood splattering Niven's neck and face. The body went limp in his arms, falling against him as the last vestiges of life parted the man's body. He wiped the salty blood from his mouth and glared down into the face of his victim – at the contorted face of a large and black female. Niven released his grip with a shudder of horror, allowing the naked body of the woman to drop like a sack of potatoes, blood gushing from her mouth and seeping from the great rent in her torso. The vomit issued from Niven's throat before he could stop it; and with bowed head he saw it splatter onto the woman's sweat soaked chest as if cover her nudity.

The silence in the barracks was broken only by the gurgling in the throat of those who sought their last breaths; obdurate, even in death. Here and there a knife blade flashed in the light from a solitary lantern and then, at last, the silence was complete.

The panting marines stood back to allow Captain Monk free passage down the centre of the room. He came up to the landward door, the remaining timbers of which swung from a solitary hinge. His bloodstained sword hung limply from his hand. Monk looked past Niven's blood soaked breeches and down upon the dead female, who's dulled and staring eyes stared back at him. 'You survived a nasty experience, Mr Niven and, for what it is worth, she would have slit your throat to the bone, given the chance.'

'I wish to Christ that she had, Mr Monk – I truly wish that she had. To kill a man is one thing – to kill a woman is a blasphemy, a curse that I shall bear for ever.' Niven covered his face with his hands, not to know that the woman's blood seeped through his fingers and ran down his cheeks as if to scar him for life.

Monk leant down and twisted an ugly fish-gutting knife from the woman's limp hand, throwing it to the floor before guiding Niven to the freshness of the outside air.

The rigged yawl that had come to collect both Niven and Pardoe came about as it arrived at the main chains of *Bellicus*. Pardoe watched as Niven's figure climbed up the larboard battens, slowly and with great labour, his head held down and his blood soaked clothing telling those who watched from above more about events on the island than any words could conjure.

'Onwards to *Eaglet*, Hellard, with all haste – our work this day is not yet done.' Pardoe sat back into the stern sheets, his memory of the attack coming back to haunt him. The assault with Lieutenant Barnes had been vicious enough, though the opposition had been taken by surprise. The rise and fall of bayonets had been swift and deadly, yet when the deed had been done the marines had found no reason to reproach themselves, nor find any remorse for the ease with which the wholesale killing had been carried out.

Niven's recollection of events on the eastern side had shaken Pardoe to the core. The French troops in the barracks had stood no chance as the marines had used their bayonets with vicious efficiency. Even the muffled scream of the female had been cut short as Niven's blade had pierced her throat, just as the men in their beds had died before they had time to realise what was happening. Now, as with Barnes' men, those marines would be guarding the barracks they had just taken with no chance to bury the dead without being seen, bodies that would smell soon enough in the coming heat of the day.

As the yawl came up to *Eaglet*'s main chains, so Pardoe bade Hellard to tarry a moment. Within seconds he had discarded his clothes and plunged into the cool water. As he washed his naked body with undue vigour, his feet constantly treading water, so Hellard rubbed Pardoe's clothes together as if in a washtub in the sea alongside; and dashed them against the gunwale with the sole purpose of ridding them of blood before the stuff hardened and tarnished them forever – and quickly, lest the smell of the stuff attracted the sharks.

The dark of the night had descended with increasing rapidity. Booth lit the deckhead lanterns in their turn, bringing light to the great cabin of *Bellicus*. Winchip stared towards Tortuga, seeing nothing through the blackness of the windows. He grunted his thanks to Booth and at the same time made up his mind to go up to the deck through the companion. It was as he came down the quarterdeck that the challenge to an approaching boat came from the larboard entry port. Hellard's strident response came without preamble. So, the attack was already over and the barracks and guns secured. It had been a swift expedition but had it been successful? It was not long since when Winchip would have stridden forward to greet his own people; but now that he was a commodore, things were different – *too* damned different for his liking. To Lieutenant Guy Percival, he said. 'Ask Captain Pardoe and Lieutenant Niven to attend me in my cabin, Lieutenant, as soon as they come on board, if you please.'

The first action of the night seemed to have gone smoothly, yet Winchip knew in his heart that it would be the next event, the cutting out, that would cost the lives of too many of his people, yet it needed to be done – had to be done. As he resumed his seat in the great cabin, so he came to a sudden understanding. He was no longer the arbiter of his own affairs. From this time on, he could never share the likelihood of death during the boarding of an enemy, just as he could never again walk the gun-deck during an action, encouraging, directing or giving advice, sharing the same smell and taste of the smoke, or pulling on a rope when the gun-crew had been all but decimated. *Capable* came intrusively into his mind in a rush that he tried to ignore – but he failed and the weary old ghost came back to haunt him once again.

Winchip sat upright in his chair at the knock on the door. 'Enter!' He waved Niven and Pardoe to chairs without preamble, his eyes brightening with a genuine smile, just to know that they were safe and well.

Niven and Pardoe entered the cabin with the freshness of the night upon them, properly dressed and with their hats tucked beneath their arms. Pardoe spoke first, as was proper.

'The guns on both flanks of the entrance have been secured, Sir. The marines are now guarding them with their lives. Captain Monk has elected to remain with them.'

Winchip nodded. 'Frankly, I would expect nothing else – how many did we lose?'

'Not a single one, Sir, everything went to plan.' Niven's grin lacked the conviction of his words but it went unnoticed.

'That is excellent news, Gentlemen and I congratulate you both – but the hard part is yet to come. The boats are being gathered as I speak. There will be twenty-five of them, each manned with a fair share of both marines and seamen.' Winchip looked purposefully at Pardoe. 'This is your expedition, Captain. Do you have a plan?'

'I do, Sir. It is somewhat vague as we may be observed as we approach. If we arrive unseen, then we shall board each of the five vessels at the same time, take them and run out to sea – though God knows, it sounds too easy to my mind.'

'And if you are seen and the alarm is raised, what then?'

'We attack in either event, Sir. Should we be seen, then I shall delay events for as long as it takes for the lookout to realise that we are not what we seem. After that it is all down to providence and the force of arms.'

'And what about the men-of-war, Captain?'

'They are double anchored under the fort. If they are awake and cut their cables, then they may catch us; but that is in the lap of the gods.'

'I can offer you no alternative, Peter. All I can do is wish you luck for I have no advice to give you and neither would I deign to.' Winchip's face hardened for a single moment. 'Bring Burke back alive if you can. I have an urge to see how well he dances on a rope.'

'I shall, Sir, short of being too late, for there are those who would dangle him from a main yard in the blink of an eye.'

'Then let them know it is my wish that he be captured alive, Peter, for it is because of that man that some of our people may die this night.' Winchip held out his hand. 'Good luck to you both.' With the shaking of hands done with, he turned to the stern windows and stared out into the blackness of the night, one hand slapping upon the other at his back as he conjured in his mind how *he* might have planned the attack. As the realisation came to him that he would do just as Pardoe had described, so he allowed his face to relax into the rudiments of a smile.

CHAPTER ELEVEN

Mayhem and Death

In the light northerly air of the late evening, the first five boats pulled towards the sloop of war, while the remainder made their way to each of the other ships; the armed barque and the two dark and benign colliers. Far across the water and under the shelter of the fortress, the two men-of-war lay at anchor, gaily showing deck lights; lights that would inhibit the night sight of their lookouts and by virtue of that, any view of events in the bay. The boats of Winchip's squadron showed no lights and all oars were muffled at the thole pins.

Pardoe sat in the stern sheets of the leading boat as it progressed towards the sloop of war, finding himself drawn slowly forward and backwards with the long and shallow pull on the oars, knowing that should the alarm be raised, they could be blown out of the water before they could even come about. His sword lay across his lap and his right hand struggled to prevent his right knee from jerking up and down like a wild thing. In the air, the smell of the slave ships toyed with his nostrils; the stink of urine and faeces, sweat and squalor, all bundled into one; but then, with a light gust of wind, the stink was gone to another place. He dashed extraneous thoughts from his mind – five minutes more and they would be upon them. The expectation of another engagement so soon after the gun emplacements had found an unwilling gap in his train of thought, the prospect of a second attack in one night playing havoc with his nerves, knowing that his chances of survival were diminishing by the moment. It was with a grunt and a tighter grip on the gunwale that he dismissed even those fears to the back of his mind; he had little to worry about with the strength of those who would be fighting at his side, just as he had a duty to instil confidence into his people.

'Are you a' right, Sir?' Hellard's hoarse whisper came down to him and it carried a note of concern.

'Cramp, Hellard – just cramp.'

'We'm comin' up to 'er now, Sir.'

Pardoe could feel the tiller bringing the boat round yet he made no move. He was preparing himself to answer the challenge from the sloop in French – but could hear only singing and raucous laughter on the light night air; and as the ship loomed above them, so the boat stopped, gripped to the chains by willing hands without so much as a bump. One after the other the boats came alongside, each gliding noiselessly through the water until the five of them were held together to form a raft of men, poised and waiting for orders. Across the water in both directions, Pardoe could see that all the boats were in position. He nodded to Hellard who was waiting with the signal. The canvas cover came off a lantern to leave the bright red glow held high in the air. Before it could be lowered so the mass of men clambered up the side of the sloop's quarter like monkeys as others found their way through the entry port. The noise was continuous, shouts and screams and the sound of pattering feet along the length of the deck as men ran forward, others turning aft towards the poop and under it, to the officer's quarters and the captain's cabin – all unopposed and with no sign of hindrance yet to come. Pardoe launched himself down the main companion with as much fear for his own safety should he fall in front of the crashing feet behind him as he was for what was yet to come. In the semi-darkness he could see men rushing towards him, their shouts of warning on their lips as they came up to him, bare torsos glistening with sweat in the light of a solitary deckhead glim. There was no sign of an officer and no uniform to signify even a petty officer.

Hellard dashed beneath the poop with a pistol in one hand and a cutlass in the other. Behind him, like a pack of baying wolves, Eaglets crammed into the small corridor, coming to a sudden halt as the coxswain split the sentry's fearful face with a horizontal swipe of his heavy knife. Hellard stepped over the screaming and writhing body of the man and kicked down the door of the great cabin, his pistol pointing before him to deal with the unexpected. As he crashed through the swinging remnants of the door, so he saw the captain, wide eyed with fear, holding before him a naked Negro, a girl whose sudden screams brought life to the momentary cameo. Hellard fired, feeling a sting on his arm as the noise of the pistols, shooting in unison, came as one loud explosion. The young captain was flung backwards, across the single table and into the stern seat, the gaping hole in his forehead spraying blood left and right. The screaming girl crumpled to a heap on the floor with legs akimbo and her arms still clasped across her chest in scant defence rather than modesty. Beyond all that, the cabin was empty.

'Back, lads, to the companion!' Hellard turned and urged them back, seeking mere haste where speed was impossible.

Pardoe shot the first man in the chest and promptly flung his pistol among those who had followed in his footsteps. He grabbed at his second pistol as he parried the cutlass of a seaman, feeling himself pushed forward as Eaglets came from behind him. He feinted with his sword and then violently thrust the blade deep into the man's stomach as the swing of the seaman's cutlass left him exposed. There was little headroom, just as there was no chance to give a rallying call to those about him. Immediately, he engaged another seaman; and in the compression of bodies about him, stabbed the man's leg, it being the only part of him that he could reach. The man screamed and fell to the deck to be dispatched by a maul from behind that split his skull with the force of the devastating blow. Pardoe retrieved his sword with alacrity and took guard immediately, fearing he was too late – but there was no opposition left to him. The crew of the sloop were throwing their weapons to the deck and retreating from them as if to deny ownership. Their hands rose in surrender as they backed towards the hull and the messing tables that were strewn with bottles, pots and cheeses. A bucket of hot stew fell to the floor with a ringing crash, sending the steaming contents in a greasy wave across the deck.

'No more, lads!' Pardoe all but screamed the words lest any man died without the means of defence. Glancing about him, his eyes settled upon the only snotty present. 'Have the dead put over the side and each of these others bound hand and foot, Mr Pickering; and then have them put into a ship's boat to be held alongside where they can stay safe or drown, as they wish. I shall see how Mr Hellard is faring.' Pardoe dashed aft without waiting for a response. There were enough Eaglets to take care of twice the number they had encountered. Too late, he realised he had not waited to ensure that no Eaglet was either dead or wounded. As he passed the wheel, so he almost clashed with Hellard, striding aft with his cutlass in one hand and a smoking pistol in the other. His shirt was matted with blood at the shoulder.

'Are you hurt, Hellard?'

'No, may the Lord bless you, Sir, there was only the captain and he was in no position to put up a fight – and that's no lie. He were as drunk as a tinker and were using a young lass in his arms as a shield – she'm a blackbird, Sir. All 'e 'ad were a pistol and he were too slow to use *that* proper.' Hellard shook his head. He'm as dead as the dodo now, his head bein' stove in like.' He looked down at his own shoulder. 'Taint nothin', Sir – just a scratch.'

'The captain's death is a pity, Hellard; the man would have looked good, dangling from a yard arm. Pardoe summed up events and decided that their battle was won – and yet so easily. 'Young Lord Pickering is having our captives put on board the boats, Hellard. See that he gets help and then let us be gone from here, we need to make sail as soon as we can, towing our boats with the hope that the breeze stays with us,' Pardoe moved aft until he saw Midshipman Archer limping towards him. 'Are you hurt, Mr Archer?'

'No, Sir, I stubbed my toe on a damned ring bolt.'

Pardoe grinned in the dull light of the lantern. 'Have we a butcher's bill to pay?'

'None, Sir, not a man wounded and certainly none killed.'

'Thank the Lord for that. Hellard is rallying the men to raise fore and mains'ls and then cut us free, so take charge, if you please – and we are towing our boats, prisoners and all.' Pardoe watched the midshipman away and then dashed for the captain's cabin, his sword still gripped tightly in his right hand to cover any eventuality.

The cabin door was hanging from one hinge and inside the small space the black female was laying crumpled on the deck, her wails more of anger than self pity. Checking that the cabin was indeed empty, Pardoe pricked the girl in the rump with his sword, fearing to touch her naked body with his hands. Her shrill scream changed his mind with haste. He grabbed her by the wrists and drew her upright, seeing a fear in her that he had never seen before in the eyes of a woman; it was as if she anticipated her death – or worse, causing her screams to change to a resigned and hollow moan.

'Do you speak English?' On hearing Pardoe's words, the girl's eyes widened to the size of crowns. 'Well?'

The girl fell to her knees and grasped his legs. 'Y...yes...I do.' She blinked many times and then pulled herself to her feet as Pardoe lifted her up by her arm-pits. He looked about him and picked up the captain's deck coat from the floor. She stood, naked except for a scant loincloth and two strings of amber beads that hung beguilingly between her firm and upward pointing breasts. He wrapped the cloak about her, relieved to be able to cover the awesome beauty of her nudity. His mind had been oblivious to the noises of the ship preparing to sail. Now, with the sudden shout of distant orders and the movement of the vessel beneath him, he was stirred into activity. He took the girl by the arm and led her firmly out of the cabin and through to the quarterdeck and the binnacle.

'Stay here. I shall come back for you.' He looked into her eyes. 'You are safe now. You have nothing to fear from me and no other man will hurt you, on that you have my solemn oath.' Only when she nodded her understanding with dewy eyes did Pardoe leave to find Archer.

It was as he passed the capstan that he heard the bugle, the sound coming loudly and clearly on the light northerly wind. The high pitched note was craving a response and seeking action. Of a sudden it stopped but only to sound the "Aux armes" – the bugle's task undoubtedly accomplished.

Already, Céleste – for that was her name – was on the move beneath him; and as he looked upwards, so the maintops'l fell with a rattle and then a thud as it filled. He suddenly remembered that name – and even saw the vessel in his mind's eye at Boston, lying silently against the mole as if hiding a dark secret. He shouted for Archer and waited patiently for the midshipman to arrive.

'You called, Sir?' Archer stood in breeches and blouse, the sweat on his face glistening in the light from the deck lantern.

'Yes, Mr Archer. I think we need a helmsman.' Pardoe allowed his smile to broaden – this was no time for admonishments. 'I shall take the wheel for the moment. Do we have English bunting with us?'

'No, Sir.' Archer said sorrowfully.

'Could you send, "enemy in sight", in French?'

'Indeed I could, Sir.'

'Then do it, Mr Archer – the French men-of-war are stirring as we speak. Put it on the forestay where *they* cannot see it and yet the commodore can.'

Pardoe took a glass from the rack and looked aft, seeing nothing except the other vessels that they had attacked, all now on the move and blocking his view. It was to be a race to the entrance of the bay. Should the French cruisers reach there first, then there would be no hope for his four prizes, or for his Eaglets. His one hope had been the sloop's guns; but that useless thought brought nothing but a resigned grin to his face.

'*Bellicus* has acknowledged, Sir.' Archer panted out the words, while beside him stood Roberts, a helmsman from Eaglet.

'Thank you, Mr Archer – take over the watch, if you please.' Pardoe turned to Roberts and nodded towards the wheel. 'Steer small, Roberts, and keep to the centre of the entrance, for there are rocks aplenty waiting for you should you fail.'

She was still where he left her, standing by the binnacle, away from the capstan where the bars were being removed and stowed as he arrived. He took up her hand with a smile. 'What is your name?'

'Kuana...Kuana of the Mandinka...from Gambia...in Africa.'

'Well, Kuana, from this moment you are free – no longer a slave. I shall...' He caught her as she fell into a dead feint, cursing himself for his stupidity. If there had ever been a case for care and caution then he had obviously provided neither. It was down to Mr Pollard now, the only man qualified to take care of the girl where he had failed. He left her where she was, tucked up in the cloak and now with his jacket for a pillow. After her spell of slavery she would have little to complain about; and yet much to mourn, being so far from home.

Pardoe once more took up a glass from the rack and looked aft. All five vessels were now running south in line stern, askew, so as not to steal the wind, their boats trailing behind them. The armed barque was closing on Céleste, of that there was no doubt, just as those behind her were maintaining their station. Behind the last collier, Pardoe could see the profile of the first man-of-war, her yards swinging as he watched, coming round to the south having left the safety of the fortress. He knew at that moment that they would not catch up with them this side of the entrance to the bay, for they were under the shelter of the mountain that encompassed the fortress and out of reach of a steady wind. With a satisfied grunt, he placed the glass back in the oaken rack and covered it with the canvas flap. Even the drag of the boats in tow would not hinder them now. He could imagine the tall tales that would ensue from the incredible exercise just completed, just as he must also expect sad tidings as the list of those Eaglets, wounded or dead, would come to be known.

'Deck a'low - flag's a' signallin'!'

Pardoe waved a hand in acknowledgment and then grabbed the night-glass, handing it to Archer. 'Up you go and see what she says, Mr Archer.' He was certain it would be an instruction to sail to the south; there was no alternative. It was not long before Archer came down the mainstay.

'She says. "Proceed south with all safe sail", Sir – that is all. Mr Dundas is putting on the acknowledgment.'

'Thank you, Mr Archer – you did well today.' But Archer was gone and out of earshot, sorting his bunting as he went.

The entrance to the bay was approaching faster than Pardoe realised. Already, the promontories to east and west were becoming increasingly defined, changing from mere shadows to distinct cliffs, equally spaced apart from Céleste, which meant a passage through the gap without a chance of scraping a rock.

The flash of cannon fire from atop the cliff was followed by a ringing crash of sound, the noise akin to the tearing of cloth as a ball passed over the sloop, ending in a mountainous fountain of water that rose into the air, a cable distance from Céleste. From the west came a similar discharge which, again, thrummed across the tops to crash into the water a cable to the east. Pardoe tensed in terror, knowing that the shots still to come would be closer – if not on target. He took up a glass and focussed it on the point, his heart almost missing a beat as he saw a dark red glow in the dark. They were heating shot, of that there could be no doubt. There was nothing to do but wait. His small flotilla could neither change direction nor could they come about. It took little time to realise that the gun emplacements had been retaken and that they were about to receive the terrible consequences – though how it could have happened he couldn't begin to fathom.

Through the glass, the stern of *Bellicus* was apparent as she faced south with *Incensed* two cables off her bow and similarly positioned before her. Together, they would offer a wall of fire to the French ships as they emerged from the bay. There was hope in the sight of them but still the fear of another thirty-two pound ball, heated to a glowing red, from either of the cliff top guns. Pardoe was suddenly aware of Dundas at his side.

'What is it, Mr Dundas – is there something more I should know?'

'Our marines are firing those shots, Sir; there can be no doubt. Were they not to fire upon us, Sir, the French would know that the emplacements have been taken.'

'Thank you for that, Mr Dundas – you are right, of course, though I wonder why I didn't think of it myself.'

'With respect, Sir, perhaps you have done enough thinking for one day.'

Pardoe laughed out loud. 'Perhaps you are right, lad – but then, so have many others.'

CHAPTER TWELVE

'A Damned Good Drubbing!'

Commodore Daniel Winchip stood at the taffrail of *Bellicus* studying the stretch of water between the flagship and the entrance to the bay. Both the flagship and *Incensed* were devoid of sail, all canvas being tight up on the yards and beyond the reach of the French dismantling shot, yet ready to let fall at a moment's notice should there be the need for a chase – or escape. As for the rigging, that had been left to fate. The sight of the four vessels sailing towards him on the meagre wind filled him with both pride and anguish in equal measure, a mixture of emotions that caused him to neither smile nor weep for them. He thanked God that the execution of the plan had obviously worked – and that the vessels had been cut out successfully; but not so the escape, for in the early gloom of dawn the two French men-of-war were already making headway and looking to catch the little flotilla before it could reach the exit to the bay. He turned on hearing a polite cough from behind him.

'Yes, Mr Costly – what is it?'

'The sloop has acknowledged, Sir – and the flotilla is continuing on a course to the south.'

'Thank you, Mr Costly. Remain in sight, if you please.' Winchip turned to Niven. 'There is little you can do here, Lieutenant. Are the guns run out?'

'No, Sir, not as yet.'

'Then let it be done; and done as we planned. Both lower and upper decks will fire a broadside at the guns of the first ship; and then continue to fire at the second whilst *Incensed* does likewise with the first. If we disable their guns, then the day is ours. All guns shall be inclined aft, as we have practiced, so that we obtain the advantage with an early start to our cannonade – all double shotted.' Winchip looked down at the deck and finally nodded his certainty that nothing had been forgotten.

'Will that be all, Sir?'

'Yes, James.' Winchip jabbed a finger in the direction of the French. 'Those ships must be destroyed or taken, I care not which. If they are not disposed of now, they will gather others about them and harry us to a watery grave given the chance – you mark my words.' Winchip stood to his full height. 'Our people are the ones to do it above all others – and you can take *my* word for that, too.'

Niven gave a broad smile. 'With your permission, Sir, I shall attend the gun-decks and ensure that our people understand.'

'Off you go, then; and may Lady Luck go with you!' Winchip grinned to himself as Niven left. With all the gun practice behind them he had no doubt that the gun captains of both *Bellicus* and *Incensed* were up to the mark and eager to show what they could do. As for the French, Winchip was well aware that their eagerness for a fight was measured by their allegiance to their captain. What he could surmise from that was precious little, except that it was common knowledge that aristocratic French naval captains left much to be desired – and knew even less about the ship around them than they did about the sea. Convinced that he was right, he raised his telescope once more and was surprised to see that Pardoe's flotilla was making good headway and that his son-in-law had directed the colliers to spread themselves in order to occupy the width of the safe exit from the bay, dismissing any thought of being overhauled by the two sixty-gun French ships. As he lowered the glass, so he could hear the marines at the fo'c's'le urging the English vessels on. Niven turned at the companion on hearing the loudness of the huzzahs with a look of fury that turned into a wry grin as Winchip held up a hand.

'Let them be, James, it will encourage them for the fight, even if does scant good for discipline.'

'Excuse me, Sir; *Responsive* has just joined the line. She is astern of *Incensed* with her guns run out.' Midshipman Claridge's face was devoid of expression.

'Thank you, Mr Claridge.' Winchip was as nonplussed as the midshipman, yet he knew what Madoc was about. The man wanted to show his worth – let Winchip know that his new captain was worth his salt. 'Our new man is not afraid of a fight then, Lieutenant.'

'And thank God for that, Sir, now we shall have the French for certain.'

'Nothing is ever *that* certain, James.'

Céleste passed *Bellicus* under full sail with even her sprits'l full bellied in the rising wind. The sound of her cutwater cleaving the meagre waves was a joy to hear, as was the straining of her rigging and the lapping wash that came across to *Bellicus* and ran down the starboard side of the flagship's hull beneath the point where Winchip stood. Even from the captured sloop, the hands waved above her bulwarks and feint huzzahs were audible on the wind. For a moment Winchip was taken back in time, to an occasion when *Eaglet* had needed to forge ahead under a full suit of sail. Minorca came easily to mind, at a time when the English line under Admiral Byng had become broken and the French ship had sought to take advantage of *Intrepid*'s demise. *Eaglet*'s bar-shot had done its work; taking down the Frenchman's rigging and tops, to leave the enemy in total disarray – and the line intact. Winchip had been in breeches and blouse then, his crevat consigned to a pocket and his sword tied to his wrist by a lanyard and held firmly in his hand. He had been part of the action, as one with his people, yet now, he stood in an ornate hat and a 'flash-gold' coat, directing from afar – it would not do – it would never do. He called to Costly as he removed his hat; and by the time Costly arrived at his side, so his coat, too, was placed in the midshipman's arms.

'Take these to my cabin, Mr Costly, they serve no purpose here – and return with my fighting sword lest it turns to rust in its retirement!'

'Aye, Sir!' Costly went off with a bound, his flushed face wearing a cheeky grin.

Winchip strode along the upper gun deck, taking in the abashed grins of his people as he afforded them a nod or a pat on the shoulder. His fighting sword was clipped to his belt. This was where he belonged – where he wanted to be.

Already, Lieutenant of Marines Moyes-Pimm was urging his men to the nettings and to the tops in deep guttural tones, while those going aloft passed up well rolled protective hammocks to the cross-trees and beyond. A barrel of a man, Moyes-Pimm stood and watched as the great guns ran out with dull menace across the lay of the deck and the gun's crew heaved at the tackles. The loblollies came and went and the barefooted young powder monkeys deposited their cartridges where directed, excited yet afeared, all the signs visible in the quickness of their movements and the speed with which they departed the scene of imminent destruction; each with eyes as wide as saucers and mouths as tight as a purser's moneybag. Lieutenant of Marines Moyes-Pimm grunted his satisfaction and returned to the fo'c's'le. His marines would do their stuff, of that he was certain. It was his captain that held his concern, stuck up on a rock with half his men across the mouth of the bay.

Winchip found Niven by the boat tier. 'Mr Niven! Have the battle ensigns sent up – and smartly, if you please.'

'Aye, Sir.' Niven shouted orders at Midshipmen Piper and Foggerty and then disappeared into the darkness of the deck and the melee of seamen about the guns.

The cheers resounded round the ship as the battle ensigns jerked open in the increasing wind and fluttered free in the first faint light of dawn, curling their tails as the wind welcomed them.

The two colliers passed on their way, dark shadows in the gloom, the smell coming upon each and every man jack as Winchip knew it would, just as the speculation about the slaves would follow, when the vessels were past and gone; any spontaneous conclusions certain to confound them.

Winchip and Niven looked at each other simultaneously. The French were three cables distance from the point; and closing on them rapidly.

Niven came back to the quarterdeck, his chest heaving. 'All is prepared, Sir.'

'Thank you, Lieutenant, she is now yours. Remember *Corrine* at the Isle de Ré in '56, when we picked up Foche. It was a time for chastisement, not revenge. You have five minutes more than I expected. Give your orders as you see fit and consult me only when you when you must.' Winchip's eyes fixed themselves on Niven's, holding his stare for a moment until his first officer realised the meaning and intention of his commodore's words.

'Aye, Sir!' Niven was about to move away when he jerked to a halt. 'The guns are firing on the French from the points, Sir – it must be the marines! Good God!' Niven pointed across Winchip's face. 'They're using heated shot!'

'But not with any accuracy, Mr Niven.' Even as Winchip spoke, so the maintopgallant sail of the second French ship burst into flame and seemed to shrivel to nothing before their eyes to leave the mast burning like a torch. 'They are firing too high, Mr Niven and probably frightening themselves to death with equipment they know little about.' Winchip smiled. 'Yet it does the heart good to see it.'

'The French are coming through, Sir and are taking in sail – they mean to make a damned fight of it!'

'Of course they do, Lieutenant, they have more guns than we do. Gather your officers around you and have the youngsters stir themselves with the cartridges.' Winchip slapped his thigh as Niven departed. It would be another five minutes before the first French ship was upon them. He would not have dared to wish for such good fortune.

The roar of the twelve-pounder from Winchip's cabin signalled the commencement of the engagement. As the vile yellow-grey smoke billowed out, so Winchip watched and waited. As the second cannon fired, so he saw the first ball smash into the roundhouse of the Frenchman with a shower of smashed timbers, leaving a gaping hole and a dangling and bloody body to boot. It was a good beginning with the range established and the first shot drawing blood; but it was the shots yet to come that would make the difference.

The inclined guns of *Bellicus* roared out, one after the other, upper and lower decks, until they fell silent. Winchip knew what would happen next, there would a broadside from each deck, of that he was certain. Already, the guns were being re-aligned, dragged across the deck to the satisfaction of the gun captains. A splintering crash from amidships of *Bellicus* threw splinters high into the air as another ball struck the mainmast a glancing blow that sent a shiver through the length of it; but that was all, there had been no broadside from the French, just impetuous fire from undisciplined guns. Somewhere above a stay snapped with a loud report.

As topmen sped to the ratlines, so the upper deck guns discharged as one, offending the ears, belching smoke that was slow to clear, absorbing the deck until the wind took it forward, sending it sneaking through the rigging like mist in a graveyard before passing into the darkness and out to sea. The upper rigging of the Frenchman seemed to come alive. A t'gallants'l spar speared its way to the deck, emitting flashes of white sail in disarray. Clews, lifts and lines trailed behind the debris, halting for a moment as it collected a stay before continuing down to the deck. Furled sail was ripped apart and, as if for a finale, the foretopmast sagged to fall back against her main.

The result of the broadside from the lower deck eighteen-pounders was less obvious, the smoke blotting the Frenchman from sight and covering the water like a blanket, hiding the great wave brought about by the rocking of the ship as it recoiled from the power of the guns. As the smoke cleared, so it became obvious that the round shot had struck the Frenchman a devastating blow, smashing and penetrating the timbers of her tumblehome and finding her gun ports, pitching men bodily into the sea or leaving them hanging from the ports, their lives extinct before their battle had begun. Winchip slapped his thigh. The next broadside would do her an even greater mischief.

On an impulse, Winchip went down the main companion taking two steps at a time. As he arrived, so Second Lieutenant Percival appeared through the smoke, sword in hand and blood defacing the whiteness of his blouse.

'Are you hurt, Lieutenant?'

'No, Sir, we lost a gun and three men with it – two into the water and the third with the surgeon, Sir.' Percival shouted the last as the guns fired once more, his worried brow telling Winchip that he wanted to be there with his people.

'Off you go, Lieutenant – and tell them that I am with them!'

Percival disappeared into the smoke as another crash of smashed timbers came from forwards. As Winchip strode the length of the gun deck, so he peered through the gun ports towards the French. There were huge gaps in her tumblehome and many of the French guns were lying idle, out of commission and unattended. Had he stayed a moment longer he was certain he could have counted those guns that remained in action on the fingers of both hands. He recoiled suddenly as a bulky figure bumped into him, dragging an injured seaman from the fray. He saw immediately that it was Munro.

'Let me help you, Douglas!' He almost shouted the words as he grabbed at the injured man's feet. 'What the devil are you doing here; you're a secretary, no longer a seaman?'

'And you are a commodore, if I'm not mistaken. Who is tending the quarterdeck?'

They lifted the wounded seaman across the deck between them, to the larboard side where they laid him down, Winchip nodding to the busy Doctor Miskin as he worked on a wounded seaman stretched out on the midshipmen's table. Percival's high pitched voice rang out a chorus of orders out of the smoke; to the gun captains as soon as the next broadside had been delivered. The order of the load was shouted in rhythmic time, each man seeking not to fumble nor slip as he performed his specific task. The next broadside crashed out on deafened ears – a dull boom

The Eaglet in the Americas

that moved the very deck itself. The powder monkeys rushed in through the smoke to deliver the cartridges for the next discharge, just as the Loblollys carried in the great eighteen-pound balls with haste and were gone again just as quickly.

Winchip looked at Munro and jabbed his finger upwards. At that, he turned and left the scene of noise and carnage and took to the companion. Douglas Munro was a step behind him.

'God, it is hell down there.' Munro wiped his brow. 'Pardon my blasphemy but I had to do something, Daniel, I could never sit at my desk and not be part of it, my word I could not. I shall always be a sailor first and a damned secretary a distant second.'

Winchip, ignoring Munro's outburst, stared across at the Frenchman, seeing her shattered tops and the damage to her tumblehome. At a glance he knew that the enemy was beaten – it only required the lowering of the French ensign to end it all.'

'She is done for, Daniel – you have won, my friend.' Munro patted Winchip's shoulder. 'My word – that was a damned good drubbing if ever I saw one!'

Winchip looked over towards *Incensed*'s opponent, seeing less damage than he expected. She was still in the fight, of that he was sure. He had no sight of *Incensed*, the smoke from the guns of Bellicus having obscured everything. He held onto the binnacle as the upper and lower decks of *Bellicus* seemed to discharge their guns as one. The broadsides were devastating in their noise and smoke; but as the echoes of the discharge diminished, so the silence became absolute. From the Frenchman, there was no reply.

'Mr Costly!' Winchip waited for the midshipman to come down from the signal locker. 'Have the guns cease their fire, Mr Costly – as quickly as you like.' Already, Costly was gone, shouting towards Niven and then plunging down the companion. Too late, the lower deck fired once more, the heavy shot smashing in the planks of the Frenchman's hull and destroying the configuration of her strake. For certain, she was done for, her last gun fired under a French captain. As if to confirm Winchip's assumption, the tattered French ensign came down her halyard in small jerks, as if even that simple task was being executed by someone close to death.

Winchip shook his head, for a defeated ship would always be a shamed ship, yet, as he shaped the words in his mind, so the sun put her head above the parapet to commence the new day.

CHAPTER THIRTEEN

The Black Pit of Hell

The ships of Winchip's squadron were brought to deep anchors some fifty miles west-south-west of Cap à Foux on the south-western point of Tortuga. The longshore current flowed placidly past the ships to form eddies and small whirlpools beneath their counters. It placed them in full view of any ship seeking to take the Windward Passage, which was to Winchip's liking and would, perforce, be to the chagrin of anything less than a French Fleet.

On the day following the battle, the early morning sun had risen to the noise of loud voices and the thud of mauls as repairs were carried out to the French men-of-war and to both *Bellicus* and *Incensed*. The eight dead seamen from the flagship were committed to the blue translucent waters with honours due, each man wrapped in a hammock, laden with a weight of round shot that would speed his corpse to the deep and clear waters of the Caribbean Sea. The French officers had been paroled to commit their own dead from the privacy of *Spartiate*, the larger of the two French ships. Those of the French who were killed were numerous; and it was to be a long and tedious ceremony to commit them all under the white flag of France with its fleur de Lys at the centre; for the moment proud, yet still resigned to its place beneath a gaily fluttering blue English ensign.

Winchip, Niven and Loxley sat apprehensively in the sternsheets of the longboat as it bobbed towards the nearer of the two colliers. As bad luck would have it, the wind came down to them, bringing with it a concoction of smells that immediately churned the stomach. Only Mr Miskin, the surgeon of *Bellicus*, gave no sign of discomfort as he sat with baleful eyes on the bow thwart; and neither did he cover his nose and mouth with a kerchief as were Winchip and Niven, both.

'We shall not go to the armed barque, James.' Winchip spoke as though he had at last come to a decision. 'Burke and Pascal shall come to me when I am ready for them.'

'They shall be going nowhere else, Sir. Mr Percival was responsible for taking the barque and he understands his orders. They are separated and in irons, without contact and are being fed and watered.'

'Good.' Winchip gave a nod of satisfaction. 'A couple of days in solitude will put the fear of God into them. By the time I get to speak to them, they will be willing to do anything I ask.'

'Willing to do what, Sir?'

'Fear not, James, I have something in mind but not yet perfected. They will swing, of that you can be certain.' Winchip spoke across the helmsman to Loxley. 'You know more about slaves than any man in the squadron, Stephen. You must be the man to guide us, for I fear we shall not like what we find, or have the knowledge to put it to rights. Can I rely on your help?'

'Of course you may, but your problem is easily solved, Daniel; but the French will not like it – that is for certain.'

'What do you have in mind?'

'Transfer all the French prisoners to one of the French ships and use the other to house the slaves, for they'll not last long in the colliers, you can take my word for that!'

'They've lasted this long, Mr Loxley.' Niven spoke as he prepared himself to take the battens as the boat approached the first collier.

'Have they, Mr Niven? Loxley shuddered and pressed a kerchief to his nose.

'We'm Comin' to the entry port, zur!' Pender swung the tiller over.

'Thank you, Pender.' Winchip put himself to rights. 'Who took this collier, Mr Niven?'

'Mr Bowes did, Sir.' Niven scrabbled for a kerchief and pressed it to his face. 'My apologies, Mr Loxley, you have made your point!'

On arrival at the chains, Winchip climbed the thick battens that were the steps, his hand clinging to the rough fibres of the knotted rope. Once through the entry port he had eyes only for Lieutenant Bowes, who's usually tanned face had turned to a shade of grey. He waited impatiently for the pipes and the unnecessary salute from Lieutenant of Marines Barnes' and his bullocks; and when that was done he exchanged courtesies with Bowes and then nodded towards the poop. To have spoken at length would have required a relaxation of the throat; and Winchip was not yet ready for that. The smell had even permeated the captain's cabin; but it was a mite easier.

Winchip laid his hat on the rough-hewn wooden table. 'Well done, Mr Bowes, yours was not a pleasant task yet you seem to have coped very well.'

'Thank you, Sir – did we lose many people in the cutting out?'

'A few; but less than I expected, thank the Lord.' 'Winchip looked out of the ship's stern window and sniffed the air. 'What have we here, Lieutenant, besides what I can smell?'

'Words cannot describe it, Sir. You must need to come with me to discover the whole picture – though under any other circumstances I would submit that you left it to others.'

Winchip grabbed at his hat. 'I wish that option were open to me, Lieutenant. Let us be at it, before I change my mind.'

Bowes led the way to the main companion, situated similarly to that of *Eaglet*, next to the boat tier; but here it was guarded by two marines with fixed bayonets. Gingerly, he descended, going down sideways lest he slipped on the filthy steps. A lantern hung from the deckhead and others were obvious down to the fo'c's'le, each giving light enough to see the horror that Bowes had feared to describe.

Winchip, following Bowes and squinting in the darkness, allowed his eyes to accustom themselves to the gloom. What he eventually saw made him stagger back with a gasp. 'My God above...!'

The black bodies, male and female, lay naked beside each other, in three rows athwart the deck from Winchip's viewpoint, all the way down to the ship's bows, becoming vaguer as the distance and increasing gloom deprived him of detail. Had he taken two more steps he would fallen amongst them, without a doubt.

'Let us have more light down here, Lieutenant. I am not given to doing God's work; but something must be done for them – and *now* if they are to live!' Winchip had heard the low groans and the odd weak cry for succour that came to him from out of the darkness.

Bowes nodded to the nearest marine. 'Get more lanterns, marine, from wherever you can find them!' He looked back at Winchip. 'It is the black pit of hell down there, Sir. There are dead ones down here, too. I left them for you to see, or I would have had them prepared for committal. As for the others, they are all shackled and will need a smithy, or a key, to free them.'

Winchip stood as high as he was able. 'Then let it be done, for they shall not stay like this for another minute if I have the means to release them.'

'There are difficulties, Sir, for there are over on hundred on this half-deck alone – and there is the fear of revolt once they are freed.'

'Are there *more*?' Winchip was taken aback.

'Aye, Sir, on the deck below, about another two hundred – below where we stand.'

Loxley spoke from behind Winchip. 'Give me the men and the authority, Daniel and I shall have this lot transferred in a trice. It will not be a pleasant task though, better done by volunteers if it is to be done with care – and I shall need sweet water, for you can be certain their casks are tainted.'

Winchip shook his head in despair. 'Have them fed and watered somehow – but do it, Stephen, even if you have to rob every galley in the squadron! By the time you have done that we shall have a smithy here. Perhaps, then, we can get them to fresh air, a few at a time, for the poor souls must be shown that at least we care.' Winchip shrugged off his concerns lest he dwelt too much on them. 'Double the marines on deck, Mr Bowes and give Mr Loxley all the help you can, for he will need it; that is for certain.

'I shall have the hoses rigged, Sir – give them the means to wash themselves, together with the deck. That should buck them up a little.'

Stephen Loxley interrupted. 'May I suggest that you have them drink first, Mr Bowes, lest they swallow the sea water?'

Bowes nodded his understanding and then looked back at Loxley. 'I have a means to help, Mr Loxley. Mr Pollard, on *Eaglet*, has been looking after a Mandinka slave girl who speaks English. She was found by Captain Pardoe on the sloop-of-war. She is now on Eaglet.'

'Then I shall go and get her and return immediately, Mr Bowes, she will be invaluable to us.' Loxley was back on the deck, through the entry port and down into the jolly boat before there could be any objection.

As Bowes went up through the companion, so Winchip spoke directly to Niven. 'Get yourself over to the other collier, James and repeat my orders – have someone get them cleaned up and put to rights; but retain some form of restriction and show the red tunics. What Mr Bowes said about revolt should not be taken too lightly.' On an impulse, Winchip turned back to Bowes. 'Some fresh air down here will help, Lieutenant. Have some men rig an awning and open the forward hatch.' Winchip turned and climbed the steps into daylight, suddenly aware that he was becoming inured to the smell.

The air on the deck proved him wrong. He faced towards the clean air from windward and took in gulps of the stuff, remaining into wind until his brain started to whirl. Refreshed, he moved to the taffrail and considered his options, realising at once that he was governed by necessities. He strode to the fo'c's'le, to Lieutenant of Marines Moyes-Pimm and his marines. Moyes-Pimm saw him and tipped his hat in salute.

Winchip was unequivocal. 'I wish you to go to the other collier with some of your marines, Lieutenant, to make your presence known.' Winchip let that sink in. 'You will answer to Mr Niven who will go with you.'

'I will see to it immediately, Sir.' Moyes-Pimm had the look of dread in his eyes and the smell of a dead fish under his nose but Winchip ignored it. Things that were sordid had little to do with the man's idea of society proprieties. Now, he was about to accept the unacceptable, if only to add to his education.

Winchip relaxed and stared into space. There was much to do and there was the still the threat of other French ships in the area. He needed to be back on *Bellicus* where he would be instantly available should there be a sighting on the horizon.

'Pender!' Winchip shouted to his coxswain through the entry port, only to find that the jolly boat was on its way to *Eaglet* with Loxley and from thence to the other collier with Niven. He put on a brave face and searched out Bowes, the man who, at this moment, had every right to make a claim on his services.

By four bells in the afternoon watch the noise of repairs had diminished to that which could be described as normal. Spare masts and a spar had been taken up to the *Frenchman*'s tops and the damaged ports amidships of *Bellicus* were once again useable, requiring only a lick of black stuff to bring them back to normal.

From the stern windows of *Bellicus*, arrived at by hailing a passing longboat laden with three water casks, Winchip watched as boats passed to and fro between one of the two French ships-of-the-line and the colliers. The slaves in the boats were huddled together, swaying back and forth in time with the stroke of the oars. At least someone had found a key or a smithy. He hoped that Bowes had delegated someone to provide the food and water, not only for the slaves; but for the French prisoners as well. The fact that Stephen had launched himself so willingly into caring for the slaves had meant a great deal to Winchip. It was as if Stephen was trying to make amends for all that had gone before, much of which should have been laid at the feet of others. Winchip slapped his thigh and smiled to himself, already anticipating the uproar his actions would bring about when it came to their arrival at Guadeloupe – but that was in the future and this was here and now. He turned away with a shake of his head. Tomorrow was another day.

Kuana sat in the stern sheets of *Eaglet's* jolly boat with Stephen Loxley at her side. She still wore the coat that Pardoe had thrown about her shoulders, to cover her nakedness in the cabin of the sloop. As the oars set into their rhythm, so she allowed her body to swing with the motion of the boat. The shock of the events of the past few weeks had dulled her brain; but not enough to prevent her realising that there was yet hope for her own salvation as well as for the Mandinkas that were with her. How glad she was that she had learned English in the Catholic Mission, though she had learned little else of the things in which she had no interest. Above all this, she had not been violated, though there had been those who had tried, only to be attacked by her fellow Mandinkas, to their cost. She wondered, too, if her parents were mourning her death, thinking she had been taken by a beast...

'We shall be there soon.' Stephen smiled and patted her hand, unaware that he had interrupted her thoughts.

Kuana looked at Stephen and held her gaze on him for a moment. How strange it was that some white men acted so differently from others. The man beside her was of the gentle type, she had seen them before, in Gambia. He was kind and considerate and so quick to react in the cause of a lady. The other one – the man who had given her the coat, was of a different breed, his sidelong eyes had searched her body in secret – and he had a wife, she could tell. She found it strange that a man can lust after a woman when he already owns one – or more.

'Steady there, easy oars!' Hellard's voice transcended all other noises.

Kuana took Stephen's hand as he helped her through the entry port of the French man-of-war. As she climbed to the deck, so she saw her fellow Mandinkas cavorting in the gush of water from the canvas hoses.

'Is this the one who speaks English, Mr Loxley?'

'It is, Mr Bowes.' Stephen released Kuana into Bowes' care and watched with delight as she hugged her own countrymen. He stood where she could see him, a source of refuge should she be overcome by events. As Bowes spoke into her ear, so she nodded her head in understanding. As he finished talking, so she held up her hands for silence. The slaves gathered around her, the women as naked as the day they were born and some heavy with child and with breasts that strained to hold their contents; and yet they showed neither coyness nor fear of those about them. Stephen shook his head in wonder at such things. He had seen many slaves, including heavy breasted women and small, screaming children, but none such as Kuana, now dressed in a captain's deck coat, acting the part of a princess. It was at that moment that he fell in love with her; a forlorn hope, well aware that he had very few of the qualities that she deserved in a man.

At last she came back to him, grasping his hand like a bow anchor lest she faltered on the battens. Her hand was cool and without the dampness of sweat as was his.

'Give way!' The jolly boat eased away from the *Frenchman* at Hellard's command and at once Stephen could feel the pressure of her next to him. She had spoken to the slaves and they had made vocal responses that meant nothing but to the slaves themselves; and as she had finished speaking, so they had chatted among themselves and asked her questions which she had answered with authority. To an admiring Stephen it had meant nothing; but the outcome was that the slaves were contented and patently at ease, whereas at one time the tension had seemed to be mounting. That was all that mattered, except that, given the opportunity, he would have transported them home to Africa himself rather than let them move on – to the terrible destiny that surely must await them.

At the end of the first dogwatch, as the great orange sun sank below the western horizon, Stephen stood at the taffrail of *Bellicus* with Kuana at his side. She had placed her hand in his and still they were clasped together, staring astern as if words would be an intrusion. The trail of the sun came down to them and the underbellies of the clouds glowed a fiery red, maintaining the memory of the heat of the day.

As time went by, Stephen became confounded by a feeling that nothing could assuage. His loins ached and his head span as he tried to find justification for his thoughts when he knew that somehow his feelings towards Kuana would be dashed in their infancy. It was with a shock that he realised Kuana was speaking to him.

'Your eyes are wet with tears that won't fall – are you sad?'

'No.' He smiled at her beautiful face, now golden in the dying sun.' I have a great admiration for you and I have no idea how I can explain my feelings. I have known you for only a day and already I feel as though I have known you for ever, in my heart.'

'At home in Mandinari we call that love and have a great respect for it – but usually it takes longer than half a day.'

They laughed together and drew closer. Stephen looked down at her, her head being below his shoulder. 'I have never known a woman, Kuana. At this moment I am afraid to say anything lest I offend you – and yet we must speak together as I have so much to say and so much to ask you.' He saw her shiver in the cooling air and took off his pea jacket to cover the deck coat that was already round her shoulders. 'Come, let us go below, it is getting colder and you must eat.'

They ate together at the midshipmen's table, facing each other across the dishes of food and the bottle of claret that Booth had supplied. It was by the light of the lanterns that Kuana eventually left him. She paused at the canvas curtain that was the entrance to the gun-room and turned to smile at him. 'Aleikum asalaam, my new friend – my Stephen.' With that, she allowed Booth to show her the way to the dispensary, where the grill in the door had been covered over, a jug of water and a basin had been put on the side and a hammock had been slung. At least she would sleep well, which is more than can be said for those French prisoners who would now be huddled together in the bowels of their ship, wondering what their fate would be, knowing that they had taken part in acts of piracy, or whether the stories of English prisons were true – or even worse, would they be hung, as pirates always are?

CHAPTER FOURTEEN

Pirates All

With the wind a few degrees abaft the beam, the English and French men-of-war had been obliged to reduce sail on angled yards to accommodate the ship-rigged colliers as the ugly slavers plied clumsily northwards, to the selfsame spot from which Winchip had agonised over the attack to be made on the place.

Winchip had been impressed by the authority with which Stephen had conducted affairs, moving from ship to ship and deck to deck, in an effort to both placate and settle the agitated slaves. There had been three births in the one day and the total number of dead slaves had risen to forty-five, many with rigor mortis when the bones needed to be snapped to affect a moveable package to the upper deck. At eight bells in the evening watch, the bodies had been slipped into the water from the longboat, out of sight and with a short prayer of committal from Mr Pollard, an operation that would have gone unnoticed were it not for the flurry of activity in the water as the sharks moved in.

Winchip rose from the stern seat and sat at his small Gillow table to complete his journal, despite the continuous sound of the last repairs being done to *Bellicus*. What he had written already made strange reading but that had never prevented him from telling the facts as they really were. With his quill sharpened he busied himself, naming those who had come to his attention and emphasising the protective part played in the piracy by the French men-of-war, consistent with Winchip's belief that the slaves and their French Navy escort had been bound for Martinique. He replaced the quill in the silver stand and steepled his hands. There would be much to write about and most of it would be written accusingly – words he may regret and might not stand him in good stead with those who condoned the sort of treatment that slavery brought down upon innocent human beings. It was only his pragmatism that stopped his anger from overflowing; and the knowledge that things would never change. He closed the journal with care, knowing that he would be adding things of a more serious nature within the hour – things that would have fatal consequences for some and a surprise for others. It also crossed his mind that the slaves would be hard pressed to survive in the plantations of Guadeloupe or Martinique, should the latter place be taken at last by the English. He laughed without humour and briefly at that. Had he really saved these slaves so that they could continue onwards to their terrible fate? He slapped the table – it was a battle he could never win, though he would leave his mark upon the place; and on the strength of that he resolved to first write to Madeleine and to Emma, though what little he dared to relate could be written on the head of a belaying pin.

In spite of his despair at having to set out for Guadeloupe with such a diverse company, Winchip at least had the satisfaction of knowing that, according to his orders, his mission would be completed on his arrival at Basse-Terre. His only problem was one of manning. He had a sufficient number of seamen to sail the English and French ships; but only enough to man the guns of one side on each of them. It had been done before and would be done again; but it could never succeed should a French fleet appear on the horizon.

At last he rang the small brass bell on the table, bringing the head of the sentry round the door as a rabbit would peer from its burrow.

'Tell the master-at-arms that I am ready for the prisoner, Burke!'

Douglas Munro was the first to enter, with both the notes of evidence and the Book of English Maritime Law gripped in his hand. He laid them on the table where he was about to sit at Winchip's right hand and then took his seat, drawing the ink stand towards him. He flipped open the lid of the ink well and laid a quill to hand.

Winchip smiled. 'This is not a court, Douglas.'

'I came prepared, Daniel, for with you in the chair it could turn into anything.'

The master-at-arms, Mr Basson, followed behind Munro but turned abruptly to face back to the door. The two marines dragged, rather than carried in, the reluctant Seth Burke. The man was as pale as death and wide eyed. Saliva was on the dark stubble of his chin and his thinning hair was awry. His clothes were dirty and in disarray and he smelt of the bilges. He stood in front of Winchip, supported by the two marines.

'Fetch a chair for Mr Burke – he spoke to no-one in particular – the man is not fit to stand.' Winchip looked to Mr Basson. 'Has this man been mistreated, Master-at-arms?'

'Not to my knowledge, Sah!' Basson looked at a spot high above Winchip's head.

Winchip waited as Burke sagged into one of Winchip's dining chairs. Winchip's agent for the last few years had changed a great deal. Gone was the gaunt rakishness of the man he once knew, though the two gold rings that adorned his fingers were still real enough. His face was almost puffed-out with good living and his clothes, now misshapen, had once shown the cut of quality.

'I have to consider sending you back to Boston, Mr Burke. There are many people there who seek the money you have stolen from them and others who seek your head for what you have done.'

'No, Sir, you cannot, for they will hang me for sure – and me an Englishman.' Burke's glazed and wandering eyes suddenly focussed on Winchip as if daring him to do such a thing.

'I shall hang you if you do *not* go back, Mr Burke! You are a thief, a scoundrel, a conspirator in the matter of piracy – and a fraudster. I think those are causes enough for a hanging, don't you? I know a magistrate in Boston that would hang you for any one of those offences and be delighted to do so.'

'God in Heaven – I am done for, Captain. What can I do to make amends?'

'It is too late, Mr Burke. Perhaps I should hang you today as the sun goes down.' Winchip looked at Mr Basson. 'Give him a meal, Master-at-arms but not too much, lest it breaks the rope.'

'Aye aye, Sir!' Basson nodded to the marines, who lifted the weeping Burke like a sack of potatoes and dragged him, yelling and swearing, out of sight.

As the door closed, so Munro turned to Winchip. 'That was a bit much, Daniel, the man's entitled to a fair trial.'

'Not in my command, Douglas. You know he is guilty, as do I – and others I could mention. Were you to return to Boston today, you would find a hue and cry for the man, baying for his blood; men who have lost their businesses and are now in debt.'

Munro thought for a moment, a shadow of a smile gathering at the corners of his mouth. 'You old devil, Daniel! You are trying to scare the man into telling you something – or giving you something, aren't you?'

'You are absolutely correct, Douglas.' Winchip grinned. 'He stole Stephen Loxley's savings, every penny the lad saved. He also made Stephen sign the transaction for the stolen slaves in his intended absence, which makes Stephen, rather than Burke, the conspirator.'

'So, what do you propose?'

'Burke shall take the king's shilling, Douglas. He will then serve in His Majesty's Navy – a free man for a few days, though I doubt he will realise what he has done.'

'My Lord, what a jape that is! I have to admire you, Daniel but were they Pascal's to sell?'

'They were the property of others, Douglas. The slaves will have come from a dozen slave ships, most of which have been sent to the bottom with the best part of their crew. There are no longer any owners alive, Douglas, except Pascal – and he obtained them through piracy. The only reason the colliers are with us is because he needed the space in which to carry them.' Winchip looked directly at Munro. 'I am sure that you will find a goodly sum of money in Pascal's baggage.'

'I shall go over to the barque and have the baggage searched, Daniel.' Munro rose from his seat and was about to depart when he turned back. 'What the devil will you do with nigh on five-hundred slaves, Daniel?' He resumed his exit with a grin when Winchip raised a finger and tapped his own nose.

Winchip rang the bell once more. 'Ask the master-at-arms to bring in Captain Pascal.'

Pascal was a giant of a man, swarthy, bearded and with a swathe of black hair tied at his neck with a floppy ribbon. His nose was beaked and large and his lips like that of a clam except that they were twisted in a perpetual sneer. He was dressed in black, though his thick leather belt had once been tan.

'Give Captain Pascal a chair.' Winchip had a smile on his face as he spoke. He stared at Pascal for a moment and then looked down at the paper before him, the sheet on which he had made a few notes and an impatient scribble in one corner. 'Are you a pirate, Captain?'

Pascal recovered from his surprise at such a direct question. 'Bless you, no, Sir. I just convey slaves for their owners – it's a lawful pursuit, Sir, as I'm sure you are aware.'

'Of course, Captain.' Winchip looked down at the paper before him. 'I am informed however, that you sold these slaves – Winchip waved a vague hand towards the window – to Mr Burke, is that so?'

'Oh yes, Sir! Mr Burke was looking to buy them from me and eventually, I gave in.' Pascal drew himself upright and cast glances at his escort around him as if daring any man to doubt his word.

'Then you would be willing to sign an affidavit to that effect and clear the matter up – for your protection, you understand?'

'Well, I don't know nothin' about signin' nothin', Sir'

'Then you had better show me your manifest and conveyance papers – just for my records you understand. You instructions from the original owners of these slaves will do perfectly.'

'I don't deal in papers.' Pascal sensed a trap and his face clouded on the instant.

'Then you are in breach of His Majesty's Maritime Law, Captain Pascal; and that is a hanging offence.' Winchip hurried on before Pascal could collect his wits. 'We shall be hanging Mr Burke at sunset this evening.' Winchip studied the piece of useless paper before him. 'I see no reason why we cannot accommodate you at the same time. '

'Damn ye! Ye can't hang a man, just like that!'

'I can, Captain Pascal, as you shall see – and from the best vantage point, at that.'

Where's this bloody affidavit then? I'll sign if ye stops talkin' about hangin' and here's me word on it!' Pascal spat on his hand and held it out to Winchip.

Winchip spat on his own hand and then gripped Pascal's, only to have it pumped up and down in Pascal's utter relief. He waited until Pascal had signed the paper that Munro put in front of him. Only then did he speak.

'Have him put in irons, Master-at-arms – return him from whatever part of the ship you have stabled him.' Only when Pascal was through the door and out on the deck did Winchip hear the bellows of blind fury emanating from the dull witted pirate. He turned as Munro entered with a large canvas bag and a broad smile.

'We have done for them both, Douglas. The only point now is do they deserve to die?'

'Let others decide, Daniel; that is my opinion. Munro sat as he spoke. 'The man with the means to find out the truth of things is the lieutenant governor at Guadeloupe. His name is Henry Moore and he is reckoned to be as fair as any man.'

Winchip nodded. 'What is in the bag?'

'The bag belongs to Pascal and you will not believe what is inside it. There is a draft on Fuller's Bank in London for twenty-thousand guineas, payable to bearer. There are also two-thousand guineas in a leather bag and both Stephen's and Pascal's signature for the slaves, cash paid.'

'So, Stephen told the truth. Pascal took the money and Stephen took the blame, that's a fine kettle of fish.' Winchip sighed; he had been right all along. 'Burke may have paid out twenty-two thousand guineas for the slaves but do you not realise that he would have got twice that much and more for them in Martinique!.'

'Good God, Daniel! 'Hang the devil, I say - and be done with it!'

'It is not for me to judge him Douglas, as you suggested, for Stephen is involved with what has passed. I shall put the facts to Commodore Moore if we see him, or to Lieutenant Governor Henry Moore. I shall abide by either's decision…'

'And say goodbye to twenty-thousand guineas?'

'A moment ago you were commending the governor!'

'Then, good luck to you, Daniel, I hope that things work out.' Munro smiled and then let out a sigh as if he were beginning to learn more about Winchip, event by event.

At one bell in the afternoon watch, Winchip sat at the great table, its highly polished surface gleaming in the light from the stern windows. It was bare, except for two shining shillings that lay almost invisible on the polished wood before him. He then nodded to Mr Basson.

Burke and Pascal entered of their own accord but with two marines astern of them. They stood at the other side of the large table, more contrite and appearing more conciliatory; and when Winchip spoke to them, so they both jerked upright and gave him their undivided attention.

You have both been found out, Gentlemen. You, Mr Pascal, have been stealing slaves from legitimate traders and then sending them and their boats to the bottom – except for the two you used to transport your ill gotten gains. You are a pirate, a thief and a murderer, all offences for which you will go before the Lieutenant Governor of Guadeloupe and suffer such punishment as he deems fit, though piracy is a hanging offence and gives the governor little option.' Do you want to go to the governor for trial or will you take the King's shilling?'

Pascal held out his hand, a broken man. Whatever he had been told while he was in irons, Winchip had no idea but he snatched the shilling from Hellard with what sounded like a moan of despair as he left the cabin between two marines.

Winchip then turned to Burke. 'You, Mr Burke are a scoundrel and a thief. There are those who would hang you at Boston and it so happens that that is where I shall be taking you eventually. However, you can gain my silence by taking the Kings shilling and lead a full life in His Imperial Majesty's Navy. What say you?'

Burke held out a hand that shook like a leaf. He had lost both his money and his slaves and his body was bent. He was crestfallen and without hope and his face was as dark as a thundercloud. As Hellard placed the shilling in his palm, so he clasped it in his hand. Hellard span him round and pushed him through the cabin door before Burke could shout the blasphemy that was on his lips. They were followed by the master-at-arms.

'What devilment are you up to now, Daniel?'

'Devilment, Douglas? – They are now under the jurisdiction of Their Lordships at Admiralty. The governor will not be interested and neither would Their Lordships want him to be. We are also at sea and, though you may not have noticed – we are at war.' Before Munro could answer, there was a knock on the door.

'Enter!'

The master-at-arms came in and remained by the door. 'Mr Burke is asking to see you, Sir. He says he has important information for you.' Mr Basson looked up at the deckhead as if disclaiming any involvement in the matter.

'Then bring him in, Mr Basson, before the man changes his mind.

Burke had obviously been within reach behind the door as the master-at-arms disappeared and then reappeared with Burk in his grip. He dragged the man before Winchip and remained holding the shaky figure agent lest he fall to the ground in his fear of being hanged.

'What is it you have to say, Mr Burke?'

Burke looked about him furtively as to give credence to what he was about to say.

'There are more slaves, Captain – lots more; and I know where they are but you must say nothing to Pascal or he'll kill me where I stand.' Burke's voice little more than a hoarse whisper and as he finished so his eyebrows rose to make it clear that he was offering one thing for another – his life for the slaves.

'I am not interested Mr Burke. I can now get the information from Mr Pascal since they are obviously his slaves.'

'He will never tell ye – they're his nest egg.'

'Then I shall have it beaten it out of him – take him away, Mr Basson!'

'No! No! Wait, Sir – they are Pascal's men, something like two hundred of 'em. His camp is on Cumberland Island, just south of Brunswick. He has over two hundred slaves there, waiting to be shipped, Sir – is that worth my life or is it not?' Burke stared at Winchip with wide eyes, waiting with bated breath.

'You have done your duty as a citizen should, Mr Burke, but it has nothing to do with other matters.' Winchip looked up at Basson. 'Take him back to the hole in which you found him, Master-at-arms.'

CHAPTER FIFTEEN

'In Peril of Our Lives'

The light of day was giving way to the evening. Already, the underbellies of the clouds were turning pink, just as the horizon to the east was darkening by the minute. The squadron of Commodore Winchip lay just below the horizon and to the south of the settlement of Brunswick that lay behind the islands that formed the coast. It was sufficiently distant from the island to remain unseen.

Winchip had shown the written paper that Burke had provided to Pardoe and Basson as the trio sat in the great cabin of *Bellicus*. When he had finished, he leant back in his chair and waited for a reaction which was not long in coming.

'Are we to go there in Eaglet, Sir?' It was Pardoe who asked the question.

'Yes, Captain but you will not be alone; you will go in company with Captain Madoc's *Responsive* which will be carrying two hundred and fifty marines under Captain Monk and Lieutenant Barnes. When your reconnaissance is done, it would of service to me if you reported to Captain Monk, for all the reasons that we have discussed. He must, perforce, be the senior in this expedition, if you understand me?'

'I understand, Sir, I would have it no other way.' Pardoe responded immediately. He had expected nothing else and was pleased with Winchip's decision. As for Basson, Pardoe and the master-at-arms had come to terms on a knoll overlooking a bay in northern France, coming home after Lagos Bay, when Pardoe would have fallen some two hundred feet had Basson not grabbed him as he was about to go over the edge. Nothing had been said to put things to rights but their respect for each other was established from that day forwards.

As the last of the light faded in the west, Pardoe and Basson stepped out of the cutter and tentatively climbed the steep sandy beach of the Island. Pardoe placed an unlit lantern among the foliage by the side of the palm, out of sight and upright lest it lose its oil. They passed under a leaning and ancient palm tree not five yards from the beach and pressed quietly onwards through underbrush and ferns until they encountered a large stand of yellow pine; and beyond that, towering above the canopy of the slender trees, a small number of mahogany trees sat in solitary splendour, their trunks dark brown and mighty in their girth with their bases protruding from black water that had the smell of rot. It appeared to be the home of creatures that never appeared but left their trace on the surface with a sudden 'plop' or a swirl of water that sent large ripples in every direction yet never showing itself. As the ground grew softer and the going got harder, so Pardoe turned to Basson and whispered. 'We need to gain height or we shall see nothing.' The night was falling upon them like a purser's blanket. 'We could climb a tree.'

'I'm climbing no bloody trees, Sir – you don't know what's up there!'

Pardoe ignored the remark and looked to Burke's piece of paper. If the man was to be believed, there was a knoll to their right, closer to the northern end of the island.

'We shall go to the right then and look at this hillock – as quietly as we can.' Pardoe showed Basson the spot on the paper, and at a nod of agreement they moved to the right and kept beneath the yellow pines, hearing his feet crunching on needles or cones, he knew not which, that covered the ground like a carpet. It was then that they came upon more water – dirty brackish water that lay about them and left the trunks of the pines projecting from it as if the area had been recently flooded. As Pardoe took another step, so something stirred up the water and concluded with a splash that spoke of something very large. They froze into statues, standing in the water up to their ankles, hardly daring to breath, lest they hasten their own deaths.

"twere nothing, Sir – and probably more frightened than we are'

'I hope you're right, Master-at-arms.' Pardoe drew himself upwards. 'Let us go to the edge of the beach and walk round, there is no other way to approach the knoll and not be seen.' It was more of a suggestion than an order but Basson nodded his agreement anyway.

Pardoe saw the knoll against the very last vestiges of the red evening sky. The hill rose steeply upwards, covered with bracken and mosses that had little substance, suggesting to Pardoe that the hill's origins lay in what was below it, limestone or coral but he had no time to ponder. After waiting a minute to assure themselves that no one else had business in what had turned out to be a swamp, they pressed on upwards to the top of the hillock with a thankful ease. They laid down simultaneously, Pardoe reaching automatically for his personal telescope. He peered down upon the canopy of yellow pine, at the same time noting that there were other small stands of Mahogany stretching as far as the fading light allowed.

'I see nothing – except trees!' Pardoe slid the segments of the telescope together silently. 'Let us look to the north.' They reached the northern edge of the knoll without difficulty and stopped in their tracks, aghast at what they saw.

The fort was alive with figures, toing and froing from the large line of huts in the centre of a great circle, lit with cooking fires that illuminated the large building furthest from the sea; a wooden palisade so large that it would take fifteen minutes to walk the whole perimeter – or the firing platform built on stilts that ran below the wall which itself which was made from yellow pine trunks, pointed at the top to deter invaders. It was a formidable place and would be a devil to take. The gate was to the south, also composed of vertical tree trunks.

It was at that moment that Pardoe saw the white men, tanned and loosely dressed, appearing to be guarding the slaves that would be Pascal's, of that there was no doubt. They were armed with muskets and prowled the interior of the fort as if to ensure that no Negro tried to escape. He turned to Basson.

'I've seen enough, Basson; it is time we were gone from here.'

'The sooner the better is what I say, Sir.' They scrambled to their feet and moved down the knoll, ever watchful in case guards had been posted on the seaward side. They reached the beach easily enough and ten minutes later they arrived at the old palm tree. Pardoe lit the lantern. He swung it three times and waited for two minutes before swinging it once more – after which time, Basson, discovering three leeches on one ankle; had used the wick to loose them off before the taper was of no further use. It was another hour before the cutter came out of the darkness, the keel hissing as it scraped the white sand.

The great cabin of *Bellicus* was as a haven to both Pardoe and Basson as they sat, each with a hot toddy clasped in welcoming hands. Pardoe had written his report on his return lest he forgot something in the meantime and now he waited as Winchip read it below the light of a deckhead lantern. The slopping of water under the counter was a continuous sound that had no intention of stopping or changing its tune. Pardoe caught Basson's eye and grinned. Things could have been very different. He wondered about the beast in the water, whatever it was. He had put it in his report; he could do no more than that. As Winchip put down the report and looked up, so Pardoe straightened his back and became attentive.

'You have done well, the pair of you. If that was all that you saw, then it is unlikely that anything else was afoot.' Winchip looked to Pardoe. 'Were the slaves in good shape?'

'They appeared to be, Commodore – but we were not to see what was happening in the slave huts.'

'Quite! What about the large building?'

'Nothing more than I mentioned, Sir, it seemed quiet all round, almost as if someone was expected and they were trying to tidy up, so to speak. Though, as I said in my report, the white men were carrying muskets and had ammunition belts crossed on their chests – they were prepared for someone, or something.'

'Perhaps Pascal was coming here after Tortuga. Is there anything else?'

'One small thing, Sir, too slight to be of importance, I thought.'

'Well?'

'The yellow pines they were using for the palisade and the gate seemed to be oozing resin akin to a spinster's candle.' Pardoe became shamefaced as he recalled what he considered to be a moot point.

'You have probably missed the most important point of all, Captain, yet you cannot be blamed as you were not aware of the importance of this resin.' Winchip had met it before. He looked on Pardoe benevolently, not wishing to show him up in front of Basson. 'That resin is flammable. Were it to be set alight, then the whole palisade would go up in flames in no time at all – my God, they have made a great error in using that particular pine for their defences.' Winchip leant back in his chair. 'You have done better than well, the pair of you. Leave now, with my thanks and ask Captain Monk to present himself.'

Winchip stood as they left and walked to the stern windows. He now had the possibility of a plan, albeit a tenuous one and fraught with danger for the slaves. He almost hoped that Monk would talk him out of it but he knew the man would clutch at any straw to complete a mission successfully – and thank The Lord for it.

Pardoe was in the bow of the first of twenty boats that approached the island and the fort with muffled thole pins. At the appropriate moment he held up his hand and then stepped out of the boat as it came onto the shallows. He physically halted the boat with his hands to prevent it coming hard upon the steep beach before the fort. One by one the marines eased themselves over the gunwales, handing muskets over before they stepped out of the boat. Silently, the beach began to fill with red tunics and tall shakos without a stumble or a curse. Monk came up to Pardoe and tapped him on the shoulder as a group of marines went past with their arms loaded with equipment.

'Shall you stay with the boats, Mr Pardoe, I would feel happier with your presence here, it being necessary to keep good order; and no pipes to be smoked lest those in the fort smell the smoke?'

Pardoe knew that Monk's request had nothing to do with good order or pipes – he wanted him out of the way. 'Of course, Captain. Anything less for you to worry about, I'd say.' Pardoe grinned and shook his head.

'It is the way of things, Captain – you understand?'

'Of course I do Mr Monk, just ensure that I don't have to come to your rescue.' Pardoe held out his hand and Monk gave it a good shake before he disappeared into the blackness. Monk had been informed about the swamp and he had not taken it lightly. Pardoe was convinced that it had something to do with Monk's plans but he couldn't fathom what, so he dismissed it from his mind. There was much to do and Monk was the man for the task, of that there was no doubt at all. Suddenly, Pardoe realised that, but for the twenty marines spread along the span of the resting boats, he was alone, except for the slop of waves as they fell in rapid succession onto the beach.

Pardoe called the nearest marine to come to him. 'These boats must be turned towards the sea and brought closer together in case anything goes wrong and our departure needs to be quick. Don't forget, you could be the ill-fated after-guard when it happens.' He nodded as the marine set out to do his bidding with a will.

Lieutenant of Marines Barry Barnes, sandy haired and tall and with shoulders like that of a prizefighter, led a file of marines round the fort to cut off any prospect of escape by Pascal's men. His column moved through the brushwood and ferns that separated the fort from the swamp with great care, one eye on the dark mystic waters of which Pardoe had spoken and the other up to the battlements should a head appear.

It was as he considered his options in respect to setting up a defensive position that he realised that Pascal had no idea about military matters. There was no cleared ground around the fort – no killing field of fire – and, by virtue of that; snipers from the undergrowth around the place could pick off any head foolish enough to appear above the palisade.

As he trudged through black water and then came back onto firm ground, so he saw that they had now almost encircled the fort. Before him, the moon was now shining on the expanse of water that had to be the estuary of the river – the very place he had hoped to find suitable for a line of defence from the water's edge to the boats, now less than a quarter of a mile away. With that he raised an open hand to bring the long file of men to a halt. He turned to Sergeant Haggler and drew him to the ground.

'Tell the men to dig in behind mounds of sand. They must lie on their sides to reload as they have learnt – and tell them that if any man exposes his head to the enemy, then *I* shall be the one to shoot him. These pirates aren't worth the life of a marine.'

'Right, you are, Sir – I'll tell them right enough.'

'Very well, Sergeant, keep them some distance from the fort but within range, for things are likely to hot up before this night is done.' Barnes suddenly started at a noise from his left. He swung round to see a marine creeping towards him, his shako awry and traces of fern stuck in his cross belts.

'What is it, marine? Speak man.'

'There's some boats round the bend, to seawards, big ones they are and they're tucked up against a quay and there's nobody on 'em, Sir.

'Are you sure of that?'

'Yes, Sir – and they stink something rotten!'

'Then go to Sergeant Haggler and have him take a squad of men for each boat and prepare to repel boarders if necessary – he'll know what to do well enough.' Barnes wanted to close his eyes and see Pardoe in front of him when he opened them: someone to take the boats offshore. Instead, he made his way down the line, ensuring that everything was set as Captain Monk and Pardoe had wished. All that was required was the sound of musket fire, the signal for action – and the dispelling of fantasies.

With a cloth soaked in lamp oil, a corporal of marines soaked the two great doors of the fort has high as he was able, knowing that it would make its way down the doors with no help from him. When that was done, he took an offered firebrand and applied it to the oil. As he stepped back, so the flames slowly licked upwards, feeding from both the oil and the sap as it rose up and spread as it went. The sap began to bubble like tar in a bucket as it caught light, until the vertical logs of the door were well alight and looked to be immersed in flame within minutes of being lit.

The sudden pandemonium within the fort could be heard as the flames licked over the tops of the spiked trunks and vanished into the air above. The first musket shot elicited a scream from the parapet and the tumult rose as slaves screamed and bellowed in a guttural language that was their own. Four marines ran at the door of the fort with the trunk of an old yellow pine but to no avail, the stout doors holding firm time after time. At last Monk called for brushwood, directing that it should be piled against the doors until they succumbed to the flames.

Sergeant Haggler checked his men as they sat quietly behind the bulwarks of the barques, for that was what the ships turned out to be, ship rigged or not, He had inspected the great cabin of each ship and had come up with papers that proved they had been overtaken by the pirates. The manifests were in English, addressed to a Captain Miller and had indicated that the ships were each sailing under 'Letters of Marque' from the Crown. What had become of the crew, he had no idea and neither did he wish to dwell on the possibilities.

As he came up through the companion, a snot rag to his nose, so he looked upwards to the top of the mainmast. It towered above him, well over the height of the palisade, as did the fore and mizzen masts of both ships. In a moment he had men climbing the ratlines. Within two minutes muskets were firing from the tops and cheers were being raised with every successful shot.

The doors at the fort entrance gave at last, the pine trunks falling inwards under a shower of sparks to bring a flickering light to even to the darkest corners of the fort; and a great huzzah from the marines who formed two lines and fanned out – under the leadership of the master-at-arms – in good order and with bayonets flashing red in the light from the fire.

CHAPTER SIXTEEN

'A Nest of Vipers'

Sergeant Haggler heard the huzzah from the marines above the crackle of burning timbers and the roar of the flames. He knew that this was the moment when heads would appear and frightened men would be in a hurry to chance their luck with the points of the palisade rather than face up to the British Marines.

'Steady, men, let the bastards get a leg astride and then shoot them dead – any moment now.' Haggler satisfied himself that his men were down from the tops and poised; and that musket barrels were pointing to where Pascal's men would appear, though it seemed that they never would.

True to Haggler's guess, the first heads appeared and then others followed, clambering between the spikes to escape the horde of red tunics that would be pouring through the gate.

The first shot was followed by a volley which soon became a fusillade. Bodies jerked upwards with screams of pain and fell back from whence they came or dropped onto the gruesome spikes to stay pinioned for ever, dead or dying.

As the noise of musket fire died, it suddenly occurred to Sergeant Haggler that the two barques could be in danger of catching fire and that they would be need to ferry the Negroes to the squadron. Without preamble, he shouted to the corporal to take charge and gathered ten men about him. The trek through the underbrush delayed them, catching at uniforms and muskets until suddenly they were out into the open and by the inlet – and with that, the quay.

Hellard sent men to loose off the cables and others to prepare the anchors, glad to see that his men knew what was required of them, gleaned from bitter experience. The two Barques drifted slowly from the quay and as soon as haggler was certain that the fire would not reach them, so he had the un-catted anchors let fall. Two loud splashes told him that the job was completed. A boat was swung over and lowered with little fuss and the task was done.

Monk had led his men into the fort with the expectation of being shot with the first volley from the pirates. That he was still alive came as a shock, as did the fact that the thirty or more of Pascal's men who still lived were already standing in the centre of the fort with their hands held high. Of the slaves there was no sign but from the slave huts a low moaning sound carried on the air like a dirge. He had his marines find cord enough to bind the pirates, though he could well understand why they had surrendered when he realised that his marines were still coming through the gate, their muskets held at the port, only to find that it was all over and that the fort was theirs. As for the prisoners, their fate was preordained. It would be a short trial and a long drop – the way of all pirates. Perhaps they had hopes of rescue – or while they were alive there was still hope.

Twelve marines had died and already they were lying outside the vacated fort, waiting to be buried in the hard sand outside the palisade. Rough crosses were being hewn from the yellow pine branches and their uniforms were being bundled for the journey back to the ships. The wounded were being carried to the barques on makeshift stretchers. Those of the pirates who were wounded were left with no option but to be taken up for passage to *Bellicus* and the promise of a hempen noose that would end their days. The dead pirates were left where they lay, candidates for a Viking's funeral – or to be taken, piece by piece, by the black wing gulls in the fullness of time.

The fire had gained in its momentum, licking round the fort like the claw of a crab, coming from both sides to meet in the middle, by which time the place would be no more than a ring of burnt timber and a mass of smoking corpses; a warning to others who might seek the same path.

'Mr Barnes – the slave huts, if you please!' Monk shouted to his lieutenant, knowing that the fire had no favourites. 'Lead them out or drag them out, it makes no difference, Mr Barnes, for they shall not burn in my name!' He watched as groups of marines ran to left, right and centre of the row of huts. Within minutes the slaves came out, women were leading children by the hand and others carried meagre bundles on their heads – their sole possessions. The men were looking right and left, wide-eyed – at the same time coaxing the women and children along as if they were sheep rather than humans. They looked about the burning fort with wide and frightened eyes as if death was staring them in the face. Monk saw the whole scene with sympathy in his heart and, as he had told his men, none was to be harmed…in *any* particular.

Pardoe was standing with the seamen about him and the marines still guarding the boats. The sound of the fort burning and the exchange of musket fire did nothing to lessen his anguish. He, like every man around him, wanted to be there with their companions, yet they could not and neither could they convey their feelings aloud. He started to pace, backwards and forwards as though he were pacing the poop deck to exercise his legs, when a figure came running along the sand towards him, stumbling now and then with the steepness of the beach and at the same time shouting Pardoe's name. He walked towards the marine, the man's tunic now clear against the light from the fort.

'What is it? What's wrong?'

The marine stopped to catch his breath. 'We have taken the fort, Sir – at a price!' The man took another deep breath and gathered himself. 'Sergeant Haggler sent me to tell you that we have found two ships beyond the fort, in a large inlet. He had them taken into deeper water lest they catch fire.'

'Well, thank The Lord for that.' It solved the problem of taking the slaves on board the ship's boats to a total lack of accommodation. 'That is good news, Marine. What of Captain Monk?'

'He is well, Sir, though we have lost some of our men. The pirates have been killed or taken and the slaves are safe.' The marine took two easy breaths. 'Captain Monk sends his compliments and suggests you bring the boats around the point so the barques can tow them to the squadron, Sir.'

Pardoe felt the wind and, trifling as it was, it would be abaft their beams and that was good enough. 'That sounds good to me, Marine. How good are you at rowing?'

The two barques came out of the darkness, each with a lantern showing on the foretopmast. As they neared the squadron, so they came into the trifling wind and the ship's boats were released to return to the vessels from which they came. The challenge came from *Bellicus* and a voice came out of the blackness in reply

Winchip sat at the great table in the cabin of *Bellicus*, waiting patiently as Booth served the claret. When all was done and Booth had retired to the ship's galley, so he leaned forward in his chair to face the three officers before him.

'You are to be congratulated, Captain Monk, on a job well done. It is my opinion that the task for which we were sent has now been completed, thanks to you and your party and there are those that shall hear of it, you mark my words.'

'Thank you, Commodore but without Captain Pardoe and Lieutenant Barnes, things might well have gone against us.'

'You are generous, Captain but that is what command and teamwork is all about.' Winchip singled out a paper from the small batch on the table before him and looked at it in wonderment. 'Your report, Captain, tells me all I wish to know, though how you managed to set light to a fort and then rescue its occupants leaves me breathless – however, the task is done, the fort is no more and you have prisoners to boot. My cup is full, gentlemen, I can say no more.'

'The prisoners are in irons on one of the slave ships, Commodore, the slaves on the other.' Pardoe continued. 'The slaves have been fed with fish broth, Commodore, which was to their liking and Mr Timms, the purser, has issued palliasses to be spread about the lower deck on which the ladies and the children can sleep. They are on loan, Sir – the purser being unwilling to take them off his inventory.'

'That is to be expected, Mr Pardoe but what about the prisoners?'

'They are on the other barque, Sir, in irons and probably very uncomfortable. They have not been fed.'

'And where are the barques?'

'They are tethered together for safety, commodore and are under guard by a small night watch, alongside the colliers.'

'And how many slaves and prisoners are there?'

'There are thirty-two prisoners and sixty-one slaves, Sir, including children.'

'Well, Basse-Terre is not that far away and we shall no doubt provision there. I think we shall leave things as they are, Captain.' Winchip rose to the scraping of chairs as those present got quickly to their feet. 'We shall meet on the morrow, Gentlemen, when things look the better for a few hours of sleep.

Tigan, the large Mandinka of the village of Mandinari on the River Gambia, rose from his place on the lower deck of the barque and shook his companions awake, with a motion of his finger to his lips, bidding them to keep silent. The group of Mandinka gathered around Tigan in the darkness, straining to hear his words above the slopping of the wavelets against the hull. When Tigan had finished, so they all looked at each other with wide grins on their faces, digging each other in the ribs to express the delight with which they welcomed Tigan's words. Quietly, they slit open a large sack of oakum, passing the coarse woven caulking material from hand to hand until each man carried a large handful. Without a sound, the slaves came up through the main companion, one after the other, to a bright moonlit night. They were forty in number, with ages stretching from youth to maturity, moving slowly so as to prevent the ship from colliding with the other barque moored alongside. They passed through the entry port and then moved across to the other vessel with but a single step through the other's port. At the companion, they stopped. The sound of snoring came up from below and from the light of a single deckhead lantern they could see the prisoners laying on the boards of the lower deck, the lamp light reflecting from their iron shackles and the great chain that ran through their leg irons to keep each man chained to the next.

Tigan made a sign. It was all that was needed for the slaves to patter quietly down the steps to the depths below and fall upon the prisoners as they slept. For a moment there was noise enough – but it was quickly stilled as oakum was crammed into the mouths of Pascal's men with such force that their faces were bulging and their nostrils dilated as they fought to breath. The men were forced to their feet and each was half dragged, half carried up to the deck above, pausing only to beat individuals into submission. At last, the prisoners were bunched by the outer port, seeking reasons from each other by eye movements alone. There was no chance of escape. One man fell to his knees and there were tears in his eyes. Tigan raised a foot and killed the man with a single kick to the head, the neck snapping with a loud click.

Tigan nodded his head and four slaves picked up the dead man and lowered him through the port, allowing him to slide down the meagre tumblehome to hang by the feet, tethered to the next prisoner standing at the port. The man suddenly realised what was happening and threw himself to the ground, only to be picked up and ditched through the port like a sack of potatoes. It took fifteen minutes to put Pascal's men over the side, the last one disappearing speedily into the depths in a cloud of bubbles that sparkled in the moonlight like fairies as they burst onto the surface…his last breath on this earth..

Winchip's face was like a thundercloud as he sat at his desk In *Bellicus*. He had heard the news at the end of the morning watch as he slept in his cot. He had dressed quickly and had assumed his seat in his cabin before he sent the sentry for James Niven.

'How did they escape, Mr Niven? Who was in charge of the watch, Mr Niven? Who was on guard duty at the time, Mr Niven?' Winchip banged his fist on the desk top. 'Somebody must have released them; and they must have taken a boat for it is too far for them to swim. I must also assume that you have had the sense to search all vessels.' Winchip stared at Niven as if he wished the deck would open up beneath him.

'I have gone into the matter thoroughly, Sir, you may be certain of that. The disappearance of the prisoners is a complete mystery, unless the barques were boarded in the night and that others of Pascal's gang rescued them.' Niven raised himself to his full height. 'There *is* no other explanation, Sir.'

'Oh, my god, James, what shall I write for Their Lordships at Admiralty, you tell me that! By this time next month you will outrank me – that's the only outcome I can see at this moment.'

'I would suggest you write nothing in your journal, Sir, for I shall get to the bottom this matter if it is the last thing I do. Have you any orders for me, Sir?'

'Have you allocated crews for the barques?'

'I have. Sir, Lieutenant Bowes has one and Lieutenant Hartley has the other and the whole squadron is prepared for sea.'

'In that case bring the anchors to short-stay and we shall take the Windward Passage while we have a friendly wind.' Winchip rose and moved to the stern windows where, for a brief moment, he could turn his back on the disaster – and the world.

Lieutenant Bowes stood at the crude binnacle of the barque *Caravelle* as Lord Pickering gave the order for the anchor to be raised to the short stay. It was his first command, albeit a stolen ship that smelt of slaves and behaved like a stubborn mule, if speculation was to be trusted. He consoled himself with the realisation that his journey in her would be as far as Basse-Terre and that would be an end to it.

The clank of the capstan coming to an abrupt halt brought his head up. The men were leaning on the bars but to no avail.

'What is it, Longdale?'

'The anchor is fouled, Sir.'

'Can we put men on the cable?'

'We can try, Sir but six at the most'

'Then let it be so, Mr Longdale but watch the mark.'

'Aye, Sir!'

As the men leant into the bars and others laboured at the long cable, so the clank of the pawls came one by one, gradually bringing in the cable without too great a dip of the ship's bow.

'Belay there!' The cry came from the man on the cat. 'Oh, my god!'

'What is it man?' Pickering ran over to the beak head.

'Will you look, Sir?' The man pointed downwards, his eyes wide and his face pale.

Pickering looked over the bulwark and found it impossible to draw his eyes away. Across the fluke of the anchor was a stout chain and either side was a manacled foot, each as white as chalk and still attached to its trousered leg. Beyond that, deeper in the water, the arms were flailing about with the disturbance and beyond that was the faint pale shapes of two heads, nodding to each other as if they had come to a firm conclusion. Pickering gagged at the sight and then vomited violently, tears coming to his eyes without his knowledge.

'What is it, Mr Pickering?' Bowes shouted loudly and then, seeing that Pickering was distressed he went forwards and looked over the side. What he saw appalled him but he had seen worse. 'I'll offer a guinea to the man who'll go down and secure a rope to the chain!' Bowes was not surprised that more than one man stepped forward. After the things that Eaglets had seen over the last years this was a guinea for nothing. Bowes patted the first man on the back. 'Make sure the rope is stout, for I do believe there is more than one man attached down there.' Bowes turned to Pickering. 'Pull yourself together, my Lord. We shall draw the men up on the capstan, have no fear but in the mean time put on the signal for a fouled anchor, if you please.' Bowes walked away, shaking his head in disbelief at what he had seen.

It was block and tackles and the main yard arm of *Bellicus* that eventually brought the prisoners to the surface, hanging like mackerel on a fishing line before they were lowered to the deck.

Winchip sat in his cabin, his fingers drumming on the table top. Niven sat opposite with his hands on his lap, wondering what was to come.

'I cannot take the prisoners to Basse-Terre, James, because they would smell the place out before the day is done. They will therefore be committed to the water without ceremony. I know who is to blame and how it was done but I cannot bring myself to do anything about it.'

'May I know who did it, Sir and how?'

'It was the leader of the slaves, James. It must have been done with stealth and in silence, made obvious by the oakum in their mouths. I must confess that I have a grudging respect for the perpetrators, as would any man with a conscience.' Winchip slapped the table with palm of his hand. 'We shall say no more about it – the prisoners were never here as far as we are concerned and that is how things will stay – but only with your approval.' Winchip sat back and looked Niven in the eye. 'What say you?'

'It has my approval, Commodore; and my word: but we do have the prisoners from the cutting out – the ones on the barque.'

'Then that is the end of the matter, though the number of prisoners on the barque was hardly enough to call a nest of vipers, Captain. However, we have no alternative. It just requires the corpses to be put over the side and we shall close the book on it – the end of a chapter.'

CHAPTER SEVENTEEN

The Mandinka of Guadeloupe

Winchip found himself once more in the great cabin of *Cambridge*, sitting in the same chair and once more enjoying the breeze from the two primitive windsails at the stern windows. Commodore John Moore sat on the other side of the table, avidly reading Winchip's journal; the only concise account of events at Tortuga and beyond. Winchip sipped his claret with deliberation, his mind conjuring a hundred reasons why the commodore would want nothing to do with the plans he had in mind. On the table was a long clay pipe, its bowl resting on a small dish, sprinkled with shreds of fresh tobacco, spilled in the filling. At last, Moore leaned back in his chair and shook his head in apparent wonderment.

'My word, Winchip, if you cannot find action, you seem to invent it. Those two ships-of-the-line will be a great loss to the French, you mark my words and, having said that, they will fetch a pretty penny for both you and your people.' Moore turned to a page in the journal that had taken his interest. 'I cannot believe that this agent and the pirate captain have actually taken the king's shilling or that you have allowed them to!'

'I think you may have done the same, given the alternatives, Commodore. It keeps them out of the hands of local government. I want the pair of them to swing; but in the place and at a time of the navy's choosing. The man Burke owes a great deal of money to many people in Boston and I want to take him back there to face them – and repay them. That is why I am inclined to keep the two-thousand guineas. When those people are repaid, then King George shall have what remains.'

'I think that is the just and proper thing to do, Winchip, while at the same time it would be sensible – and safer, to hand in the more valuable draft to the prize court. Keep the two-thousand guineas by all means and if that falls short, arrange with the prize court for you to make promissory notes in their name. You are a trusted and well known servant of the Crown, Commodore and 'twould be a brave man that questioned your integrity.'

'You are very kind, Sir.' Winchip knew he had been listening to common sense. 'I shall do as you say – but I submit that Burke should return with me, for, likely as not he has ruined more than a few men at Boston.'

'You will have no argument from me, Winchip. What about the man, Pascal, have you anything in mind for him?'

'Yours is the senior vessel, Commodore. I thought you might care to do the honours, once the court has had its say.'

With a smile on his face, Moore said. '"And so die all pirates", is that it?'

'Something to that affect, Commodore. One has to give serious thought to all those innocent seamen, murdered at his hands.'

'I shall give it a great deal of thought, Winchip; but, until then, I promise nothing.' Moore sipped his claret. 'What shall you do with the slaves?'

'I have a mind to free them, Commodore. They have no owner and technically, they must be free men already – though not for long, I'll warrant.' Winchip gathered himself to ask the important question. 'How does one buy land in Guadeloupe?'

'Ah, I see your drift, Winchip. You mean to invest, I take it?'

'I would like to, Commodore and I have just the man to get a place started. I must, however, engage an agent here, in Guadeloupe if my plan is to succeed. Can you recommend a good one?'

'In what commodity would you invest?'

'Sugar and molasses seems to be the popular choice.'

Moore stood, prompting Winchip to do likewise. He went to the stern windows and stared towards the south-east with his chin upraised as if out there lay the font of plenty. 'I shall give you an address, Winchip, if you will allow me to. The man has been my agent for many years and knows as much as any man about planting in the West Indies. Any monies are safe with him and his advice is worth its weight in gold. He will also deal with the prize court should you wish to fight shy of them.'

'I am obliged to you, Commodore, I could ask for no more than that.' Winchip was downright thankful.

'Then it shall be done. I shall reach Guadeloupe before you and I shall send an officer cross to you when you get there, a man able to tell you all you require to know. Should you wish it, he can see your slaves securely housed and fed, until such time as your man gets settled. Although it may cost you dear, the results will prove worth it, on that you can rely.'

'Then I shall wait upon your officer, Commodore and relieve myself of a great burden.'

Winchip sat on the stern seat of his cabin, perusing the contents of his journal to ensure that he had left nothing to chance or question. Satisfied, he leant forward and replaced the book on the Gillow table. The French Officers and all their seamen had been sent ashore, into the hands of the Navy Office with whom Winchip had deposited his claim to the prize court and the draft on Fullers Bank. It was as he reflected the benefits for his people that the knock came on the door.

'Enter!'

Stephen Loxley entered the cabin wearing brown ducks and a white linen blouse that was stained with perspiration. On Niven's advice, he wore a sword, clipped to his belt.

'Good afternoon, Brother-in-law, you asked me to call upon you.'

'Yes, Stephen, I did – please sit down.' Winchip waved a hand towards a choice of chairs. 'How would you like to live in Guadeloupe, until it is safe for you to return to England?' Winchip knew his question would come as a shock but there was no other way to put it.

Loxley laughed. 'Are you determined to be rid of me as well, Daniel?'

'No, I am not.' Winchip smiled. 'I am suggesting that you become a planter, here on Guadeloupe. I have sugar in mind and you shall have the slaves to help you get you started.' Winchip drew a chair up to the table and sat directly opposite Loxley. 'Soon, an officer will be coming over from *Cambridge*. He will be a great help in the enterprise I have in mind. It is up to you whether you take advantage of my offer to take a part share in a plantation.' Winchip pointed to a chair and filled a glass with claret. 'This is what I have in mind...'

Stephen Loxley found Kuana at the taffrail. She was alone, humming a Mandinka song that her mother had taught her; one that had been passed down through the ages. She wore a plain cotton tunic that Booth had made for her and a pair of slippers made from seal skin that one of the loblollies had shyly presented to her. The clothing was not flattering but it served her needs and returned her self respect.

As soon as Kuana saw Stephen, she came down to him and took one of his hands in hers. 'Where have you been, my Stephen, I looked for you everywhere?'

'I have been with the commodore, he wanted to see me.' He saw her garb and nodded his appreciation. 'I have much to tell you and even more to ask of you.' He couldn't avoid his broad smile. He faced her full square and held her upper arms in his hands. 'How would you like to live here, you and all your people, on an island nearby called Guadeloupe?'

'Do you mean as slaves?' A crease furrowed her brow.

'No, Kuana, I would never let you be a slave – not while I live. Your people shall work for me and will be well looked after and shall live in huts that I shall have made for you.'

'*You* will have made?'

'Yes, Kuana, for I will be with you, helping to plant the crop, whatever it turns out to be.'

'What shall I do, if you do all the work?'

Stephen smiled at her naivety. 'I hope you would want to help me to run the plantation – and perhaps, one day, become my wife.' His heart twisted itself into a knot, waiting for her response.'

As she stared at him, mouthing words that wouldn't come, so the tears came, tumbling down her dusky cheeks as if they would never stop. 'Do I have to wait?'

'I love you, Kuana.' He held her close, feeling her body shake with her crying. He put his cheek to hers and whispered in her ear. 'I want us to be together – for ever.'

'B...but you will be my master – you do not have to marry me, for I will be yours alone, whenever you want to take me to your bed.'

'You will be my wife, Kuana. It will be you who decide when, or if, you wish to come to my bed.'

'Then I am thinking that marriage is a good idea.' Her hand went to her mouth as a thought suddenly struck her. 'How many wives will you have – will I be the head wife?'

'Just the one, Kuana, for I could never love anyone as much as I love you.'

'And will my people be free?'

'No, Kuana. If they were free, then they would be taken up by the other planters and made into real slaves. They shall be my workers; but not for money. They will, as I said, be well looked after, for I know that that is how you would like things to be. They will also be well housed to maintain their pride. They shall be the 'Mandinka of Guadeloupe' and all that that implies – I can do no more than that.'

'Then that is enough, my Stephen.' She leant her face upwards for a kiss and found herself lifted from her feet.

As the port of Basse-Terre loomed large, with its high and threatening volcano and the great fort to the south of the place, so Winchip gave permission for the salute. The signal minion gave out a ringing blast of smoke from her barrel which received echoes from the mighty rocks and walls of the fort itself in return; the sounds merging as if a great sea battle were raging. Already, a cutter had appeared under sail, as if out of the rock itself, a huge jack draped from her stern staff as she sped downwind towards the anchorage. Winchip's broad pennant jerked off the truck and the foretops'l of *Bellicus* pasted itself against the foremast to lose headway in the light north-westerly wind.

The parched sails came off Bellicus like washing from a line and were into gaskets within minutes. Only then, under the watchful eye of the cutter, was the first anchor let fall – dropping into the calm sheltered waters as a stone would fall into a mill pond.

Winchip waited for a call to the governor's office but none was forthcoming. It was an hour later that a call came down from the tops, coming through the open deck light as clearly as a matins bell. The knock on the cabin door came a moment later.

'Enter!'

Niven came into the cabin wearing the dress of the day; blouse and breeches and a sweat stained crevat. 'There is a boat approaching, Sir, with a master and commander on board.'

'Is the man here already? Thank you, Lieutenant; he shall, like as not, be from the governor's office. Have him shown to my cabin, if you please.'

As Niven disappeared, so Winchip hooked up his large shaving mirror and put himself to rights, noticing that his face was like burnt umber, it had become so dark. By the time the knock had come on the door Winchip was at his desk with a lemonade jug before him and two glasses, upturned on a silver tray.

'Enter!'

The marine guard opened the door and stood aside for Niven and the officer to enter.

'Sir, may I introduce you to Captain Forsyth who is attached to the governor's office?'

Winchip stood. 'Thank you, Mr Niven; I shall call if I need you.' He held out a hand to the ginger haired and periwigged Forsyth. 'It is a pleasure to meet you, Captain, please take a seat.' Winchip gestured to a chair and sat down himself, feeling a trickle of sweat coursing down his back as he did so. 'Is this a courtesy call, Forsyth, or do you come officially?'

'Essentially, Commodore, I am here to inform you that you are required as a witness in the case of the man, Pascal. The case is to be heard in the forenoon, at four bells.'

'Thank you, Captain, I shall be there.' Winchip left it at that, having no wish to join in conversation about the trial, nor its possible outcome, with a man who had no vested interest. He waited for the Captain to continue.

'I also come in response to a request by Commodore Moore, Sir. I believe you are seeking advice in the matter of procedure. I am also told you have slaves to house and fodder, land to purchase and a need to approach the prize court, is that correct?'

Winchip smiled. 'It certainly is correct, Captain, in every detail, though how you could respond to my needs so quickly, I have no idea!'

Forsyth found a self effacing grin. 'We look after our own, Commodore. We have only been on this island since May; and it is imperative that the planters we have here are all inclined towards the English. We are in the process of ridding ourselves of the French as they are likely to act as spies. We have land available at this very moment if that is not rushing you; on Grande Terre, our adjacent island, together with a house of some size?'

'I am told that I need fifty hectares initially, together with a house and with an option on extending the land – but I hasten to add that I haven't a clue what I am talking about. Do you take lemonade?' Winchip turned the glasses up and poured. 'I think it would be wise to have my man join us. He knows a great deal about slaves but very little about planting sugar, which I believe to be a bourgeoning commodity; but that is arguable, I must admit.' Winchip rang the little brass bell, knowing that he would be lost without Stephen's presence.

'You may do very well, Commodore. Sugar is in much demand, as are molasses and rum, itself. May I suggest you consider buying one-hundred hectares while the land is cheap and sugar is so easy to sell?'

'You can suggest what you will and I am sure my man will see the wisdom of it.' Winchip looked up as the sentry came in. 'Pass the word for Mr Loxley – and sharply.'

Winchip stood at the taffrail of *Bellicus* and looked out over the expanse of clear blue sea as if he were seeing it for the first time. He was gathering a memory to take home with him, so that when he spoke of Stephen to Madeleine he could be sure that he was painting the correct picture, for that, indeed, was what it would be. The great mountainous ridges that travelled the length of the island were majestic, wreathed in jungle clad gullies that ran down to the sea where the torrential seasonal rains had cleft the rock and let nature do the rest. To the south, the great fort guarded the river inlet to Basse-Terre, the thriving town that sat on the banks as if she, too, had been hewn by nature. It was the volcano that was stunning, standing apart but looking down at Basse-Terre with smoke issuing from its tops like a newly lit bonfire. He stared at it aghast; at the very immensity of it, praying that it would not erupt while the squadron was at anchor; and that the sulphurous smell of it would disappear with a change in the wind.

He had gone with Stephen and the Mandinkas to see the land on Grande-Terre. In Culpepper's sloop-of-war they had sailed gingerly through the gut that separated the two islands. In accordance with directions they had come upon the wooden jetty of the plantation named 'Ciel et Terre', if the crude and worn letters painted on the notice board were read with care. The place had produced sugar, together with the inevitable molasses that would eventually become rum. The storage houses were solid and the refinery appeared to be in working order. The house was of red brick, two storeys high and with many windows, most with their glass intact; and the slave quarters were neglected as one would naturally expect of woven bamboo and grass. As to taking in the whole estate, it was far beyond his understanding, where to him one-hundred hectares had been an imaginary figure; it turned out to be as far as the eye could see.

With the sight of the sugar fields there came upon him a great sadness. The sugar crop foliage lay wasted upon the ground, left to rot as the French were banished from the island. Stephen Loxley shook his head in sorrow and then suddenly he brightened; 'There is much to be done, Daniel, yet it will give us work aplenty until the new crop is planted.'

The Mandinka – for that was what Loxley had agreed they could be called – had picked their way through the tangle of bamboo and grass to assess what could be done. Kuana's people were on home ground, seeing to the repairs as if they were back in Gambia and there had been a storm the previous night.

Winchip smiled at his thoughts and slapped his hand on the taffrail, remembering events as he recalled them from his memory. He had forgotten about the skirts and the pantaloons that the Mandinka had been wearing. The squadron sailmakers had been responsible, working long hours to bring some self respect to over four-hundred naked souls. Winchip could have embraced every event in turn as they came to him; the willingness of his people to do right by the slaves – when, for that day, all else was of little importance. He heaved a deep sigh. It would be the last he would see of Stephen on this voyage; but he vowed he would return – hopefully to bring the lad home.

CHAPTER EIGHTEEN

The Hanging

Winchip came out of Government House with a heavy heart. He was well used to death in all its forms, except that of hanging. Pascal had stood between two marines in the small courtroom, his face defiant and his demeanour, sour. Winchip had given his evidence and had produced his orders and journal for the four captains to read. His account of the condition of the slaves on their discovery had brought gasps from the colourful plebeian crowd, yet hardly a wince from those officers who sat in judgement of the man. Only in relation to the ships and seamen that Pascal had sent to the bottom did the bench wriggle in their high chairs, casting glances between each other that spoke far more eloquently of Pascal's imminent guilt than any official sentence of death could have done. Yet the sentence came in all its sobriety, curt and to the point; to be hanged at the noon bell on the morrow, on board His Majesty's Ship *Cambridge*, within sight of the town and as a lesson to those who were of a mind to break the laws of His Majesty King George the second, God bless Him.

Winchip had no idea that *Cambridge* would be chosen to carry out the sentence, yet upon reflection, it were better done on a ship that would soon depart and be unlikely to return, rather than to sully a ship from the home port. Pascal's limited period, serving as a seaman, was short lived indeed; but the rough hessian rope would soon see him off, sufficient to wipe away the defiant sneer that had come on his face as the sentence of death was read out. The man now had less than twenty-four hours to contemplate the wisdom of his bravado – a far shorter time than those poor slaves had, made to lie in their own faeces in mortal fear for their very lives – and then there were those who had found peace as they succumbed; their flesh already sagging on their bones when they were at last discovered.

Suddenly, Winchip remembered a task he needed to perform. Now that Pascal was gone from his thoughts, he knew he should write an affidavit for the magistrates at Boston before his memory faded. Burke had much to answer for but it should not be left to the mob to dispense justice. He had already decided that he would leave fifteen-hundred of the two thousand guineas in the hands of the court for Burke's creditors, upon which they could make a charge in writing. In that way there would be no mysterious additions to the debts that Burke owed and neither would the navy need to pay the difference. The other five hundred, stolen from Stephen by Burke, were already with his brother-in-law to see him through, until the first harvest and perhaps beyond.

He walked down the street with the positive feeling that he had discharged Admiral Saunders' orders to the letter. His only hope now was that the admiral would still be of a mind to send him home, superfluous to his needs; perhaps to be one of the ships that made up the daisy chain of men-of-war returning to England that had been Saunders' idle fancy.

Winchip's squadron came round the southern point of Guadeloupe at four bells into the forenoon watch the next day, from the east where they had sheltered in a north-westerly blow the previous night. Commodore Moore's Squadron was already anchored some way out to sea, though *Cambridge* had already come close inshore for her rendezvous with death. Her sails were furled and in plain harbour gaskets. She was lying to two anchors and a block and tackle was ominously affixed to the end of the main yard that faced to the shore. A rope had been roved through it, now hanging limply down as if the operators had gone to dinner. Ship's boats were plying towards the flagship to act in attendance, just as hoys, wherries, bum boats and cutters were milling about, jousting for the best view of events, each vessel packed to the gunwales with would-be spectators. From the brightness of their clothes and the number of colourful parasols that flashed in the sun, it would seem that a hanging in Guadeloupe was a spectacle to behold; an occasion for celebration, though Winchip could fathom none of it.

Peter Pardoe, too, had cause to wonder at the air of festivity as he watched from the stern sheets of *Eaglet*'s cutter. He had been called to witness the demise of Pascal, as had Bowes, who sat next to him. They each swayed with the pull on the oars, Pardoe's sword held upright between his legs and Bowes' clasped firmly by the middle as it lay across his knees.

'You would think that we were going to the fair, Matthew.' Pardoe pointed to a red-sailed cutter that held a bevy of women, all gaily arrayed and wearing the clothes of the gentility. Such was the density of their garments, that there was no sign of the helmsman. Among them, two feckless dandies cavorted and showed off and, as the ladies giggled behind useless fans, so their gyrations became even more effete.

'They'll be going for a swim if they're not careful, Peter – and we'll be the ones to fish them out.' Matthew Bowes shook his head in despair.

From the entry port of *Cambridge*, the challenge came to their ears.

'*Eaglet!*' Hellard's response echoed against the tumblehome of the flagship.

Pardoe took the battens with care, his hat threatening to pitch into the water. As he came through the port, so the twitter of the pipes began and a cloud of pipeclay accompanied the salute from the marines. He made the deck and raised his hat to the first lieutenant before inclining it towards the saluting marines and the stilled boatswain. He had arrived in one piece – he could ask no more than that.

'Would you please take your place at the boat tier, Captain, together with your lieutenant?' The young lieutenant ushered them along as more officers appeared at the port and the pipes twittered once more.

Pardoe beckoned to Bowes and together they joined other officers at the appointed spot. It was directly beneath the block and tackle, under which the rope was lined up to forrard along the deck. The other end hung vertically downwards, fashioned into a noose that hung suspended some four feet from the deck, turning slowly in the light air. The shadow of the thick rope lay almost below it, suggesting to Pardoe that noon was nigh.

A sidelong glance evinced a smile from Pardoe. The brutality of the sentence, let alone the execution of it, still warranted the chaplain of *Cambridge* to stand piously next to the Commodore with his book of prayer to hand, staring forward as the captain of *Cambridge* read out the charge and the findings of the court. As he finished, so Pascal arrived at the companion steps to be turned forrard, towards the hanging noose. That the man was drunk was certain, an act of mercy that Winchip would never gainsay him. His gait was awry and only the support of the seaman on each side of him allowed him to keep his feet. The sad trio passed Pardoe not three feet away and the smell of rum filled the air as if it were the moment of 'Up spirits!'

The row of men that lined the rope appeared from nowhere, one left and one right, all the way to the end. The captain finished talking and the chaplain took the moment to offer up a prayer, taking an age to deliver it as Pascal began to wilt at the knees. Pardoe realised that the silence of expectation had come over the hitherto noisy crowd on the sea of boats, just as he assumed that somewhere beyond the walls of the fort someone was holding Pascal's life in his hand – in the shape of a burning slow match. At last, the chaplain's mournful voice came to an end with a hasty and impersonal genuflection. The ship's boatswain shouted an order and the rope was gathered up and allowed to hang loosely from the tackle and drape from the hands of the seamen. Pascal was taken up and his arms tied behind him. The noose was widened and passed over his head, tightened sufficiently to hang firmly upon his shoulder.

Time stood still. Pascal started to moan and the seamen started to shuffle their feet – then even that stopped. Only the screech of errant gulls, swooping among the rigging, could be heard. It was if the noon gun would never ring.

The discharge came suddenly for all that, the echo from the walls promptly blotting out the boatswain's order. Again, the order was given and the men turned about and trudged aft, lifting Pascal off his feet and drawing him up towards the yard arm in a series of hasty jerks as the seamen at the rope lost their rhythm. For a moment Pascal was benign, hanging by the neck with his body swinging as though he were already dead. One leg twitched and then the other, until suddenly the man was thrashing out with his legs, left and right; savage grunts and gurgles coming from his throat that sought to be but never became, a scream.

The cheers from those in the boats blotted out any further noise from Pascal and it was only when his legs stopped kicking and his head was bent by the coil to an impossible angle that the rope was belayed and the man allowed to swing gently in the freshening air.

Pardoe released his hand from the hilt of his sword, only to see the pattern of the grip engraved in his hand and fingers.

It was over.

Winchip stood at the taffrail of Bellicus in blouse and breeches, the sun on his face and a light breeze playing with the ribbon on his queue. He needed the space and the moment to reflect on the day. It could be years before he saw Stephen again and yet he had once more left him in a better position than when he found him.

He had gone with Stephen and the Mandinkas to see the land on the island of Grande-Terre. In Culpepper's sloop-of-war, they had sailed gingerly through the narrow gut that separated the two islands, the ship packed to capacity on both upper and lower decks, yet the journey was short and the sea as calm as could be hoped for. In accordance with the directions he had received, they had eventually come upon the wooden jetty of the plantation named 'Ciel et Terre', if the crude and worn letters painted on the notice board were read with care. The place had produced sugar, together with the inevitable molasses that would eventually become rum. The storage houses were solid and the refinery in working order. The house was of red brick, two storeys high and with many windows, most with their glass intact. The slave quarters were neglected as one would naturally expect of bamboo and grass. As to taking in the whole estate, it was far beyond his means, where, to him, one-hundred hectares had been an imaginary figure, so it turned out to be as far as the eye could see.

With the sight of the sugar fields there came upon him a great sadness. The sugar crop lay wasted upon the ground, canes awry and the foliage left to rot as the French were banished from the island. Stephen Loxley shook his head in sorrow and then suddenly he brightened; 'There is much to be done, Daniel, yet it will give us work aplenty until the new crop is planted.'

The Mandinka – for that was what Loxley had agreed they could be called – had picked their way through the tangle of bamboo and grass to assess what could be done. Kuana's people were on home ground, acting as though they were sharing in a huge adventure, gambolling like children in their new found paradise, seeing to the repairs as if they were back in Gambia and there had been a storm during the previous night. A far cry from when they had been rescued. With death on their minds and hope gone from their hearts, they had been a sorry lot that had crawled up into the sunlight, eyes blinking and limbs hurting, knowing that there were those of their friends below who would never see the sun again.

Winchip grimaced at his thoughts and slapped his hand on the taffrail, remembering events as he recalled them from his memory. He had forgotten about the skirts and the pantaloons that the Mandinka had been wearing. The squadron sailmakers had been responsible, working long hours to bring some self respect to over four-hundred naked souls. Winchip could have embraced every event in turn as he recalled them; the willingness of his people to do right by the slaves – when, for that day, all else was of little importance. He heaved a deep sigh. It would be the last he would see of Stephen on this voyage; but he vowed he would return – hopefully to bring the lad home.

As Pardoe was piped on board *Eaglet*, so he found sanctuary in the familiarity of his surroundings; he had been commanded to witness the hanging – there was nothing voluntary in it. He went straight to the great cabin and sank himself in Winchip's depression in the stern seat with a sigh. He sat there for a while, trying to erase the vision of Pascal's gruesome figure swinging below the main yard. At last he stood up with his head bowed to avoid the deckhead. He removed his sword and hat and then discarded his coat. He would walk the deck and let the wind do what his mind could not, for it was air he needed – and plenty of it.

He was about to take another turn at the taffrail when Midshipman Charles Dundas approached him. The well built fifteen year-old fingered his hat.

'A signal from the flagship, Sir: "Prepare to make sail".'

'Thank you, Mr Dundas, acknowledge the signal and then inform the master, if you please.' So, the Commodore wanted to be away from the place as much as *he* did. He should have expected it.

'All hands up! Topmen up to loose gaskets!' The cry through the trumpet came from Second Officer John Hartley, officer of the watch, his bush of sandy hair now the longer for the growing and gathered into a queue, tied with a black ribbon.

'Another signal from the flagship, Sir..,' Lord Guy Pickering looked at Pardoe as if his captain had seen death and escaped it. '..."discharge the salute and proceed to sea, due north".'

'Thank you, Lord Pickering, inform the Master, if you please.' Pardoe could have cheered. He had come to hate Guadeloupe, the place having first attracted him; but now he was cursed with bad memories of it. He would remember it for its volcano and the stink of sulphur in his nostrils even more clearly than he would remember the arrogant Pascal and his inevitable demise. There was also Loxley, now furnished with the means to make his fortune. Above all, he also had the woman with him – a woman to whom he, himself should be giving no thought whatsoever – but he had been and she would remain in his mind for a long time to come. Kuana had been the stuff of his dreams; a release from the pale and the ordinary, the mundane and the expected. She had been a *real* woman, whatever the colour of her soft and beautiful skin and her dark, sultry eyes. He shrugged his shoulders and looked out to sea, thinking about what might have been. Better that he forgot her – cast her from his mind – and that was exactly what he did.

CHAPTER NINETEEN

The Revenge of the People

The snow had come with the dawn; a driving snow that gathered where it lay until the hoses sent it gushing through the scupper drains. Only now was the snow easing, the large flakes replaced by driving sleet as the afternoon watch ended with eight bells ringing out, two by two. The wind had been from the south-west since dawn, coming onto *Eaglet*'s quarter as she plied to the north, in the van of the squadron.

'Nine knots by the log ship, sir.' Midshipman Godfrey Archer looked pleased with himself as though he, the messenger, had affected *Eaglet*'s best speed since leaving the islands that made up Guadeloupe.

'That is good news, Mr Archer.' Pardoe afforded the sixteen year-old a nodding smile then took in compass and wind as was his habit. The sky was leaden, as it was when dawn broke and the beam sea came upon them as an oily swell, making the ship roll like a drunken sailor. There was also the hint of a sea mist, distorting the horizon and seeming to close in on them with every turn of the sand-glass. With the deck canted over and the snow finding lodgings on yards and rigging alike, he had felt it necessary to remain on deck. Now that the snow was gone and the sky was beginning to lighten, it only required the wind to abate for him to go below for a well earned rest.

The passage from the south had been speedy and uninterrupted, aided by the current of the great stream that emanated from the Gulf of Mexico and would continue into the Atlantic as the North Atlantic Drift, deflected towards the wide ocean by the craggy shores of Newfoundland.

Christmas had come and gone, as had the New Year, the two events tumbling one upon the other so quickly that it seemed they had been gone for months instead of weeks.

Pardoe was well aware that his father-in-law intended to deliver Burke up to the Navy Office in Boston where justice would be seen to be done. They had dismissed the thought of delivering him to the magistrate at the royal courts, in the fear that Burke would be hung before his debts could be paid. They had crossed the fortieth line of parallel at noon the day before, which meant that New York would have been lurking in the mists to the north-west. Soon, Martha's Vineyard would appear before them – or they would sail blithely past.

'The lookouts have been changed as ordered, Sir.' Lord Guy Pickering blew his aristocratic nose with gusto.

'Thank you, Pickering, stand by me, if you please. I am anticipating a change of course from the flagship with this mist drawing closer – to the north-east, unless I am mistaken.'

Winchip came onto the quarterdeck from a comparatively warm cabin. His concern was growing for the lee shore ahead. He had made some calculations which had made light of his worries but he needed to be sure. He knew that his son-in-law would have a midshipman in the tops but the mist in the warmer waters was drawing in by the minute. He had decided to err on the side of caution before even signals would be impossible. He took a glass from the rack and tucked it under his arm. Guy Percival was at the binnacle as officer of the watch. He straightened his back and glanced at wind and compass.

'Our course is due north, Sir and the wind is out of the south-west, beginning to ease.'

'Then it is heaven-sent, Mr Percival.' Winchip glanced at the wind pennant. 'Send a general signal while we may, "*Eaglet* to wear to the north-east – remainder in succession, three points by three".' Winchip raised his glass towards *Incensed*. A few moments later the signal was being bent on; the responses coming in rapid succession at the dip. Winchip looked to the east, to where

Culpepper would be hull down. He saw her sails as a small flash of white on a disturbed horizon.

'*Deck alow - land to the north-west!*'

Culpepper acknowledged with a wave and turned to Winchip. 'Could it be Martha's Vineyard, Sir?'

'That is more likely than not, Mr Percival, in which case we shall be in port this very night.' Winchip slapped his thigh. '*Eaglet* has done even better than I expected, Lieutenant!'

Sheltered from the rising south-westerly, Winchip's squadron lay at anchor in the naval anchorage at Boston. *Bellicus* and *Incensed* assumed the position they had left those few months ago, guarding the entrance to Boston harbour. Culpepper, bearing the cross of being the junior, lay at anchor on a deep bar further out to sea. The threat of snow had passed, to be replaced by a fine drizzle and a temperature that was warm, even for early April.

Boston Harbour was much as Winchip had left it, with smoke hanging in the air from countless chimneys. As he sat in the stern sheets of his barge, Winchip could see at first hand that there had been little change in the busy port. The quays were busy, as were the jetties, with boats hastening to and fro in an effort to beat the oncoming dusk. Two Indiamen had been loading and two Southampton Class frigates were moored against the stone mole. His eyes were drawn to an armed slaver, discharging her cargo onto the long quay that seemed to have grown even longer than when they left. On an impulse, he saw an opportunity to save much time and trouble.

'Take us into the steps by the slaver, Pender; I have an urge to speak to her captain.'

'Aye aye, Sir.' Pender pushed the tiller across and then spat out the juices from his plug of tobacco to jet over his shoulder with a flourish born of habit.

In undress uniform, Winchip climbed the weeded steps. Behind him, two of his marines followed with their muskets strapped across their shoulders. Behind them came two more marines, holding the manacled Seth Burke between them. The once shaven Burke now had a beard; and Winchip prayed that it would be sufficient to disguise him until he had handed him over.

On the quay, Winchip almost stopped in horror as he saw the slaves being lined up and shackled round the neck – it was as if they were back in Guadeloupe on one of the colliers as the slaves had risen above the level of the deck. The smell was upon them and Winchip almost gagged as it became pervasive, almost omnipresent and by virtue of that, inescapable. They were mostly females, some clad in scraps of cloth about their waists, while others were without a stitch to provide modesty. All were shivering where they stood as their heads were put in yokes and the hands that had been protecting their modesty were snatched up and joined to the yokes by leather straps. This in turn was attached to the next slave by a long rope and so on, down the line, keeping the slaves together in twos with no chance of escape. Two of the females held babies, their hands being left free for the purpose, each child with a skin far lighter than that of its mother and obviously born on the journey. Other women showed signs of advanced pregnancy and even their hands were put into the straps. There was a sound in the air that was more of a drawn out sigh than a lament; and Winchip was quick to realise that it was the whimper of victims too frightened to cry out in their misery.

He had seen enough. He had wanted to inform the man that Burke had returned, so that he could pass the information on to interested parties but he abandoned his ill-considered plan in its infancy, the man would see little reason for him to pass the word if it meant sharing whatever money Burke would have on him. He turned on a sixpence and beckoned the marines to follow him. He would go to the Naval Office where he should have gone in the first place.

The Naval Office was behind the hard, a building of brick with some substance but with no real air of permanent occupation. A marine stood to each side of the large black door and as Winchip approached, so they came to attention and saluted.

'I am Commodore Winchip. I am here to deliver up a prisoner to the senior officer.' Winchip wished he had assigned the task of delivering Burke to another; but there was much at stake and much to be discussed, besides the need for the authority of his rank.

One of the marines opened the door and ushered Winchip and the party inside. The vestibule was warm and in the room beyond a large log fire could easily be seen. Without waiting to be invited, Winchip bade his marines to wait where they stood and strode into the inner sanctum. A post-captain sat at the large desk perusing papers before him. Two lieutenants were leaning across the table as if conferring on a point at issue. The post-captain saw him first and stood up with alacrity.

'Sir, I was not told we had a visitor. Had we known...'

Winchip interrupted the man. 'It is of no matter, Captain. My name is Winchip and my squadron is already sitting in your harbour, unable to attract your attention with signals.' Winchip strode up to the desk, well aware of the looks of horror between the captain and his officers. 'I have a fugitive with me, in the vestibule. His name is Seth Burke, a one time slave trader from this town, now turned pirate. I wish to hand him over to you.'

'That is a civil matter, Commodore, nothing to do with the navy.' The man's nerve held fast.

'What is your name, Captain?'

'Dominic Harris, Sir – at your service.'

'Well, Harris, this man Burke was taken on the high seas in an act of piracy. His fellow conspirator has been hanged on board His Britannic Majesty's Ship, *Cambridge*, in Guadeloupe.' Winchip dumped the leather bag full of guineas onto the desk. In there are fifteen hundred guineas. Perhaps you would like to contact the magistrates to ensure that this money is used to pay the man's debts for there are many in this town to whom he owes money and whose claims and criminal allegations are already set before the magistrates. All I require is a receipt for delivering him up – and your personal guarantee that the matter will be dealt with immediately, so that I can proceed with my squadron to Vice Admiral Saunders in the Gulf of St Lawrence.' Winchip drew breath and put a hand to his waist as he stared the poor man down.

'Sir, with respect, I cannot try the man in a naval court. I have insufficient post-captains to hand.'

'How many *do* you have?'

'One, Commodore, and I am he.'

Winchip gave Harris credit for finding self confidence where there had been confusion and uncertainty. 'Very well, then it must be a civil court – but the money shall be paid out by you as soon as the court has delivered its verdict. Every claim must be verified and receipts made and signed. Any shortfall will be paid by the Prize Court on application.' Winchip had tempered his attitude now that he knew what was likely to happen. 'The monies must be paid out to his creditors in this town *before* Burke is hanged, lest he has left a will, which, of course, would be applicable should the benefactors come to the surface, have I made myself clear?'

'I now know exactly what you have in mind, Sir – and I shall do all in my power to obey your wishes. I can offer no more than that.'

'Thank you Captain Harris – but get the man hung as soon as you can. I have all the evidence and affidavits that you are likely to require on the flagship, which you are welcome to visit at your earliest opportunity.'

'Thank you, Sir.' Harris turned to the taller of the two lieutenants. 'Take the man into custody, Phillips and then call the Watch.'

Winchip turned and beckoned the marines in the vestibule to come forward with Burke. He then turned back to Harris. 'I expect you to do your duty, Captain; and I would like the receipt for the prisoner to give Burke's condition as satisfactory.' Winchip urged the marines forward with a gesture of the hand, satisfied that Burke was to some degree presentable. He thanked God that the man had not been beaten about; but his morale had been broken, that was for sure. It was almost as if the once arrogant Burke had already accepted that he would be hung by those from whom he had stolen money in the town that he had pillaged In fact, he had lost all hope.

For three days the squadron had cleaned ship, scoured casks, and provisioned for sea. At the mail office, Winchip had collected a letter for himself, from Madeleine and another for Pardoe with Emma's writing on the face for sure. Winchip had opened the missive at the earliest moment, only to find that Jonathan had died as he expected and that Beth was now caring for Richard. It was with a stout heart that he recalled his days with Jonathan as his coxswain. They had spent many years together and he had much to thank the man for – and to remember.

It was on the fourth day that Burke came to trial, his guilt firmly established by twenty witnesses to his felonies and a jury of his peers. It was noted with concern by Winchip that the scaffold had been erected near the hard in anticipation of the verdict before the trial had even ended. At one end of the beam that ran the length of the platform were both a trapdoor and a ring through which the rope would pass before a double knot arrested its descent. At the other end was an open iron cage, hanging from the beam, a gibbet in the shape of a man, down to the separation in which each leg would be placed; a frame in which Burke's body would be suspended until the gulls had torn the flesh from his bones and the eyes from his head. For Burke to be aware of his imminent disposition before the event sent shivers down Winchip's spine. It was a case of cruelty over compassion, where his victims had chosen to ignore compassion in favour of that which was abominable.

The claimants had come by the dozen, each waving a piece of paper with which payment was certain to be made, whether it was a bill or a promissory note, it made no difference. The queue had lengthened during the fourth day and at the raising of a 'pilot jack' on the Naval Office staff, the claims would be refuted or paid; and false claims referred to the magistrate. The queue had shortened accordingly.

Winchip was determined to pay his respects to Post Captain Harris. The man had done what he promised to do and had arranged things well. To Winchip's surprise, the man had arranged with the magistrate that, should Burke be found guilty, he would then be required to undergo questioning by the Naval Office with regards to the piracy of the slaves, the destruction of the slave ships and the deaths of the crews who sailed on those ships – all for the purposes of having a complete record of events. The magistrate had agreed, which allowed time for the payments to be made before the man was hanged. Burke may have gained a few hours of life – but many others had regained their livelihoods, no matter how small. All it required was for Burke to be taken to the scaffold and the noose to be placed around his neck for the matter to be done with, once and for all.

Winchip went to the mizzen shrouds and rested his glass on a ratline. He had a perfect view of the scaffold and could even see the gibbet turning in the wind. He was about to withdraw when a movement caught his attention. He put his eye to the glass once more and saw Burke being dragged towards the steps of the scaffold. The crowd followed behind, a motley group of townsfolk by all appearances, all taking the short journey to the scaffold to relish the demise of a felon. It may have been anathema to Winchip but he could sense the rhyme and the reason – it was justice, pure and simply – as well as: 'There, but for the grace of God, go I'.

Burke was dragged up the steps of the scaffold and his arms bound behind him. He was staring about him as if he were in a nightmare and probably praying to his maker for the first time in his life. As the noose went over his head, so he tried to avoid it, ducking and weaving until he was manhandled to a stiffness that deprived him of movement. The noose went on and was tightened, with the coil ending behind his ear – and then he was gone, through the trapdoor and into space, his head brought to the upright by the snatch of the rope. The parson had been surprised and robbed of his moment of prayer as Burke kicked and struggled for his life – but to no avail.

Winchip lowered his glass and blinked his eyes to regain his rightful focus. He placed it back into the rack with care and closed the protective leather flap. He had no wish to see Burke placed in the gibbet. That would come with time, when the ghastly sight could be inspected by the ghouls who had cheered Burke's demise.

Winchip moved through to the great cabin and took out his journal from the drawer of his desk. He had much to say and plenty of time to write it. When he was done he would go across to the Naval Office and see Harris as he had promised himself so to do. Harris had struck Winchip as being a man of many parts but exercising none of them; a waste – and a circumstance that required attention.

Captain Peter Pardoe stood at the binnacle and waited for the signal to raise the anchor. At present it was at 'short stay' and the capstan was already manned. Catting the damned anchor would require to be done after the ship had fallen off the wind, much to his annoyance.

He had watched the execution from the mizzen shrouds; and only a few minutes before, he had seen the lifeless body of Burke being stuffed into the cage that was the gibbet, much like the one on the road to Penryn, at the crossroads. That one had stunk after a week, so what price working downwind on Boston's hard once the weather warmed up?

'A signal from flag, Sir, "raise anchor – course west by north – Eaglet in the van". That is all, Sir.' Archer looked pleased to have remembered it all.

'Thank you, Mr Archer. See the anchor catted as soon as we are on course, if you please.'

CHAPTER TWENTY

Petite Tempête

The fifteenth of May dawned with a tableau of yellow streaked cloud that prefaced the coming of the sun, which, when it appeared, glistened with such intensity that it hurt the eyes. The light wind was from the north, yet it had enough warmth in it to make one believe that spring was looking to become summer.

Pardoe rested his glass on the mizzen ratlines and took in the rocky point of the Isle de la Madeleine on the larboard beam. He anticipated a call from the tops at any time, remembering that it was at this point that he had been challenged on their arrival in the Americas. Two hours later and still there was no sign of a squadron frigate.

'Deck alow! A frigate on the larboard bow! She'm challengin'!'

'Bend on our number, Mr Dundas – my god; she's a sight for sore eyes!' Pardoe raised the glass. The frigate was bearing down on them, moving to the east to come about and present her larboard entry port, probably needing to deliver a message in person. 'Mr Hartley! Prepare to receive a visitor.' To Mr Ramblin, he said. 'Come up into wind if you please, Master.'

A lieutenant clambered through the port and then raised his hat to Hartley. Pardoe waited patiently by the capstan. The lieutenant came up the deck to him and once more doffed his hat.

'Welcome on board *Eaglet*, Lieutenant. I take it you have a message for Commodore Winchip?' The lieutenant would have known all he needed to know with the simple act of identifying *Eaglet* and seeing a squadron in the offing.

'Thank you, Sir. I am First Lieutenant John Trelithic of the frigate *Charmouth*. You will not know it but the French have sought to blockade Quebec. They have a large squadron of ships in the upper reaches of the St Lawrence and Admiral Saunders has long since departed to engage them.'

'How the devil did they get past the outer frigates, Lieutenant?'

'They didn't, Sir, the French force has been up near Montreal since Quebec was taken. The admiral went up-river less than a week since, and we have heard that he is chasing them upstream, though some may have escaped and are likely to come downstream.' The lieutenant looked crestfallen.

Pardoe realised that berating the lieutenant served no purpose. 'Report to *Bellicus*, immediately, Lieutenant. Commodore Winchip will require to be told every detail of what has happened.'

'Aye, Sir!' Lieutenant Trelithic tipped his hat and was gone in a flash, no doubt thanking God that another English Squadron was to hand and he had not been deserted.

With the departure of the lieutenant, Pardoe had the ship remain in position, facing into wind with the squadron bearing down on him. He felt the need to be angry but found he could find no blame without knowing all the facts; facts that his father-in-law would wheedle out of the lieutenant in no time at all.

The four captains sat at the table in the great cabin of Bellicus as Winchip waited for the coffee to be served. Booth placed the tray in the centre of the table and scuttled behind his partition and thence to the galley as he had been ordered. Once the coffee pot had been circulated Winchip raised a hand for silence.

'The French are blockading Quebec from the Montreal side, Gentlemen and appear to be well entrenched, upstream from the city. Vice Admiral Saunders has taken his squadron up the St Lawrence and is chasing the French back to Montreal. We shall support him by protecting his rear. There is certainly no way in which any of the French ships can return down stream unless we let them pass, which is not our way...' Winchip waited for the laughter to subside. '...*Eaglet* shall take the van – and shall also take on board a pilot who is going across to her now.' Winchip nodded to Pardoe. 'We shall act as we find, Gentlemen. However, please keep your eyes on *Bellicus* at all times.' Winchip took a sip of his coffee. 'I have no wish to tie your hands during this confrontation but there are times to act individually and times to act in unison, if you catch my drift?' Winchip smiled as he received nods from each of the captains. He was well aware of Pardoe's spontaneous reactions to events and he had no wish to restrict his son-in-law's movements beyond what was absolutely necessary. Winchip looked at Nathanson and held his gaze. '*Incensed* and *Bellicus* shall act together. We may attack or we may act as blockships, I know not which, though in acting as blockships we have no intention of going aground, I can assure you!' Again, he waited for the laughter to subside. 'So, there we have it. Whatever we come across, I expect every man to do his duty.' Winchip drained his cup and left it at that. There were no questions and neither had he expected any.

The pilot was on board Eaglet when Pardoe returned. The big man stood behind the wheel, talking with Mr Ramblin. He came forward as Pardoe approached.

'My name is Charles Le Blanc, Captain, a Jersey man for my sins.'

'My name is Pardoe and I am very glad to see you, Mr Le Blanc. Shall you take the helm or should the master oblige?'

'I shall take the helm when it matters, Sir. Your master, Mr Ramblin will be busy enough controlling our speed, for that is the killer here. We have many alterations of course to make to avoid going onto the mudbanks or the shore. To run onto the mud banks at speed is to loose your ship for sure, for you will never get off again short of an almighty flood.'

'Then how are we to do battle with the French?'

'By using my knowledge of the river, Captain, for it gets more dangerous and more difficult each day we move upstream. Until we get to 'Trois Pistoles', we shall have the main channel but then we shall come across shallows and mud banks as well as deep water. After that you will need all the help I can give you, though James Cook has navigated this river several times and has recorded his seasonal findings of which, thank God, I do have a copy, though I seldom need it now.'

'Well, that *is* good news, Pilot.' Pardoe's comment was sincere, for without the man he would be lost. 'We shall set our course, if you please; and be guided by you from this moment onwards.'

Once through the Straits of Honguedo the river opened up into a great basin with no end to the waters but only the rising hills on three sides to indicate its circumference. Eaglet had continued in the van, her lookouts changing with every other toll of the bell. The breeze had continued from the north; an adverse wind that helped to control the speed of the ships plying against the gentle current. It was only with the setting of the sun that the air got colder. For the first night they anchored in the river proper, in the small cove at Saint-Anne-des-Monts on the southern shore with the northern shore invisible, lying over twenty miles across the water. It was a pretty place, below the hills, surrounded by a green sward dotted with dwellings that fostered countless sheep, intermingled with some cattle that were as black as beetles.

It was with sadness that Pardoe ordered marines to the deck on night watch. He trusted the crew as far as one dared – but this was a land of plenty with space to carve a living and there was a battle in the offing. With this in mind the order had been one of common sense – no more than that.

The next day dawned with weather similar to the day before. As they progressed, only the terrain had changed as the hills increased in height with small mountains beyond that. It was as eight bells rang in the forenoon watch that Charles Le Blanc directed the squadron to the other side of what still appeared to be a very wide river. Not a question was asked; but towards the bank, the shimmer of choppy waters glinting in the sun gave a hint of the pilot's reasoning and the presence of shoaling. Only Mr Ramblin had nodded his appreciation of the move, puffing on his clay as he took in all that was going on about him and made notes with the stub of a pencil.

'Deck there! Ships ahead – they're French!'

Pardoe raised a hand in acknowledgement. 'Signal to flag – "enemy frigate in sight", Mr Dundas.'

'Come to quarters, Mr Hartley and load but don't run out. I have no wish to capsize the ship with the first simple manoeuvre.' Pardoe turned to Bowes. 'Put Archer in the tops, Matthew, he'll know a Frenchman when he sees one – and then we shall know what we are up against. Also, send the information to flag as they will have seen nothing as yet.'

Archer snatched a glass from the rack and slung it across his shoulder with a length of fish-line. He was back within two minutes. 'Flag acknowledged our signal and it *is* the French, Sir. There are two fifty gun ships with a frigate well ahead of them. There is also a bomb ketch. They have all turned into wind.'

'Very well, signal to flag exactly what you have told me.'

Pardoe stood next to Le Blanc, needing the moment to think. He certainly wasn't about to charge upstream with battle ensigns flapping in the wind.

'You have the frigate at your mercy, Captain. He has the northern channel at the moment but he is drifting. You have only to close on him from mid-stream and he will on the mud bank for sure.'

'It can't be that easy, Pilot?' It ended as a question.

'It can, if you leave it with me, Sir; though my orders will have to be obeyed to the letter.'

'Then carry on, Pilot, if you please.' Pardoe turned and looked aft, seeing that *Bellicus* was a good four cables behind them. He saw that Le Blanc was in a deep discussion with Mr Ramblin and Pardoe felt better for that. At the moment his ship was not under *his* command and it worried him. In the end, he afforded Le Blanc as much faith as he could muster. It was Mr Ramblin who gave the first orders and it was Longdale, the master's mate who yelled the orders through the trumpet. He started as Le Blanc spoke to him directly.

'Have men ready to open the larboard ports, Captain – so as to make them think you are about to fire on them.' Le Blanc turned away without waiting for a response.

'All hands up to wear ship!'

The French frigate was as far upstream as *Bellicus* was astern of them. Topmen were scrambling up the shrouds, far more than normal and already men were mustering on the deck, ready for the heave. Longdale was shouting orders to those in the tops and both Hartley and Bowes were attending the deck, putting men to the ports to do Le Blanc's bidding. The scene was set, needing only the order for the ship to wear to starboard, towards the oncoming *Frenchman*.

'Take up courses!' Pardoe suddenly realised with great clarity what Le Blanc had in mind and he marvelled at the plan. It would take a great deal of courage to complete the evolution and pass through the wind but he knew his water as well as he knew the ground. Longdale was exhibiting a complete understanding of what he had been ordered to do and was still shouting his instructions for coming through the wind. He was not to know that the Eaglets had done it once before, near the Isle d'Oléron, three years ago at the time of Minorca. The French ship had been the *Corinne,* too cocky for her own good and now a wreck on the rocky shore of France.

For a moment nothing happened; and the French frigate came closer and closer until it was only a cable distant from *Eaglet*.

'Wear ship – open ports!'

Le Blanc turned the wheel, passing the spokes from hand to hand, trimming his turn to his total satisfaction and, as the ship came round, so the ports flew open as one, tipping towards the water below but not enough to allow it entry. Pardoe slapped his knee as the *Frenchman* put her helm over, taking the moment available to her to square with *Eaglet*'s guns if only to defend herself. Le Blanc held the turn as Pardoe expected, prepared to come through the wind and complete the circle to come back into safe water. No wonder there had been so many topmen aloft. As for the French frigate, her fate awaited her.

There was a flurry of action in *Eaglet*'s tops and a smart trim of the yards as she came through the wind, turning downstream towards *Bellicus,* now two cables distant.

The French frigate may have gone to quarters but not one of her ports opened. Her captain must have braced himself to face a broadside that would never come. The ship crossed the stream and moved away, towards the shore, suddenly showing a flurry of action in her tops as if a great realisation had come upon her captain – but it was too late.

Eaglet was through her turn and was facing back into the channel when the Frenchman ran onto the bank. Her foremast went by the board and her mainmast followed, dragging down rigging and seamen alike in the wake of the collapsed masts. The mizzen mast remained upright, her gaff as taut as a drum in the northerly; but it served no purpose.

Pardoe looked aft and shook his head with wonder as *Eaglet* completed her circle. Soon, the ship was facing upriver with her helm restored on her original course. He moved from the binnacle and offered Le Blanc his hand.

'You have my gratitude and thanks, Mr Le Blanc; that was an exceptional evolution!'

Midshipman Archer touched Pardoe's arm. 'Signal from flag, Sir; "Well done – clear the way", Sir.'

'Let fall the courses!'

Already, the French frigate was to be discounted, her bows driven high onto the mud and her stern windows almost under water. Already, boats were being swung over.

Eaglet had gone out into the stream after her incredible manoeuvre. The stranded French frigate passed astern as Eaglet moved across the flow. Already, the boats of the Frenchman were crammed with men, while others shouted from the slanting deck. She had been a fine vessel – once; and a large one of thirty-two guns. For a moment Pardoe wondered if they would try to tow her off and shook his head in despair at their fruitless efforts and the blind stupidity of their mad efforts to attempt the impossible. Her name had been *PetiteTempête*.

Pardoe now only had eyes for the French men-of-war, now less than half a mile distant. The ketch was a clumsy vessel, loitering into wind further upstream. Winchip had told Le Blanc to clear away and that was what the pilot was already doing. It was now the turn of both *Bellicus* and *Incensed*, coming up towards *Eaglet* like a brace of leviathans.

Eaglet's tops'ls caught the wind that was on her starboard beam and then the mains'ls followed with a succession of thuds. Eaglet was plying her way on the southern side of the channel, out of the way and free from the dangers of the lee mud banks. Pardoe looked over to Le Blanc, seeing the man laugh as he chatted to Mr Ramblin. Pardoe had witnessed an action worthy of his father-in-law during *Eaglet*'s early days. He hoped and prayed that he, too, might one day have the courage to make those decisions to which he had borne witness so many times but had yet to find the opportunity.

CHAPTER TWENTY-ONE

'Pickle 'em in Brine'

Winchip had decided in his mind that Admiral Saunders had already raised the siege of Quebec. What he could see coming down the wide channel towards him were the escapees from a lost cause – there could be no other reason. He raised his glass, assessing the distance to the French as close to half a mile. They had made no move to draw away from the shore, for that was what it was rather than a bank, with the river being so wide. As for the beleaguered frigate they could do little but pick up her complement, some in boats that were floundering in the current and others who were being carried downstream, waving and screaming for rescue that would never come to them in time. For a fearful moment he wondered whether the French knew something that he didn't, which immediately precipitated an earnest desire for a pilot; anyone who could fathom the channels between the hidden banks of sand and mud. He had seen the French frigate run onto the shoals, or the mud bank as the pilot had referred to the hidden traps; and that had been half a league from the shore. Suddenly, he remembered the Le Blanc's last words before he had gone over to Eaglet. He had distinctly told him that the present channel was safe for the next hour. He slapped his thigh as his mind cleared. For now he would maintain his course for as long as he was allowed to; and leave others to follow their noses. He called to Percival who ran to his side from the binnacle.

'Lieutenant, I want you to maintain this course until the last moment, no matter what happens. Make a signal to *Incensed* to do likewise with her opponent before it is too late – and order battle ensigns, if you please.' As Percival dashed away so Winchip raised his glass once more. The French were moving quickly in line astern, three chains apart, with both stream and wind to help them. He wondered how long it would be before the enemy decided that *Bellicus* was in no mind to be driven off her course.

The sudden arrival of Midshipman Piper disturbed his train of thought. He almost rounded on the lad but instead, he asked. 'Well, Mr Piper?'

'Incensed has acknowledged, Sir and battle ensigns are being hoisted.' As Piper said the words, so the shadows of the great jacks came and went as they fluttered across the deck and a roaring huzzah came from all quarters of the ship.

'Find Mr Niven, Mr Piper; and have the ship come to quarters. Guns loaded and run out on the larboard side only, round shot all, to fire as they bear – and to keep firing whilst they have something to fire at!' He smiled at the lad as Piper ran forward, his voice having broken after years of continual squeaks.

'Hands to quarters, all hands up!'

He raised the telescope again, now able to see the first *Frenchman* in detail. As he watched, so her ports opened and her larboard guns ran out, two rows of black snouts that looked menacing enough from where he stood. So, she was going to pass down the starboard side of Bellicus. She had made up her mind and the die was cast – unless Winchip moved quickly. As he continued to look through the glass, the sun suddenly burst free from the sombre clouds that were scudding across the sky. In that instant he saw the sharp lines in the water that defined the channel, depicted by the change in colour of the water. The channel ahead showed itself in the deepest blues and greens, whilst elsewhere the water was lighter and greener. He slapped his thigh with delight, while a quiet corner of his mind called for caution. The water beneath the French was dark enough and she was still afloat. He had learned a lesson and he was not about to dismiss it out of hand.

'Mr Niven!' Winchip shouted as hard as he could and was relieved to see Niven turn towards him. 'Run out the starboard guns and load with round shot – leave the ones to larboard!'

Niven reacted without question before his sentence was completed. The larboard guns were secured and already the breechings were off and the tackles taken up on the starboard side. Winchip moved across to Walter Blackstock, the master.

'Put your helm over, Master, we shall pass them on their starboard side, if you please and as close as you like!'

'Aye, Commodore!' The master pushed the helmsmen aside and took the wheel himself, testing for the slack and then waiting for the moment. Suddenly he was dragging the spokes round, pulling on them until he could turn the wheel hand over hand, bringing the rudder across just sufficiently to serve his purpose.

Winchip watched the jib of *Bellicus* slowly pass across the foremains'l of the *Frenchman* from right to left and beyond, events happening so quickly that he was afraid Mr Blackstock had overdone it. At last, there was clear water in front of *Bellicus*, dark blue mingled with deep green showing depth enough; and the distance between the two ships was now a mere chain and still the *Frenchman* was maintaining her course as if she suspected that *Bellicus* would change her mind yet again. Niven was poised by the forward gun, his sword glinting as it rested upon his shoulder. How Munro was faring on the lower deck he had no idea but he would certainly have his hands full.

A great shadow passed over the fo'c's'le of Bellicus, cast by the fores'ls of the Frenchmen as she came into the line of the sun.

'Fire!'

Niven's voice blended with the sound of the first discharge and the huge cloud of acrid yellow smoke that blew backwards, directly across the deck in the light north-easterly. The next gun fired and then the next, the sound of splintered wood and the cries of men bringing the reality of death to the event, their screams rending the air with every shot. Winchip watched with horror as one of *Bellicus*' great guns was knocked sideways, its crew scattered about the deck, writhing and screaming as fate sorted the dead from the wounded. That the French had found time to load and fire even one starboard gun showed that there were experienced seamen aboard. Already, the Frenchman was beam to beam with

Bellicus, yet still the guns of his flagship were firing, the foremost gun bouncing backwards on its breechings as it fired its second discharge. Winchip heard the whine of a musket ball as it passed nearby and, looking upwards, he could see Monk's marines in the tops, returning the fire, protected by hammocks as they fired and reloaded.

Suddenly, the Frenchman was past and gone. Already, Niven was giving orders, the displaced gun being handled by ten men and a hastily placed block and tackle. Mr Abraham Perry, the gunner, kept his orders short and clear and soon the gun was back on its carriage and being loaded as if it had never gone astray.

Winchip saw the wounded – and worse – being taken below, a place he would be quick to visit when this business was done.

The second French ship was almost upon them, another thirty seconds and it would begin all over again. Winchip looked aft to see that Nathanson was following his example and taking the outside water, avoiding all thoughts of mudbanks. As he watched, so the first guns were fired, one after the other into a crew who had endured one cannonade and may not have the stomach for a second. Quickly, he looked away, noticing that Niven and Percival were checking each gun and encouraging the crews as they drank their fill from the water bucket rather than the puny ladle. The powder monkeys had done their work and the buckets for the slow match were refilled and back in their place. Blood was being assuaged with water; washed into the scuppers and out through the drains.

Then, the second ship was upon them, following its companion for fear of the shoals and not risking a deviation as Winchip had done. *Bellicus* fired first, the smoke once more blowing out across the deck in a putrid yellow cloud, made all the more real by the sudden brightness of the sun. The guns roared out, one by one, down the line. Large timbers flew from the enemy's bulwarks and her gun ports were reduced to splinters as the great guns discharged one after the other. Any new damage to *Bellicus* merely added to the damage already received, while those of the gun crews who had suffered injury were limited to ugly splinters, large and small, that flew through the air like barbed spears.

Winchip watched as *Incensed* fired her guns in turn, issuing clouds of yellow smoke that obscured everything but sound. The guns roared out and the red and yellow spurts of flame diminished as the smoke gained apace, blotting out the hulls to leave billowing sails in clear air to strain at angled yards; and the solid thuds of the guns, until even those stopped. So, the *Frenchmen* had forced a passage; but not without cost. Perhaps they would meet again – but not this day. Her name had been *Protectrice*.

Winchip went down into the darkness below decks and found his way aft to the orlop deck and to the cockpit, guided by the cries of the dying and the moans of those who were less badly wounded. He found the surgeon, Walter Bartholemew, straddling a man whose arm was smashed above the elbow, the useless limb flopping about as the seaman blasphemed and cursed those who tried to restrain him as he tried to protect it from the large knife in the surgeon's bloodstained hand. Only when an assistant straddled the patient's body and gripped his good arm was the surgeon able to slice away at the flapping skin and the useless detritus that prevented him sewing up what remained. Winchip moved about the other wounded with a word here and a gesture there, simply to let them know he was among them – and cared.

Winchip found his coxswain at the boat tier. As Pender knuckled his forehead, so Winchip drew him aside.

'There will be no committal, Coxswain. I shall not see a committed body that I have sent to the deep finish up on a riverbank for all to see and for the animals to fight over. They shall be put in brine until we are at sea again, when we shall send them down with full honours, as they deserve.' Winchip looked Pender in the eye. 'Am I clearly understood?'

'Aye, Sir and they shall thank you for it and that's no lie.' Pender nodded his head.

'Then see to it, Coxswain – and as soon as you can, if you please.' Winchip turned on his heel without waiting for a reply. He knew the job would be done and the bodies immersed together in an old water cask, though for how long they would have to remain so, he had no idea.

He climbed to the crosstrees with a glass and stared ahead at the vast expanse of water ahead of the ship. To his delight, he could see the channels, some small and others wide and deep. The channel they were using continued onwards, wide and safe, though it needed watching. For now, they were in deep water and would be so for as far as Winchip could see. As the sun ducked behind a cloud, so he looked again at the now familiar water and could still see the same channels, less clear – but there nevertheless.

Winchip was in no mind to finish an engagement that could put him on a mud bank. His task – and duty – was to ensure the integrity of Admiral Saunders.

After an exchange of signals and with the coming of night, the small squadron had anchored in the lee of the Isle aux Coudres, a substantial island on the northern shore of the great St Lawrence River where repairs could be done and the wounded cared for, no matter how long it took.

Winchip completed his journal and closed the book with a sigh. Wiping the nib of the quill, he replaced it in the stand with the others. The repairs to *Bellicus* and to *Incensed* seemed to be endless. On the third day the sound of the mauls and the adzes continued to dominate all other sounds, as did the shouted orders and the blasphemous curses – just as the insidious smell of tar permeated the decks as the loggerheads stirred the surfaces of the heated tar-butts. With the windows facing to the east, the lighted stern lights of Bellicus seemed bright against the darkness of the horizon. They cast down their light into the after part of the cabin, giving out that golden glow that only burning tallow can provide. He jerked suddenly awake, aware that he needed sleep. In a moment of sentiment he took the likeness of Madeleine and Richard from his inner pocket and propped it against the ink stand. As usual, she stared into his eyes – as she did from every angle – there was no hiding from her and neither would he want to, his only wish being that she was there, with him, sharing the moment – even making love together. He sighed and undressed by the clothes closet. In his nightshirt and night-cap he went to his cot, praying that he would be allowed a few hours of continuous sleep.

It was during the forenoon watch the next day, in a bitter northerly, that the squadron entered the Montmagny Channel that would lead them past Quebec and onwards, towards Montreal and Rear Admiral Charles Saunders. No sooner had *Eaglet's* course been set, a cry came down from the tops, warning of ships upstream. Pardoe prayed that they would be English. A moment later, Archer arrived on the quarterdeck.

'It is a large squadron, Sir. I think it may be Admiral Saunders.'

'Thank you, Mr Archer. First, you will send up the challenge – and as soon as you like, young man.' Pardoe smiled as Archer cursed himself for his stupidity. He was up the ratlines like a monkey as Dundas bent on the bunting.

'Deck alow – 'Tis a flagship and English at that!'

'Relay it to flag, Mr Dundas; "flagship in sight".

Pardoe shook his head. They had come full circle and yet so much had happened in between. His mind went back to Kuana and what might have been if common sense hadn't won over lust. He knew he would have such thoughts again but they all came back to his beautiful Emma in the end.

'Flag has acknowledged, Sir and instructs us to bend on "despatches for flag".

'Very well, Mr Dundas, see to it if you please.' Pardoe stared in the direction of Admiral Saunder's fleet. Were they to be sent home from this enigmatic land? He hoped they would be, for the place was unsettled and unstable, one could feel it in the bones. The slaves, too, lent little credit to those who dealt in them. Humanity was standing on its head – certain for a fall.

'Flag has acknowledged, Sir.'

Winchip bobbed along in his barge as it approached *Neptune*, the ninety-gun flagship of Rear Admiral Charles Saunders. Tucked inside his uniform coat, the events of the past few months were encapsulated in a sheaf of papers and his journal. They said little about those who had died in the process or of the horrors of slavery; but his words told the facts and that was all that mattered.

Pender gripped the chains so that Winchip could climb on board. The drum and fife band was there once more, as was Saunders, standing as large as life as if nothing had occurred since they had last met.

After a brief exchange of niceties, Winchip passed his journal and papers across the great table. He attacked the dish of coffee before him with decorum, sipping the nectar as a cat would guard her milk. There was much for the admiral to read and not all of it pleasant. He knew he would be held to answer for the hangings, just as Winchip knew that Commodore Moore's despatches would give credence to his words and actions. Winchip had written his reports in chronological sequence, allowing one incident to justify another. As for the outcome, it would read as though he had marched through Admiralty Orders without regard for protocol, always a dangerous habit unless the end justified the means. He sat upright as Saunders spoke at last.

'I must confess, my dear Winchip, that I gave you your orders in the belief that no man could untangle such a web of deceit. I was obviously wrong. I shall be sending dispatches across to you in due course for Their Lordships at Admiralty. In telling them that the Navigation Acts are being upheld as much as is humanly possible and that the slave pirates have received their just deserts, I shall be mentioning your name in no uncertain terms and on that you have my solemn oath. You have lifted a burden from my shoulders that I have neglected for far too long.'

'You are too kind, Sir.' Winchip stopped at that, his surprise at Saunders' words leaving him speechless.

'Your squadron will go into Louisburg for repairs and victualling immediately and from there you will go home for a well deserved rest, as will your people.' Saunders gave a sardonic chuckle. 'I lost *Diana, Lowestoffe* and *Vanguard* upriver at Pointe aux

Trembles, Winchip. My family will have to wait for me to redeem myself in Their Lordship's eyes before I see them again.'

'And what of the French, Admiral, how did they fair?'

'A damned sight worse than we did, Commodore; *Atalante* and *Pomone* were lost to them, together with many smaller vessels. They are finished up there, Winchip. Amherst will winkle their army out quickly enough and that shall be an end to it.'

'That is good news, Sir and very welcome. It almost makes one proud to be part of it.'

Saunders let out a hearty bellow, acknowledging Winchip's well aimed dart at another branch of England's forces. Then he stood and held out a hand. 'Give my love to England and let her know that we serve in her name – all of us, be we navy or army, it matters not.'

'I shall, Admiral – and will expect your orders and despatches in due course.'

CHAPTER TWENTY-TWO

Retribution

There was a flurry of salutes to Winchip's broad pennant as the squadron left the naval anchorage at Louisburg, on Breton Island. The only addition was the old second-rate, *Pernicious*, on her last voyage to the Nore and her eventual break-up. She was commanded by Douglas Munro, in his first ship since 1756. His last had been a frigate at the time of Minorca, before he became an aid to the Governor of Gibraltar. It was a far cry from a ship of twenty-eight guns to one of ninety but Munro had the benefit of her original officers and most of her original complement. If there were any blessing attached to his new and temporary command, it would be his unconfirmed promotion to 'post' that would serve him best, seeing him to a higher rank as a matter of right, provided that enough Admirals, Commodores and post-captains died or retired before he did.

Winchip stood at the taffrail of Bellicus and trained his telescope aft, to scan the shoreline that was fast disappearing at the end of the ship's wake. The light south-westerly had warmth in it and it suited his purposes. He had much to consider and even more to remember about the Americas, yet they still meant little to him. The place was bourgeoning, of that there was no doubt and that alone was sufficient to warrant anomalies, political friction, lawlessness.., he could have continued; but to even give consideration to the slave situation was to finish in confusion. As for the on-going war between England and France, it was already a victory for England. He knew that the states of America would soon act in unison for a federal government rather than British rule. The idea would fester and grow outside politics until even a small incident could bring the present incumbents to arms – that, and a man to lead them. He slapped a hand down on the taffrail, sending a pair of gulls screeching into the air from his window sill below.

'Excuse me, Sir, we are clear of the environs and need to determine our easting.' Niven stood to Winchip's side, his hands tucked behind his back and his body relaxed to infer that he was in no rush for the information.

Winchip turned to face him. 'I wish our easting to be on the forty-ninth line of parallel, James.'

'Aye, Sir but we did agree the fiftieth, if you remember. Have you had a change of mind?'

'I have, James. When we met those two *Frenchmen* on our way up the St Lawrence, one of them killed two of our people and wounded several more. We gave the first one a carronade they will talk about for years to come and we hurt her badly. I believe that the two of them are returning to France and making what repairs they can at sea. I also believe that they have a conflict of minds as to who commands them – or they would have straddled the channel in the St Lawrence and taken out our tops, take my word for it. Had we gone about, there would have been a good chance that we would flounder in all the mud and sand about us, for I had little knowledge of the river at that precise time and only later did I manage to read the colour of the waters with some accuracy.'

'Are you bent on catching them, Sir?'

'I am, James. I am convinced they will take the forty-ninth and then wear to the south-east to avoid the Western Squadron.'

'Damn me if we shan't do it, Sir, though the second-rate *could* hold us up, weeded as she is.'

'Then Captain Munro shall lag behind. She is large enough to look after herself and, besides that, she is fully provisioned.'

'The forty-ninth it is then, Sir, I shall put up a general signal.'

'Thank you, Captain.' Winchip looked astern to find that the Americas were gone from his sight, though they would still be visible from the tops. He turned with a mind to go to his cabin and found Pender hovering for his attention.

'Well, Pender, what is it?'

'The committal, Sir – we are at sea now.'

'But not in British waters, Coxswain – not in British waters. The lads are comfortable enough where they are for now, wouldn't you think?'

'I would, Sir, I would!' Pender fingered his brow, turned and was gone, his face a picture of joy.'

The Atlantic Ocean meant more to some than to others, depending upon each one's taste of it in different weathers. Some would tell the truth of it; of the mountainous waves and the terrible squalls and the ships they had seen go down with all hands, while others would speak of fine weather and the doldrums and of whales and blue skies, at the same time scoffing at those who sought to exaggerate the might of such a placid sea.

On the twelfth day of the crossing, *Eaglet* found herself taking in sail as another squall came up from the south-west.

Pardoe stood at the binnacle in his tarpalling coat, his face running with water as the rain came once again. He cast an eye at the helmsman and at Mr Ramblin, gripping his clay pipe in his teeth with the bowl pointing downwards. Even in the rain, smoke was emanating from the upturned bowl in small puffs. Pardoe grinned and turned away, expecting nothing else from the man for all eventualities.

Eaglet was in the van of the squadron, a league ahead but with her purpose taken from her for the moment as the visibility came down to the immediate environs of the ship. Dusk was upon them and, with that, a small hope that the squalls would diminish or go altogether. As if in answer to his prayer, the rain ceased and the last rays of the sun glinted brightly from behind him. He turned with shaded eyes and slapped his knee. They had just experienced the last of the squalls, as evidenced by the now cloudless sky; and more, the sun still had some heat in it.

'Deck alow! Two sails ahead and both French!'

'They'm ships-o'-the-line – on the larboard bow!'

Pardoe waved a hand in the air and turned to Dundas. 'Signal to flag, Mr Dundas, "two French ships-of-the-line on the larboard bow".'

'*They'm on our course!*'

Pardoe caught Dundas's attention and received a nod of understanding.

'Are they French, Peter?' Bowes was out of breath.

'They appear to be but you can wager they'll add sail now that we're in sight.'

'Flag has acknowledged, Sir.' Dundas stood in clothes that were shedding vapours in the last of the evening sun.

'Thank you. Up to the tops, Mr Dundas where you can better dry your clothes, Pardoe turned away with a grin on his face. To Bowes, he said. 'Why do I think that this is no coincidence, Matthew, you tell me that?'

'It's those two Frenchmen from the St Lawrence, isn't it?'

'Exactly, that is why we are on the forty-ninth and not the fiftieth.'

'Then we had better not lose them, Sir!' Bowes grinned and was gone before Pardoe could respond.

Winchip slapped his thigh. 'Damned if I wasn't right, James!'

'What do we do, Sir, are we to attack them or follow them home, for as sure as damn it we shall not lose them?'

'We shall put them into Lampaul, James, at Ushant. They shall not know it but we will herd them into that port or they shall have to fight us and we have a second rate on hand to avoid that.'

'My word, Sir, you have the mind of a politician and the brain of an admiral – always one step ahead and knowing what to do when you get there.'

'I shall take that as flattery, Lieutenant.' Winchip did all but laugh. 'Munro can remain in their wake. Incensed and Bellicus shall remain to the north and keep nudging them southwards. They shall not complain as long as they are pointing towards France. When we are nearer to Ushant we shall come at them from the south and they will add sail to dash into the harbour like rabbits down a burrow. However, should we meet with the Western Squadron, then things must be allowed to take their natural course. If we meet with one of the inshore cruisers, then we shall attack the *Frenchmen* and be done with it. Bend on signals to that affect when or if the time comes and we shall deal with events as they happen but in the mean time have *Eaglet* and *Trial* show stern lights; and keep in touch with the French lest they try to lose us in the dark.

'Aye, Sir.' Niven saw in his commodore an uncommon vindictiveness that smacked of revenge.

Pardoe stood at the beakhead rail. The sky was dotted with stars and the south-westerly wind was carrying the whole squadron forward at a good pace. With the full moon astern of the chase, he could see the dull white light of its reflection in the stern windows of the forty-gun *Frenchman* ahead of him. She carried no stern lights – a sure sign that she sought to escape rather than fight. They had been sailing on a compass bearing slightly south of east for several hours and Pardoe was certain that Ushant would be seen by dawn. In the meantime, he decided to snatch two hours sleep before the sky lightened.

Matthew Bowes decided to wake the captain at five bells in the morning watch. The sky was beginning to lighten in the east and only the planets were left to twinkle in the early light of morning. The French ship was on *Eaglet*'s starboard bow as it had been for hours since; and *Bellicus* was on the starboard quarter as before and looked to remain so until this business was done with. *Eaglet* was carrying a full suit of sail, with stays'ls being added in the night as the *Frenchman* started to draw away. Bowes was about to call a midshipman to wake the captain when Pardoe appeared beside him.

'I think we can dispense with the stern lights now, Matthew.'

'*Deck there! A small island ahead – and Ushant on the larboard bow!*'

Bowes called to Archer. 'Signal to flag, Mr Archer; "Ushant on the larboard bow".'

A good two minutes passed before Archer returned. 'Flag has acknowledged, Sir and signals us to maintain station to the north, within sight.'

'It looks as though we have played our part, Matthew. Have us brought to north-east, if you please.' Pardoe looked to the north, to see Trial obeying similar orders. Only a fool would fail to realise that his father-in-law meant business.

'Come to south-east, Master.' Winchip stood near the wheel of *Bellicus* with a glass to his eye. 'I have her name, Mr Blackstock, it is *Protectrice*, the one we fought on the St Lawrence. We shall make them run for the harbour at Ushant, Mr Blackstock, or be sunk where they stand.'

'They'll run right enough, Commodore, or go down with the ship for there's no beach hereabouts.' The huge cliffs of Ushant bore witness to Mr Blackstock's words. Even the harbour was but a large cleft in the cliff, running for a good half mile inland and four chains in width.

With *Eaglet* and *Trial* well out of things, *Bellicus* continued to the south east. Once the French ship realised that a run to the south was out of the question, she wore to the north east and added sail.

Winchip slapped his thigh. 'She is ours, Master!'

'And so's t'other, Sir, she's followin' behind her partner!'

'The master is right, Sir, we have the pair of them.' Niven clapped his hands and then stared ahead, his hands on his hips. 'I never believed they would do it.'

'Nor me, James.' Winchip stared at the disappearing ships. 'Send in *Eaglet* and *Trial* and have them bring us a report of what is in harbour – and caution them about going in too close for there may well be large guns in there.'

'Aye, Sir.'

South west of Ushant, at the harbour entrance, Pardoe was able to see into the bay that led to the village of Lampaul and the extensive harbour. The cliffs to either side loomed large above Eaglet and his only prayer was that there were no guns looking down at him. As the great cleft continued inland, so it narrowed.

Stone houses were tightly packed against the cliff face to the rear of the lengthy hard. There were fishing boats aplenty, crowded together as though the days work was yet to start, and two French frigates beside a bomb ketch. The two French men-of-war were turning into a wind that was blowing directly down the great cleft towards the harbour as he looked, with figures already beginning to free the anchors and take in sail. Their mains were taken up and before long they were sitting squat upon the water with bare yards. He lowered the glass for a moment and then replaced it to his eye. He had not been seeing things; there were gun placements at either end of the hard, each with two embrasures. It was not a heavy defence but it could do much damage to a frigate, given the opportunity.

'Trial is coming onto our larboard quarter, Sir.' Dundas stood waiting as if he had asked a question and was waiting for the answer.

'Thank you, Mr Dundas – now, keep your eye on the flagship, if you please.' Pardoe looked for and found Bowes at the boat tier. 'Mr Bowes!' Pardoe waited. 'Mr Bowes, I'd like you to fire a ranging shot towards the harbour.'

'Aye, Sir.' Bowes was gone in a flash, his cheeky grin replaced by the look of a man about to tempt fate.

The twelve-pounder fired unexpectedly, a surprise as always, the echoes rebounding from the cliffs about them as if they would never stop and the smoke billowing out to lay upon the water until the wind sent it tumbling forwards in a low cloud. The suspense lasted but a few moments, until one of the houses beyond the hard received a direct hit, taking down the whole of the front wall in a cloud of dust and timbers. Smoke began to emerge from the ruin, spiralling upwards as it increased in volume until the south-westerly turned it to the north-east and flattened it.

'They are well in range, Peter but then, so are we.' Bowes stared towards the harbour as if expecting the two men-of-war to discharge their broadsides at Eaglet.

'You are right, Mr Bowes, we have no more business here.' Pardoe turned to Mr Ramblin. 'Take us away, Master, lest we suffer the consequences.' Already, the French men-of-war were putting over their boats to pull their ships clear rather than risk putting sail on them in the adverse wind. Pardoe saw their reasoning but it offered them no escape from the English squadron. Five minutes later and the ships were under tow, their dangling anchors not yet even catted. Pardoe noted that they were beginning to straddle the narrow bay and that lines were being thrown from one's bow to the other's stern. They were going to defend their position, of that he was certain.

'See us away from here, Master, as quickly as you like!' Pardoe saw that Trial, too, was making preparations to leave. 'Signal to flag, Mr Dundas, the French are preparing a defensive position.'

CHAPTER TWENTY-THREE

The Loss of a Legend

Winchip and Niven stood on the quarterdeck of Bellicus, each with his hat dangling from his hand in the rising south-westerly. Winchip could see down the length of the inlet to Lampaul and the situation was exactly as Pardoe had just described it. The cliff rose up in steps as if carved by a giant and at the top a stone wall continued round as if to stop sheep from plunging over the edge. There was not a single English ship in the inlet; and neither was there likely to be with that amount of fire-power staring them in the face. It was nothing short of a stalemate. It was the last thing he wanted or expected. The only thing for certain was that they would not escape, and yet neither was he prepared to blockade the place. Winchip was about to speak when Midshipman Piper coughed behind him.

'What is it, Mr Piper?'

'A signal from *Pernicious*, Sir, they have sprung some planks forrard and require pumps, Sir.'

'Acknowledge, Mr Piper and bend on "Captain to repair on board", if you please.'

'Aye, Sir.' Piper all but ran towards the gaff halyard.

'What can happen next, James, you tell me that?'

'How expendable is she, sir?'

Winchip turned and looked Niven in the eye. 'Are you thinking of a fire-ship?'

'I was, Sir...tentatively, I hasten to add.'

'Has she any brass cannon?'

'None, Sir, they were taken off her at Louisburg.'

'And what about powder, what is the state of her magazine?'

'A full magazine; the less air the less likelihood of an explosion.'

Winchip went to the mizzen shrouds alone, his hands gripped tightly behind his back, contemplating the consequences of putting a second rate to the torch. It was not an easy decision, even though the rate of exchange seemed to warrant it. For almost quarter of an hour he agonized over the decision he would have to make. At last, he raised himself up and strode purposely back to where Niven stood, a look of anticipation pasted on his face.

'By God it is worth a go, James, my word it is! Two forty-gun ships, two frigates and a bomb-ketch, all trapped. It would be her last fling, James. Winchip tucked his hat beneath his arm and pointed towards *Pernicious*. 'She would bring truth to the meaning of going out in a blaze of glory.' He lowered his hand as a cough came from behind him. He knew it would be Munro. He turned and acknowledged Munro's salute. 'Douglas! Thank you for coming across.' Winchip again pointed a finger towards the ships at anchor and those that were tethered together. 'I am of a mind to send your command down there as a fire-ship, Captain.'

Munro's answer was unequivocal. 'You can have her with my blessing, Sir. The old tub is beyond her usefulness – short of a blockship; and according to her master, she is quite capable of taking a detour without so much as a 'by your leave.' As for the present, she is leaky in the bows and taking in more water than we can handle. '

'Thank you, Douglas; I hope you repeat that at my court martial. We shall take off her whole complement and dress her in a full suit of sail. With a small crew, we can point her and let the wind do the rest, for even if she ricochets off the cliffs she will finish up where we want her to – right in among the French, who, I must add, are tethered together in a lover's knot.' Winchip spoke to James Niven directly. 'Get her officers to help you James and when all is done, then spread her people about the ships. Keep no secrets, Captain. Every man has a right to know why his ship is being sacrificed – if they haven't guessed already.'

'Aye, Sir.' Niven, already working things out in his mind, said, 'some of the crew should remain on board to set the fire. If it is set too early then the sails will catch fire for sure.'

'You are right, Lieutenant.' Winchip was beginning to enthuse about the whole concept, though he had doubts that Their Lordships at Admiralty would see things in the same light. He turned to Munro. 'Have her boats towed behind her as well, Douglas, for I'll not see a man lost when he can row home. The enemy will be well occupied saving themselves rather than waste shot on a few boats. Also, make sure that every man jack can swim.'

'Aye, Sir, I shall see to it.' Munro turned and was gone.

'Excuse me, Sir.' Midshipman John Costly stood patiently next to Niven with his slate beneath his arm.

'Yes, Mr Costly., what is it?' Niven looked down upon Costly.

'The wind has backed to an easterly, Sir and gusting. Mr Blackstock suggests that a storm may be brewing.'

'Thank you, Mr Costly. Remain where you are for a moment.' Niven orientated Ushant in his mind. 'That means a difficult passage for the old lady, Sir; she'll have what wind there is ten points before her beam. Better I let her master know, I think.'

'I agree, James. Have Mr Costly catch Munro if he is not already gone. If he has, then send a signal for they shall be too busy preparing the ship to heed the wind.'

Eaglet lay close to the entrance of the anchorage with only her bow in sight to the French. Pardoe waited for the great event from the beakhead rail, noting with concern that the great guns at each end of the meagre stone hard were protruding through the slots in the stonework of the embrasures. They would try their damnedest to sink the old *Pernicious* once they realised what was happening but they would have small chance of success before they were engulfed in flames.

'She is coming round *Bellicus* now, Peter.' Bowes had the deck and had seen Pardoe come up through the companion.

'Ah, yes and under tops'ls and t'gallants, that's a sound idea. She'll catch the high wind with her yards over like that and her lifts lowered.'

'God, she's ponderous slow.' Bowes shook his head.

'The wind is chasing all about the place in there, Matthew. Look how the water ripples as the wind changes.'

Pernicious had straightened with the use of the tiller. As it moved into the bay, so the top pintles and the top of her rudder showed how far over the wheel had been spun to drag her round the corner of the great cliff. Behind her, trailing from her stern by lengths of line, five of her boats bobbed gainfully along, waiting for occupants once the ninety-gun ship was on her way.

The smoke rose with a suddenness from amidships and then at the bows, coincident with her main hatches. Soon, the smoke was replaced by flames that licked upwards and spread sideways like wildfire, now licking the mainmast and touching the shrouds. The smoke increased again and the flames came afresh, licking out of the companions and seeking fuel as they grew.

The first resounding blast of a shore gun brought a huge fountain of water near the old man-of-war's bow. Then came a second, striking her beakhead and sending timbers high into the air. A third shot and a fourth echoed out as the guns fired in rotation and then a whole broadside struck *Pernicious*, momentarily halting her in her tracks and sending her trailing boats into a merry dance with the stern wave. Yet her momentum carried her onwards, although her course had altered. She would now come onto the hard and into the ships before it at the skew – a coincidence that would raise terror in the hearts of all who saw her menacing sideways approach.

'There, Peter!' Bowes pointed a finger. 'Our people are leaving the ship, they're jumping – look there!'

'And there goes Captain Munro – good man!' Pardoe gripped the rail as he watched her people jumping from the chains and the entry port alike. There was a flurry of water splashes as the swimmers made for the boats before it was too late. One after the other, they climbed into the boats and cast off the lines with the swipe of a knife, in each boat the ones already on board were helping others up and over, dragging the sodden souls to safety. The last to climb over a gunwale was Munro, taking a last look about him as *Pernicious* moved away like a lumbering ox. As the men in the boats waved to those who watched from the squadron, so the crews waved back and cheered and cheered again.

'They are not waving for the pleasure of it, Peter. I do believe they have a problem.' Bowes leant forward, his brow quizzed as the hand waved frantically. 'My God, Peter, they have no oars.' Bowes screamed, 'The stupid bastards haven't put any oars in the boats!'

'Raise the anchor, Mr Bowes and be sharp about it!' Pardoe turned and ran aft to the binnacle, shouting orders as he went. Mr Ramblin was there, waiting for him.

'All hands, all hands up!' Longdale put the trumpet back on the hook and raced for the shrouds, taking the ratlines two at a time.

As sails were let fall, so Mr Ramblin turned the wheel back and forth until it bit. We've steerage way, Captain.'

'Thank you, Master, there is nothing for me to say, except that we need to be there with those of our people.' Pardoe pointed a finger and then let his arm drop, his anger boiling within him with no chance of being expressed.

'As you say, Captain.' Mr Ramblin shrivelled the helmsman with a look that had melted many men, enough to cause the man to jump back with a start as the master gripped the wheel.

Only *Eaglet*'s t'gallants caught the wind, the tops'ls refusing in the lifeless air, yet it had been enough to move the ship forward and to answer the helm.

Pardoe remained at the binnacle and watched in awe at the sight of *Pernicious* on fire. The flames had climbed her masts and caught her yards with only the poop free from the conflagration. The noise of timbers bursting and the flames crackling was painful to the ears and refused to stop. The smoke had reached the cliff-tops and was being flattened by an easterly wind, denied access to the protected sanctuary of the anchorage.

Eaglet shuddered and Pardoe was thrown to the floor as the ship seemed to stop in her tracks. He scrambled to his feet and helped up Mr Ramblin, all the time worrying that the ship had hit a rock. He regained the binnacle in time to be thrown onto his back as another sickening crunch came from forward, causing the ship rock where it stood and the helm to spin like a wild thing.

'What in the name of heaven…?' Another crash from forward made the ship lurch. As Pardoe placed his feet to counter her return to the upright, he suddenly realised that the ship had made no such movement beneath him. He knew at that moment that she had been hit by the great guns beside the hard, the ones he thought would be rendered benign by virtue of the fire and the gun's inability to see Eaglet in the smoke and flame. He had been wrong and now he was paying the price. He leapt to his feet as Bowes came aft.

'What is the damage?'

'We are sinking, Peter, there is no hope for her, we have been hit three times in the bow and the water is pouring in. I have ordered the boats over and they are bringing them to the chains where Hellard is in control.'

'Thank you, Matthew – and what about the others, the ones from *Pernicious*?'

'They have joined with us, Sir and their boats now have oars.'

'Right, then get them going, Matthew, back to *Bellicus*, if you please.'

'What about you, Peter?'

'I shall come in due course, Matthew when I have a mind to.' Pardoe turned about and moved up the quarterdeck, his head hung low.'

'You will come now, Sir!' Hellard had strode up behind his captain and now stood like a rock behind Pardoe and when his captain turned about, so he punched him on the point of his jaw.

'Well done, Hellard though I think you may have to answer for it when all this is done.'

'I've done worse, young sir and I'm still here.'

'And thank God for it, I say. Come on, before we get left behind.'

Hellard hoisted Pardoe over his shoulder and strode to the larboard port, closer to the water than he had ever seen it. As a great bubble of air burst at the ship's tumblehome, so Pardoe was passed across and both Hellard and Bowes joined him.

With a loud crack and with a scream of tortured timbers, the mainmast of *Eaglet* fell to starboard, the great splintered stump leaping into the air before sliding over the nettings into oblivion, taking shrouds, lines, stays and yards with her.

As Hellard put his foot on the topmost batten at the entry port and pushed to clear the boat, so *Eaglet* began her slide to the bottom, increasing speed as she went until her stern windows passed them by in a rush of air and a great gurgle for a death rattle. Hellard fell backwards into half a dozen arms as the boat was forced away from the sinking ship and then drawn back into a whirlpool as if it had an urge to rejoin *Eaglet* in her plunge to the depths.

Winchip watched in horror as *Eaglet* slid beneath the waves. He had witnessed every moment of her demise and now that she was gone he had lost his point of reference. He could neither weep nor scream his despair and yet he wanted to do both those things. Instead, without comment to those about him, he walked to the taffrail and raised his telescope to his eye. *Pernicious* had done her job well. All the French ships were afire. Their magazines had blown up in their turn and their crew had chosen to drown rather than be burned to death. The hard was now ablaze from end to end and the powder rooms of the embrasures had blown their own installations to kingdom come. The rugged path that wound its way from the village to the cliff top was a line of colour as the inhabitants struggled upwards, their belongings occasionally falling from their grasp to bring others tumbling to their death as they lost their footing on what was no more than a goat track.

The roofs of the simple stone houses were now on fire, small pyramids of flame that gobbled up all in their path, sometimes blowing up as some forgotten combustible was discovered for what it was.

The boats were coming in now, one at a time, clinging to the chains of whichever boat was nearest, before being sent out again and again. Winchip had no idea how many of his people had perished but he would not be long in finding out.

'She did her job, Sir, God bless her.' Munro stood in his wet clothes with a puddle already forming on the deck at his feet.

Winchip turned on his heel. 'Douglas, thank God you are safe!' Winchip shook the man's hand – one person looked like another in the panic and confusion. 'And Peter is he safe?'

'Aye, Daniel but he took one on the jaw from Hellard.'

'What *are* you talking about?' Winchip spoke as a deep rumble of thunder came from overhead.

'Your son-in-law was all ready to go down wi' his ship until Hellard decided otherwise and now he'll have to suffer the loss of a tooth or two at the hands of Mr Pollard.'

'God preserve us from romantics, Douglas. I shall talk to the lad and remind him of what he has left behind in Falmouth, that'll sober him up somewhat. Damned semantics, does he think he would be remembered as some hero from Shakespeare?' Winchip looked up and down at Munro's sodden clothes. 'You were a damned fool to go with her, Douglas. I wonder what might have happened if we'd had a rain storm as they were trying to light her up.'

Munro put a hand on Winchip's shoulder, flattening the gold braid of his epaulette. 'I know you loved that ship, Daniel but don't let it linger, there's too much else that needs your attention and let us face it, a ship *was* just a ship.'

'Today, I disagree with you, Douglas and in many years time my answer will still be the same.' Munro was not to know that every nook and cranny of the ship was known to him and that memories could be revitalised by a glance at a chair or a dent in a cushion; even a spot at the taffrail, anything he chose could hold a memory, bring her presence to mind and seeing her, for Madeleine had been part of Eaglet, just as she was now part of him.

CHAPTER TWENTY-FOUR

The Homecoming

Winchip stood abaft the double wheel of *Bellicus*, in the shadow of the poop, totally distraught at the devilish stroke of misfortune that had brought about the demise of *Eaglet*. Thankful as he was that his son-in-law had survived the catastrophe, he was well aware of those of his people who had gone down with her. She had sunk because the oars for the boats had been missing – a careless sin to be laid at the feet of the boatswain when all was said and done – but *he* was feeding the fish off the Island of Ushant – the 'Storm Island'.

The diminished squadron had made a hasty retreat from the environs of Ushant. In all, thirty-two seamen from different ships had lost their lives in the waters about the island. Twenty-one had been from *Eaglet* and the others from *Pernicious*. The loss had been sufficient for Winchip to regret that he had not taken a chaplain on board at Gibraltar when he had had the chance. He was not one for the interference that a chaplain could cause on board ship and he was not truly religious; but come the day of judgement, he would be as quick to get on his knees as any man in the King's Navy. There were, however, many among his people who felt the need for religious guidance and comfort and he should have respected that. He resolved to correct the situation and was glad that the matter had come to his mind that very afternoon, at the time of the lengthy committal, well south of the Lizard, when the two sailors tucked up together in their cask of brine had joined their comrades in English waters.

'Excuse me, Sir.' Lieutenant Hartley, late of Eaglet, waited at Winchip's side, the look on his face expressing regret at having disturbed the commodore.

'Yes, Lieutenant what is it?'

'The 'Lizard' is reported on the larboard bow, Sir – you asked to be informed.'

'Thank you, Mr Hartley – tell me, would you care to remain with us in Bellicus?'

Hartley looked stunned by the question but quickly recovered his composure. I could think of nothing finer, Sir, especially if she is to remain your flagship.'

'Then you shall be her fourth officer, young man unless Their Lordships say differently.' Winchip smiled – but not benevolently for Hartley had earned his position.'

'Thank you, Sir.' Hartley put two fingers to the rim of his hat and turned on his heel.'

Winchip knew there were others who needed to know their position, deprived of their ship and left out to dry. He would go to his cabin immediately and see to it, for work was now to be his consolation, plenty of it and with a purpose. He had no wish to arrive home with the temper of a bear or the countenance of a mourner. However, he wanted to gather his old crew about him and Hartley was just the beginning.

The squall at Ushant had brought warm air with it, as well as rain and the odd peal of thunder. As Winchip entered the great cabin so Booth brought him a dish of coffee. The air of the place was tainted with the aroma of beeswax, lamp oil and coffee; friendly smells that sat well with him. His journal stared back at him as if to remind him that it required completing, a task he had avoided, that had now come back to haunt him. The knock at the door came unexpectedly.

'Enter!'

Costly allowed half his body to penetrate the cabin. 'Black Head is on the larboard beam, Sir and the tide is on the last of its ebb.'

'Thank you, Mr Costly. We seem to have an angel on our shoulder.' He would have laughed at Costly's bewilderment if it wouldn't have embarrassed him.

Winchip sat at the Gillow desk and opened his journal. Whatever he wrote, it was going to end up as an indictment of his inability to command. To be bested by a series of unfortunate events was never – and never would be – a plausible excuse for failure. His head spun as he scanned through the pages of the last seven months. They had been to so many places and had come into contact with so many different – and foreign – people; and so many events, most of which would be remembered with horror, they had been so gruesome. The Americas had been a place apart; a burgeoning country with a poor helmsman – England, a circumstance which may change sooner than Parliament and Mr Pitt realised.

Whatever he wrote would be the truth, as always. He could do no more than that. He was about to come home to 'Santander' to see Madeleine and the ever growing three year-old, Richard and nothing could be allowed to spoil that.

Culpepper's *Trial* came to larboard as she passed beneath Pendennis Castle and once into the mouth of the Fal she came about, to anchor opposite the Falmouth Quays and out towards Flushing. As she settled on her anchorage in shallow water, so Nathanson's *Incensed* came up into the south-westerly, in deeper water, displaying her salt encrusted tumblehome with a touch of panache, her sails coming off her as her bow anchor went down with a splash. The second anchor would be sure to drop, to insure her against the unexpected.

Winchip stood at the taffrail of *Bellicus* as she came round Pendennis, his hat beneath his arm and with the warm south-westerly playing on his face and ruffling his black forelock. As the salt caked ship approached deep water before coming onto the mouth of the Fal, so he light-heartedly cursed the church for obscuring his view of the house. *Bellicus* came about in the deeper water so that his view was at last presented to him, for this was not *Eaglet*, when he would be in a position to wave to her and she to wave back in return – done through telescopes – a mad arrangement. She would know already that *Eaglet* was not with them, just as Emma would be fretting, searching through the trees with Madeleine's glass. He knew, too, that Munro's Alice would be with them and that they would come down to the Quays together, panic in their eyes and with beating hearts and would remain so until Pardoe and Munro stepped from the ship's boat with their broad smiles and with their arms held wide.

Madeleine sat askew at the desk in the withdrawing room as she penned a letter to her husband. She found it difficult to write words that would not be a repeat of things she had already told him. Try as she might, new expressions of her love for him seemed to be wearing thin and new words simply would not come. She wiped the nib of the quill and replaced it in the silver stand, promising herself that she would try again later to express herself as she would wish. She look across at Richard, standing on the window seat with his nose to the large window, taking up the space that Madeleine had used for an hour each day, hoping that *Eaglet* would appear. She took up her sherbet and sipped the cool, fruity liquid with relish, finding relief in it as it cooled her inner body. She decided on the spur of the moment that she would walk in the garden and then sit on the terrace, where Emma and Alice sat, Emma reading and Alice busy with her sampler. She sighed, soon, it would be summer; and then, perhaps, her Daniel would be home – and home for good if he were to be true to his word. She took Richard by the hand and he jumped down to the floor. Together, they went into the hall and then out through the front door and into the warm May sunshine.

Emma was on the top terrace, engrossed in her book until the noise of Madeleine's shoes on the gravel caught her attention. 'I thought you were writing a letter, Madeleine.' Emma laid the book face down on her lap.

'I found it hard to bring freshness to my words; I do declare that they kept coming out as before, earnestly meant though they were.'

'Then you must invent some new words or consult the dictionary, for I have the same trouble.'

'But the words must come from the heart, dear Emma; they should flow in tune with one's thoughts.'

'If that were so, Madeleine, we would be likened to old harridans, for sometimes my heart has a mind of its own.'

Richard tugged at Madeleine's hand. 'Papa's ship, mother.'

'He will be coming home soon, my darling.' Madeleine smiled down at him, seeing in him a great likeness to his father.

Richard pointed his finger again, this time high in the air; high above the roof tops of the houses behind the quays, high enough to denote distance, even as far as the Carrick Roads. 'Papa's ship.'

Madeleine followed his gaze; and seeing no *Eaglet* she looked way. A moment later she realised that Daniel's ship now had far more guns. Her eyes riveted on the stern of the large ship-of-the-line and her hand went to her mouth. It was Daniel's ship, as bold as brass, yet it looked so drab, so covered in salt that it glistened white in the sun.

'Emma! Is that your father's ship – please tell me that I am not mistaken?'

Emma rushed to Madeleine's side. 'Ugh, it is so dirty, it cannot be.' Her shoulders sagged. 'Besides, *Eaglet* is not with her...' Emma's words faded as she spoke, the connotation of what she had said vying with the assumption that the ship was her father's. Her face went as white as a sheet. 'It cannot be.'

'Papa's ship.' Richard's finger still pointed, his face beaming with his smile.

Emma collapsed to the ground with a sigh; and as Madeleine crouched down next to her so she, too, almost fainted at the horrific implication of *Eaglet*'s absence and that Peter had not come back to them.

Winchip fretted at the entry port of Bellicus. He wanted them to hurry, to get the jolly boat to the chains and he a chance to get to the house before they realised that *Eaglet* was not with them. At last, Hellard looked upwards and nodded. Munro and Hellard were quickly down the battens and Winchip made his descent, his sword seeking to pitch him into the Carrick Roads. He climbed into the stern sheets without preamble and nodded his assent to cast off.

At the Quays he took the weeded steps throwing caution to the winds, allowing that, were it not for the helping hands of Munro and Peter, he might not have survived the wet seaweed and the worn and slippery timber of the steps.

'Run ahead, Peter, for they will believe nothing except your personal appearance, mark my words!' As Pardoe set off through the 'ope' and up to Church Street, Munro and Winchip relaxed. They would have run, too, had dignity not prevented them.

As Emma struggled to her feet, so Madeleine put her hands to her mouth and stared at the figure running up the terrace path. That it was Peter, there was no doubt but she found it impossible to speak lest she burst into tears of joy. It was Peter's shout that did the trick.

'Peter!' Emma took Madeleine's hand and pulled herself to her feet. Without another word she ran down the path with her ribbons blowing in the wind and then threw her arms about his neck as they closed with each other.

Madeleine walked to the bottom of the path and waited at the old iron gate, under the yew tree that prefaced the commencement of the cemetery. She was not fit to go into the street, dressed as she was. With the crunch of shoes on gravel, Alice came down to her and Madeleine held out her arms to bring her to a stop.

'Are they back?' Alice took the few steps down to the street path and looked along Church Street. She turned and beckoned Madeleine. 'They are coming, they're by Wynns, I can see them both – though where is *'Eaglet'*?'

'We shall find out, Alice. They will tell us when they are ready and not before.' Madeleine suddenly found the thought of waiting unbearable. She turned to Alice and held out her hand. 'Come, Alice! I say damnation to the gossips, dressed as we are. Let us go to our men!'

END

ISBN 1-41204537-1